PENGUIN BOOKS

Zoe Sugg, aka Zoella, is a vlogger from Brighton, UK. Her beauty, fashion and lifestyle vlogs have gained her millions of YouTube subscribers, with even more viewing the vlogs every month. She won the 2011 Cosmopolitan Blog Award for Best Established Beauty Blog and went on to win the Best Beauty Vlogger award the following year. Zoe has also twice received the Best British Vlogger award at the 2013 and 2014 Radio 1 Teen Awards and the 2014 and 2015 Nickelodeon Kids' Choice award for UK's Favourite Vlogger, and she was named Web Star for Fashion and Beauty at the 2014 Teen Choice Awards. In summer 2016, Zoe launched her exciting new book club with WHSmith.

Books by Zoe Sugg

GIRL ONLINE

GIRL ONLINE: ON TOUR

GIRL ONLINE: GOING SOLO

**Follow Zoe on Twitter and Instagram
@zoella
www.zoella.co.uk
www.girlonlinebooks.com**

Girl Online
GOING SOLO

ZOE SUGG

PENGUIN BOOKS

PENGUIN BOOKS

UK | USA | Canada | Ireland | Australia
India | New Zealand | South Africa

Penguin Books is part of the Penguin Random House group of companies
whose addresses can be found at global.penguinrandomhouse.com.

www.penguin.co.uk   www.puffin.co.uk   www.ladybird.co.uk

First published 2016

001

Typeset in 13.5/16 pt Garamond MT Std by Jouve (UK), Milton Keynes
Printed in Great Britain by Clays Ltd, St Ives plc

A CIP catalogue record for this book is available from the British Library

HARDBACK
ISBN: 978–0–141–37217–4

INTERNATIONAL PAPERBACK
ISBN: 978–0–141–37219–8

Penguin Random House is committed to a
sustainable future for our business, our readers
and our planet. This book is made from Forest
Stewardship Council® certified paper.

To my lovely viewers, readers and fans, thank you for all your continued support and for sharing my love of Penny and her story. I hope you continue to follow your dreams until they become a reality.
If I can do it, so can you!

Brighton
Station

The
Flour Pot
Bakery

NORTH LAINE

Snoopers Paradise

Blakers
Park

FIVE
WAYS

The Royal
Pavilion

to KEMP
TOWN

Choccywoccydoodah

THE LANES

The
Creperie

JB's Diner

Boho
Gelato

BRIGHTON

BEACH

The
Pier

Map illustration © mapsofjoy.com, 2016

15 September

Where Is Noah Flynn?

A small interruption to regularly scheduled blogging!

If you're a regular *Girl Online* reader, you know I love answering your questions, either in the comments or via email. Despite most of you being super cool and asking about normal things like my new school year and how I go about getting organized for my up-and-coming coursework and exam deadlines . . . I've also had my inbox flooded with questions about Noah Flynn. More specifically: Where is he? What is he doing? Why did he leave The Sketch world tour?

Now, this isn't just happening here on my blog but on every social media account I have, and even in real life too! So I feel it's time to set the record straight about what I know.

If you're a new reader of my blog, you might not be familiar with the fact that Noah and I used to date (emphasis on the 'used to'). Long-term readers may also know him as 'Brooklyn Boy', and although I haven't written about him in a while – or us, for that matter – his recent hiatus has left a lot of people wondering about him.

So, deep breath, here's the truth: I don't know either. I know as much as you do, and all I can hope is that he's OK and happy, whatever he's doing. His management issued this statement:

'Due to juggling a heavy workload alongside personal matters, Noah has made the decision to leave The Sketch world tour a month ahead of schedule. He sends his apologies to his fans for any disappointment caused and thanks them for their continued support.'

And that's all I've got. Unfortunately, being a friend of Noah's doesn't automatically mean I have him GPS-tracked, so I can't log into some app on my phone and see where he is (although I'm pretty sure my mum does this for me and my brother). All I can say to you is that I know Noah, and he wouldn't have made this decision lightly. But he is also a very strong guy and I'm sure he'll be back before we know it.

I hope this answers your questions and that we can resume life here on *Girl Online* as normal.

And for those of you who might not have a clue what I'm talking about . . . I'm sorry, ha ha! Also, Noah, if you're reading this, text me back or I may have to send out a private investigator to track you down.

Girl Online, going offline xxx

Chapter One

The moment I finish the blog post, I hand over my laptop to Elliot. 'Do you think this is good enough?'

His eyes scan the screen and I worry at a hangnail on the edge of my pinkie finger.

'Looks fine to me,' he says after a few agonizing seconds.

His confirmation granted, I grab the laptop back and hit publish before I can change my mind. Immediately I feel a burden lift off my shoulders. It's done now. I can't take the words back. My 'statement' is officially out there, even though it's ridiculous that I even need to make a statement. Heat rises in my cheeks as I realize how angry this situation is making me . . .

Elliot coughs – loudly – interrupting my train of thought. His lips are bunched up into a corner, which makes my heart drop because I know he's worried about something. 'Have you really not heard from Noah since mid August?'

I shrug. 'Nope.'

'I can't believe him. Brooklyn Boy is letting us down.'

I shrug again. It's about the only gesture I can muster. If I think about it too hard, all the emotions I've been struggling to hide will come bubbling to the surface.

'All I have is this one text.' I take out my phone and pull up the message. 'See?'

> Sorry, Penny. It all got a bit too much.
> I'm quitting the tour and taking a break.
> I'll be in touch soon Nx

I don't know what Noah's definition of 'soon' is, but it's been well over a month now and I haven't heard a peep. I have sent numerous texts, DMs and emails, all with no response. I also didn't want to seem like some desperate ex-girlfriend trying to track him down, so that slowed to a stop recently, but it still sends a gut-wrenching flicker through my mind every time I think about the fact he hasn't responded.

'Well,' Elliot resumes, 'you've done the right thing by putting your story out there and getting people off your back. Who needs that kind of drama, right?'

'Exactly.' I shuffle down to the end of the bed and grab a hairbrush off my desk. My eyes wander around the selfies pinned to the mirror as I run the brush through the knot of newly sun-kissed auburn tangles; there are pictures of me with Leah Brown, Elliot and Alex, even one with Megan. Most of them are obscured, though, by cut-outs of my favourite photographs from magazines – inspiration for my portfolio – and my A-level revision schedule, carefully high-lighted and colour-coded so I know exactly what I need to do. Mum made a joke that I spend more time colour-coding than actually studying, but it helps me to feel in control of something. Everything else in my life seems just beyond my reach – Noah, my photography career, even my friends . . . Everyone is preparing for life beyond sixth form. Even though I've got a huge head start with my internship with François-Pierre Nouveau – one of the hottest photographers on earth – I feel like I'm standing still while everyone is running around me. Where do I go from here?

'Do you think he's found someone else?' Elliot peers at me over the rim of his glasses with an expression I know all too well: the 'this is never going to go down well with Penny' expression that he likes to surprise me with every now and then.

'Elliot!' I throw the brush at him, which he ducks easily. It hits the back wall and lands on a pile of laundry.

'What? He's single; you're single. It's time for you to get *out there*, Pen. There's more to life than just Brooklyn.' He gives me one of his exaggerated winks and I roll my eyes. If there's anything that makes me feel more agitated than Noah's silence, it's the thought of Noah with someone else.

Needing to change the subject, I ask Elliot, 'How's Alex anyway?'

Elliot raises his hands to the sky. 'Perfection, as always.'

I grin. 'You guys are too cute, if not slightly sickly.'

'Did I tell you he's moved on from the vintage shop? He's working in a restaurant now.' Elliot beams with pride. 'I can't wait until I'm finished with sixth form and we can move in together. I mean, I spend most of my life at his place anyway. When I'm not here, of course.'

He smiles, but it doesn't quite reach his eyes. I lean over and grab his hand. 'Your parents will come around . . .' For weeks now, it's been non-stop fighting in the Wentworth household. Sometimes we can hear them shouting through the thin walls of my attic bedroom; those nights are a little awkward.

Now it's his turn to shrug. 'In my opinion, they should just put themselves out of their misery. We'd all be happier if they'd just split up for good.'

'Penny!' My mum's voice echoes up the stairs to my bedroom.

I turn my phone over and check the time. 'Oh nuts. Come on, Elliot – we're going to be late! I can't miss my first lesson.' I scramble off the bed and start throwing books into my bag. I quickly check my face in the mirror, and it's only then that I realize I only brushed one side of my head before throwing the brush at Elliot. I grab a hairband from my desk and gather my hair – tangles and all – up into a rough top-knot. It will have to do.

Elliot's ability to turn a dark cloud into a ray of sunshine always amazes me, and when I turn round he's back to his bright and bubbly self. He hooks his arm through mine and then grins at me. 'Race you for a chocolate croissant?'

'You're on.'

We take the stairs two by two, laughing and bumping into each other as we go.

'What are you two nutters up to now?' Mum tuts as we jump down the bottom step before nabbing a warm chocolate croissant each out of her outstretched hands. 'Don't forget – home by seven for Tom's birthday.'

'No problem!' I say, already halfway out of the door, knowing full well I have chocolate in places a well-put-together sixteen-year-old shouldn't have. I would've never forgotten my big brother's birthday, but I know why Mum's reminded me. I've taken to hanging out with Elliot after school around Brighton, snapping photographs of him for my portfolio. He's like the perfect model for me: so super self-confident he's never afraid to stand in the middle of the street in a pose, even if there are people walking by. 'Maybe I should start a blog,' he said to me one day. 'Then I could show off all these photographs! Even the ones you don't like are amazing.'

'You should,' I replied. 'It would be great for your fashion work too.'

'I'll think about it' was his response, but he's never actually gone through with it. I suspect the thought of *having* a blog is more appealing to Elliot than the thought of all the work that goes into it. He's always rolling his eyes at me when he sees me on my laptop yet again, but he also knows that's what it takes to maintain it. And, since my long period of absence from it last year, I'm more determined than ever to make it a success.

Outside, there's a chill in the air that reminds me autumn is on the way, even though it's still only September. This time of year is my absolute favourite; the leaves start to turn golden and wither away after their summer of hard work, and the sun seems to shine a lot more clearly as the mist from the summer heat disappears. Everything just seems a little brighter and fresher – a clean slate for the new school year. A clean slate. That's exactly what I need.

I snuggle closer to Elliot and link my arm through his. 'We'll have to cut our modelling session short tonight,' I say. 'The only bad thing about Alex leaving the vintage store is that we can't borrow any more fun costumes!'

I think back to my favourite photograph of Elliot: he was wearing his normal clothes (skinny jeans, a burgundy T-shirt with a chunky-knit cardigan on top) along with a pirate hat with a huge feather sticking out, and he was balancing on one leg on an upside-down bucket we'd found on the rocky beach. He looked like a pirate king of Brighton. Albeit one with *really* good fashion sense.

'Back to your mum's wardrobe it is!' Elliot says with a dramatic sigh. I laugh. It's true: Mum does have a ton of weird and wonderful accessories from her drama days.

I leave him at the bus stop and he gives me two extravagant kisses on the cheek – something he picked up from Paris and then honed at his internship at *CHIC* magazine. 'See you later, *dahling*,' he says, then lowers his voice. 'And don't fret too much about Noah, promise?'

I blush. 'I promise.'

It's only a short walk to school from the bus stop, but I miss Elliot's company as soon as he's gone. His absence gives me an ache like I'm missing an arm or a leg. I'm missing an Elliot – and it hurts. I don't know what I'm going to do if he and Alex end up moving to London next year. The thought makes the chocolate croissant repeat on me and I swallow to keep it down.

My phone buzzes, and I immediately forget my promise and think that it might be Noah. But it's not him. It's Kira. 'Where are you?' the text reads. Then I look at the time. I only have five minutes until my first lesson – and I'm supposed to be doing a presentation in history class with Kira. Oops.

I pick up my pace into a run, race up the steps and through the double doors of my school. Just inside, two new Year Seven girls are bent over their phones, giggling at something on *Celeb Watch*. Immediately I feel my anxiety rising like a tide in my mind, in case it's me they're gossiping about – but this time it isn't. It turns out that Hayden of The Sketch has broken up with his girlfriend, Kendra. When one of the girls looks up at me, she frowns – but there's not a hint of recognition in her eyes. It's just because I look a bit like a weirdo staring at them. I hurry past, my heart beating quickly inside my chest. I don't even turn any heads any more.

I breathe a sigh of relief, letting the anxiety wash away. Noah and I are officially yesterday's news. I'm just a normal girl, living a normal life in a normal school. It's what I've wanted ever since the end of the tour.

Isn't it?

'Penny! GOODNESS ME, there you are.' Kira comes running up to me, snapping my train of thought before it can get too long. She launches into a run-through of our presentation, so I let her pull me through the school hallways and back into normality.

Chapter Two

'Hang on, just one more.'

'Penny, it's five to seven . . .'

'I know, but the light is perfect . . .' I take one last shot of Elliot, silhouetted against the darkening sky. This time we're not by the beach but in Blakers Park, situated in front of our houses and near a row of cute pastel homes. Living up on the hill means we always get a great view of the park, with the sea behind it, from our adjoining attic bedrooms. There is a clock tower in the park that Elliot and I have spent many sunny evenings sat underneath reading and taking photos. Elliot's making exaggerated shapes with his body, jumping up into stars and bending over into backward bridges. I'm on my tummy on the grass, shooting from a low angle. If you didn't know it was Elliot, you might not even recognize him in these photos. I manage to catch the setting sun beneath the arch of his back, rays of light blurring any detail – but it makes him look ethereal, like light is bursting out from inside him.

'OK, I'm done,' I say, putting the camera down. I sit up and check my phone – there are no worried texts from Mum, so I assume that Tom is probably late.

'Lemme see,' says Elliot, who drops out of his backbend and on to the grass. I lean over to show him. 'Oh, Penny, these are amazing! Your best yet. Those had better go in the gallery.'

'Oh, it's definitely going to be the centrepiece! I'm going to call it *Elliot and the Sunshine Bend*.'

'Maybe you need to work on your titles a bit, P.'

'Point taken.'

Elliot's fantasy for me is that I'm going to have a giant gallery opening one day – a solo show, not like the time my photographs were displayed with the rest of our school's photography GCSE class. His vision of my gallery is always somewhere grand – like London or New York, or even somewhere far-flung like Shanghai or Sydney. His grand dreams for me always make me grin, but also make my anxiety flutter. At the end of my amazing internship with François-Pierre Nouveau, he let me know that I might be able to hang a set of my photos in his gallery – *if* they ever met his high standards. I'd been sending some of the pictures I'd taken of Elliot to Melissa, F-P Nouveau's office manager, who I'd really connected with. She told me that – while they were good – something was missing. 'I just don't see any of *you* in these pictures,' Melissa had told me. 'You're almost there. Work on finding out what you're really passionate about, a subject you really love, and then you'll nail it. Your photographs need to have a voice. Something . . . uniquely *Penny*.'

I don't want to let her down, so my goal is to practise, practise, practise until I can find out exactly what is 'uniquely Penny'. Because my dreams for me are just as big as Elliot's. I want to take photographs for the rest of my life. I've never been more determined to make it happen than I am now.

Out of the corner of my eye, something catches my attention and I look up sharply. 'Noah?' I whisper, before I can stop myself.

'What? Where?' Elliot follows my eyeline, but there's no one there. Whoever it was has disappeared down the hill.

'I could've sworn . . .' But what did I see? A beanie hat, slung low over long dark hair. A familiar swing to his walk. It could have been anyone. 'Never mind,' I say quickly.

Elliot's not fooled. 'It's OK, Penny. I wish he were here too. But someone who *is* around is Tom. Let's get back, shall we?'

'Definitely.' I know I'm being silly – Noah is probably in New York, or maybe LA – anywhere other than in Brighton. I just wish I knew something about where he was or what he was doing. Then at least I wouldn't be driving myself crazy.

'Come on, slow poke!' Elliot shouts at me. I've fallen behind as we walk up the hill towards home. That's the problem with Brighton – it's almost *all* big hills, and our houses are halfway up one of the biggest ones.

'I hear Dad's cooking one of his famous lasagnas tonight!' I say as I catch up.

Elliot groans. 'Oh god, what's he going to put in it this time?'

'*No* idea. Remember that time he added pineapple to one of the layers to make it Hawaiian style?'

'I actually liked that one! I was more thinking about that time he heard that in Mexico they use chocolate in their sauces, so he melted a bar of Dairy Milk into the bolognese!'

'That was pretty gross,' I concede. 'Maybe I should tell him to stick to breakfasts.'

'Nah, you know I love your dad's experimenting, even if it doesn't always work out. I mean, who thought putting ready salted crisps on top of a lasagna would make it so delicious and crunchy? He should patent that recipe. Move over, Jamie Oliver!'

All the talk of food makes time seem to disappear, and before we know it we're back in front of my house. Elliot doesn't even look at his front door but follows me straight through mine. A rich smell of herbs and frying meat greets us as we step inside.

'Something smells amazing!' Elliot calls out from behind me.

Dad appears in the hallway, wearing a lopsided chef's hat. 'Tonight it's lasagna Greek style! Feta! Oregano! Lamb! Aubergine!'

'So it's moussaka?'

'Oh no.' Dad waggles a spatula at me. 'It's still going to be a lasagna. And wait until you see what it's got on top . . .'

'Please, please, please not olives!' I wrinkle my nose.

'Even better . . . anchovies!'

Both Elliot and I groan.

'Hello, happy people!'

'Tom!' I turn round and squeal as my brother pushes open the door, followed by his long-term girlfriend, Melanie. 'Happy birthday!'

'Thanks, Pen-Pen!' He throws his arm round me and ruffles my hair.

'Hey! Stop it,' I say, shaking him off. I skip past him to Melanie and give her a big hug. 'Hi, Mel, how are things?'

'Great, thanks, Penny. Can't wait to try what your dad's been cooking up.'

I laugh. 'Should be interesting, as always!'

The next few hours are a blur of food and laughs, wrapping me in a warm blanket as comforting as Mum's old woolly cardigan, which I take with me whenever I have to get on an aeroplane. The Greek lasagna turned out perfectly (even if I took off all the slimy little fish and passed them to Tom) and now everyone is relaxed round the table: Mum talking to Melanie about her next wedding (a *Cabaret*-themed affair in Soho), Tom and Elliot laughing at one of Dad's jokes.

An idea strikes me. I slip out of my seat and pad out into the hallway, grabbing my camera, which I'd left next to my backpack.

When I return, I turn the lens on my family – capturing their smiles and laughter. This is something 'uniquely Penny'. It's everyone I love, all in one room.

I look down at the photograph again. Well . . . *almost* everyone.

17 September

Seeing Ghosts

Thanks to everyone for their support on the last blog. Sorry I had to close comments – it was getting a bit out of hand. Maybe, though, we can get through this together? You guys always have the best advice.

For me, right now, the hardest thing to deal with is the ghosts. I don't mean actual ghosts (at least, I hope not) but the shadows – the imprints – of the missing person that are left all around in my everyday life, ready to spring out at me at any moment and stop my heart all over again.

Every time I walk round a corner there's another reminder of him. Even though I'm sure he must be far away from where I am, I keep thinking that I see him in a crowd of people just ahead of me. Once I even stalked some poor boy down the street, and when he turned round – of course it wasn't him. It was just someone else with dark hair.

Am I going crazy? You know that saying that goosebumps happen when someone walks over your grave? That's the same feeling I get – shivery, cold, a little bit scared – and it always makes me feel a bit pathetic. What can I do to drive the ghosts away and feel normal again?

Girl Online, going offline xxx

Chapter Three

After publishing the blog post two days ago, three main pieces of advice stood out from all the comments:

1. Surround yourself with friends and family – Done.
2. Distract yourself: get out and do more exciting things, until the memories of him start to fade away – That maybe I can do more of.
3. Move on – Yeah, that's Elliot's main advice too. And yet somehow I don't think it's going to happen.

So I decided to try method number two. And, in order to distract myself, I accept an invitation that's been sitting in my text messages for a couple of weeks now. Megan has been asking me to come up and visit her in London at the Madame Laplage School for the Arts, where she's in the sixth form. It's a really prestigious place and I'm super proud of her for getting in. It was such a big deal that she even featured in the local newspaper under the headline: SCHOOL-GIRL WINS PLACE AT ACADEMY FOR THE STARS. Loads of famous actors and actresses have graduated from there ('As Megan never fails to remind you,' says Elliot), but it's not just drama for which the school is famous. There's also musicians, dancers, artists – probably even a few photographers. She also has to live on campus, so in a way it's like she's already gone off to uni. Despite her crazy and sometimes arrogant ways, I do miss her.

'COME UP AND VISIT ME,' shouted one of her most recent texts. 'You'll love it.'

Elliot had rolled his eyes at that. 'She probably just wants someone to brag to about her "starring role" in *Les Mis* or whatever play they're doing.'

'*West Side Story*,' I corrected him. Megan had posted on Facebook earlier that day all about how she was going to play Maria in the school's first big show of the year at Halloween.

'Rehearsals are intense,' she wrote to me, 'but if you come up on a Saturday after eleven we all just chill out in the common room and I can introduce you to everyone.'

OK – I'll do it

Elliot tutted, but I could see even he was glad I was getting out and doing something different and a little more out of my comfort zone.

Now it's Saturday, and it's one of those bright, beautiful September days that makes London sparkle as if someone's given all the buildings a good wash. As I step off the train, I can't help but think about how far I've come in only the past few months. There's no way that I would've taken a train on my own into London before this summer, let alone a train and a tube journey, but I now have the little strategies in my back pocket that help me to keep my anxiety under control. Not completely – I know it will be something that stays with me in some way for the rest of my life, and it can rear its ugly head at any moment. But as long as I rule, challenge and accept my anxiety – and not the other way around – I know I'll be OK.

Madame Laplage School is on the banks of the River Thames, and Megan meets me at Embankment Tube station so that we can walk down together.

'Penny!' She waves at me from outside Starbucks, a coffee in her other hand. I never knew her to drink anything other than milkshakes or Coke, but then this is now 'grown-up' Megan. 'I hope you don't mind I got myself a drink,' she says. 'You don't like coffee, do you?'

I shake my head. 'I'm all good.'

'Great.' She loops her arm through mine and leads me across the bridge by the station. I can see St Paul's Cathedral as the river sneaks round the bend, and I stop to take a picture. Megan sidles into the frame and drapes herself across the railing.

'Wait, take a picture of me in front of the National Theatre,' she says, gesturing to the big concrete building that is near her school. 'Maybe one day when I have my lead role in a fabulous play at the National you can sell this picture for millions.' She cackles in a way that makes me reel with slight embarrassment and I snap the picture. 'Lemme see?'

I turn the camera round to show her the photograph in the little screen. She squeals. 'Oh my god, that is so great, Penny! Maybe you should do my headshots.'

I smile back, matching her wide grin, but something feels off. Even Megan isn't normally this bubbly and excited. I would put it down to too much coffee, but I don't think that explains it all.

'How's everything going at school?' I ask, once we've crossed the bridge.

'Oh, the school is just *amazing*. Did you know that a big Hollywood couple are going to send their kids here? It's all hush-hush according to *Celeb Watch*, but Madame Laplage is the *only* place for proper Shakespearean actor training. And the professors are just unbelievable. Did you know that they even have a monologue specialist? You should see the dancers too . . . I have never seen so many hot guys in one place.' She winks at me.

As she continues to walk and talk, I notice that she still hasn't answered my question. I know all about the school already. I just don't know how things are going for *her*.

*

Madame Laplage School is in a huge old Edwardian terraced building, the kind that was probably divided into several tall and skinny houses once upon a time. But a lot of the walls have been knocked through and are now painted with bold, bright murals by the art students. I look through the glass pane of one door and I can see the polished wood floor and mirrored walls of a dance studio.

Megan continues to talk a million words a minute as we climb a set of stairs. We stop on the third floor outside a door that says DRAMA COMMON ROOM on the outside.

'Now, don't freak out, Penny, but some of the girls in here know about you and Noah and they're all mega jealous, OK? Don't worry – I'll make sure they stay cool, but, like, don't make it a bigger deal than it needs to be.'

'Uh . . . I won't,' I say, frowning. 'Trust me, the last thing I want to talk about is Noah.'

'Good. All right . . .' She takes a deep breath, as if to ready herself. Then she opens the door.

The first thing the common room reminds me of is the green rooms I've been in backstage at concerts. There's certainly a lot more going on than in our sixth-form common room back at school. There's that same chilled-out vibe: guys lounging on worn-down sofas, girls slouched with their legs over the arms of their chairs. One of the guys even has a guitar, which he's tuning in the corner. And everyone is really attractive. I wonder if I've somehow stumbled on to the television set of *Glee*.

In fact, it's almost exactly how Megan has described it – I'll have to go back and tell Elliot that she wasn't bragging at all. It actually *is* as creative and crazy and free-spirited as she made out.

Megan waits until I've taken everything in, then she grabs my hand. We walk over to a group of girls who are sitting at a table reciting lines to each other. It takes a moment before they register that we've been standing there. I look questioningly at Megan, wondering why she isn't just saying hello, but she's focused on one of the girls.

'Oh, hi, Megan,' says a tall redhead, her hair gathered up in a high ponytail. She barely lifts her eyes in Megan's direction, and her lips are pursed together in a tight line.

'Hey, Salena,' says Megan. Her voice is so high it's almost a squeak. I've never seen her like this before. 'This is the friend I was telling you about. You know . . . Penny Porter.'

Salena turns her gaze on me and smiles. The smile transforms her face, making her seem bubbly and warm.

'Penny!' she says. She reaches round behind her and grabs the back of a chair, swinging it to a stop next to her. 'Do you want a seat?'

'Oh, uh . . .' I look at Megan, who pushes me straight down into the chair. 'I guess that's a yes, then!' I say with an awkward laugh. Megan darts across the room to the only other free chair and drags it over to the table.

Salena's gaze stays fixed on me. 'This is Lisa and Kayla. They're in Drama Year One, like me.'

'Like Megan!' I say brightly.

She nods. 'So first of all, I have to say, I *love* your blog.'

I blush, my cheeks heating up. I still can't get used to the thought of actual people reading my blog, even though the numbers on my page statistics show me it must be true. 'Thanks . . . I've been doing it a while now.'

'I know! I mean, you're just so authentic.'

Beside me, Megan is nodding enthusiastically to everything Salena is saying.

'And of course we're gutted about . . . you know,' says Kayla from across the table. Her eyes are huge and round, and her hair is cropped short.

'Thanks,' I say again, not sure what to add. 'Are you guys excited about *West Side Story*?' I ask, hoping to change the subject. 'Megan is such an amazing singer. Did she tell you about our school's production of *Romeo and Juliet*?'

Salena opens her mouth, but Megan stands up abruptly. 'Well, I'd better continue giving Penny the rest of the tour. See you girls later.'

I give them all a small wave. 'Nice to meet you. Bye.'

'Nice to meet you too, Penny. Feel free to come back here any time. I would love to pick your brains about my blog.'

'Oh, sure,' I reply. 'Ow.' Megan yanks my arm, pulling me up out of the chair so I bump my knee on the table. She drags me into the centre of the room. 'Hey, what's up?' I ask.

'I didn't want to talk to those girls any more; they were a bit boring. I told you they would be – always nattering on about Noah and the blog.'

'They weren't that bad . . .'

'Anyway, there's loads more people I want you to meet, and more of the school to see too. You *have* to see our main stage and the dressing rooms and my room.'

We're just about to leave when a hand taps me on the

shoulder, making me jump. I turn round to see a gorgeous guy staring at me. I immediately think he must want Megan, but when I step aside he reaches out and stops me with a touch.

'Excuse me, but . . . are you Penny Porter?'

Chapter Four

I blink at the six-foot vision standing in front of me, his sparkling, sea-foam almond eyes, his dirty blond, slightly wavy hair perfectly quiffed to the side. He beams at me with gleaming teeth, waiting for me to respond, but as his smile begins to slip I realize I've just been gawking at him. More specifically, at his loose-fitted tank top that shows *much* more pec than the average garment.

'Kneeshirt,' I blurt out, my brain not registering the question he's just asked me but coming out with some random mumble that I think was supposed to be *nice shirt*. My mind is screaming at me at this point. *Make words, Penny, HUMAN ADULT WORDS.* 'I mean, aren't you cold?'

'No, but you sound like my grandma.' He breaks into a soft laugh and holds out his hand to shake mine. He has this casual Scottish accent that sounds so dreamy I almost need shaking back into reality. 'Name's Callum. Nice to meet you. It is Penny . . . right?'

I take his hand in mine and notice how unbelievably soft it is, his nails perfectly manicured.

Finally, I manage a normal smile. 'Yes, Penny is right! Do I know you?' I frown, racking my brain trying to recall meeting him before now. I'm sure I would remember someone who looks like something angels carved out of the Scottish hills.

'We haven't met before, but I know you. Well . . . I know your photographs. You got my dream internship working with FPN and I *had* to look up your work to see who beat me to the post. I was impressed.'

I can't help blushing under his praise. He knows me from my photography? I didn't think that was possible.

'What brings you here anyway?' he continues. 'Are you studying? I don't think I've seen you in any of our seminars.'

Megan is getting irritated at this point and shuffling her feet; clearly a conversation between me and Callum isn't what she had scheduled in for her tour. 'No, Penny isn't studying here. I am, though. Megan, nice to meet you.' She jumps in between us and holds out her hand to shake Callum's, tossing her glossy brown hair. He takes it and smiles politely back at her. Before I get a chance to reply to Callum, Megan jumps in again. 'I'm actually just giving her a tour of the school. I'm hoping she will be visiting me lots while I study here. When I'm not too busy rehearsing, of course.'

'Of course!' I grin at Megan, but my eyes are drawn back to Callum's like they're magnets. 'You're studying photography here then, I take it?' I chip in, before Megan can say anything else.

'My second year – it's a cool place,' he replies. He sinks back so that he's leaning against one of the sofas. For a moment, the world seems to fade except for his aquamarine eyes. It's as if only Callum and I exist, locked in each other's gaze, everything else in slow motion. It must have only been a split second, because suddenly colour rushes back in as one of the music students starts strumming a tune I recognize – 'Elements', straight off Noah's last album.

That's when it hits me. For the whole time (OK, the whole one minute) I've been talking to this guy, I haven't thought about Noah at all. Everything feels electric – a feeling I thought I'd never get again, ever since Noah and I parted ways. I notice too that he has a camera slung over his shoulder on what looks like a customizable strap with stickers and scribbles in the leather. He smiles broadly as he spots me checking out his gear.

'It's a nice camera, right? It's vintage.' He swings it round his shoulder so I can get a better look. I ooh and aah approvingly.

'You must really know your stuff!' I say.

'I love photography, but, hey, only the best of us get to hang with François-Pierre Nouveau, right?' He jabs me lightly on my arm and I feel my face blush hot. He's laughing, and I nervously join in. Why is Callum McCutie making me feel like this? It's like I'm thirteen all over again. I mentally shake it off and try to be slightly cooler. I also feel Megan's big toe press down firmly on mine, and I know it's time to go.

'Anyway,' I say, 'nice to meet you. I'm sure I'll see you

around at some point. I'll tell François-Pierre you say hi.' I turn on my heel and start walking away, grabbing Megan as I go.

Callum laughs and salutes us as we walk away from him.

Is going slightly jelly after meeting Callum a normal reaction? Maybe it's a sign that deep down I'm starting to get over Noah? Maybe my heart is ready to be dusted off and get back out into the scary world of boys again?

There are a lot of *maybes*, but it's better than the *nevers* that were there before.

Megan leads me through corridor after corridor, where we pass singing, art and ballet classrooms. My jaw drops at just how much stuff they have access to. Practice rooms, musical instruments, studios, libraries. For all her bragging, Megan really has entered the big league now.

We cross the campus and she takes me inside her halls of residence. It's not quite what I expected: it's small and the ceilings are fairly low, making the light quite limited. Not good at all for photos. Megan is sharing her bathroom and kitchen space with two other girls. One, a dancer, is from Italy, and the other is from San Francisco, doing modern art.

She takes me through to her bedroom, which is in an even worse state than mine – clothes are tossed everywhere and theatre posters cover all the walls.

'Are your room-mates nice? Do you get on with them?' I sit down on the end of Megan's single bed, which is pressed up against her desk area. She pulls out her office chair and takes a seat next to me.

'Sure. I mean Mariella doesn't speak a lot of English so our conversations are a little more difficult. She studies interpretive dance though so I often just gesture what I'm trying to say by dancing, and I think that helps.'

Poor Mariella. I imagine Megan dancing in frustration, arms and legs akimbo while trying to offer Mariella a cup of tea, and I stifle a giggle.

Megan takes out her laptop and starts scrolling through her Facebook. 'I don't really see the other girl much. She's very indie, hangs out in Shoreditch a lot, and her friends all have beards and man buns. I'm just not sure I like the whole man-bun thing? What do they hide in there?'

'All their secrets?' I say peering over Megan's screen. She's hovering her mouse over her direct messages although there are no new chat notifications. Odd. Normally Megan is buzzing from every device she owns. She senses me peering and slams her laptop shut.

'You know what? Let's head back to the common room and grab some food and chill. There's not much to do here; it's too quiet.' She grabs her handbag and slings it over her shoulder then messes up her hair and applies more lipstick.

'OK,' I say. I'm surprised by the butterflies that flutter in my stomach at a single thought: *Maybe Callum will still be there.*

Back in the common room, it's a hive of activity – but no hunky Scottish guy. Beautiful young people swarm round the table-football table, weirdly good at such a niche hobby, and there are two groups harmonizing a cappella songs back and forth like a scene out of *Pitch Perfect*. To say I'm out of my comfort zone is no exaggeration and suddenly the sofa I'm sitting on feels like it's sucking me into its pillowy depths.

I wonder if it's too late to get out of there.

But then Callum walks back in, one of his friends in tow. His friend is also tall and attractive, with a head of thick, curly dark hair, but he doesn't have nearly the same magnetic pull for me that Callum does. I sit up a little straighter as he plonks himself down on the sofa next to me and his friend perches opposite, next to Megan.

'Didn't think I'd be seeing you again so soon.' He throws his bag off his shoulder and on to the coffee table in front of us, relaxing down into the seat. God, his accent is amazing. I want to pull out my phone and record it for Elliot, because I know he would go equally wild.

I grin. 'Megan thought we should make the most of the cafeteria before I head home. I'd heard the cheese and Marmite toasties here are unbeatable.' I hold up my sandwich, then realize that waving a half-eaten cheese toastie in front of someone's face is probably not normal behaviour. His mouth twists as he struggles not to burst out laughing and I try to diffuse the awkwardness by ramming the rest of the toastie in my mouth.

Unfortunately, all that does is give me giant chipmunk cheeks and I have to try to eat the toastie without opening my very full mouth, to avoid showing him a pile of chewed-up Marmite and cheese. Attractive.

I'm grateful to him for turning away for a moment, leaving me to recover my dignity. I chew as fast as I can, swallow down the rest of the sandwich, and manage to calm some of the red in my face by the time he's turned back to look at me. On his lap is his photography portfolio plus an A4 folder of black-and-white photos that look as though they've just been developed in a darkroom. I even think I can smell the chemicals on them from the developing.

The noise in the room gets a little louder as Callum lifts his eyes to meet mine. I take a deep breath. *Don't let anxiety ruin this. Please.*

'Oh, sorry, do you mind?' Callum asks, mistaking my rising anxiety for irritation. 'We have a big project due already and I want to get it perfect.'

'No, please, go ahead,' I say, glad for the distraction. At least it gets Callum's attention off me for a moment, and allows me to recentre myself.

I focus on the photographs he's laying out across his lap. They are portrait shots, so haunting they send a shiver down my spine. The detail in them is like nothing I've ever seen.

'What do you think?' he asks. 'I'm not sure it's *quite* right yet.'

'Some of these shots could give you nightmares!' I say with a laugh.

He blushes. 'I know, they're a bit gothic, but to be fair they *are* destined for a Halloween display. What lens do you use for portraits?' He smiles, and his teeth are so straight and white they almost blind me. He has a little freckle on his top lip next to his cupid's bow and I melt a little more. It takes all I have not to scream out: Who *is* this guy and where has he come from? He *can't* be human! HE *CAN'T* BE!

Focus, Penny. Photography. I can do this. 'I use a prime lens for portraits. I find that the detail it gives is amazing, but not as harsh as a macro lens, especially if you're shooting analogue. Do you shoot with film or digital?'

'I shoot in both; I think you can get great shots with both mediums.' His tongue sticks out of the side of his mouth as he works his way round the page, glue in one hand, photos in the other. 'It really depends what angle you want to go for, I guess. Some of my favourite photos have been taken with a seven-quid point-and-shoot that I developed in Boots. I'm all about capturing the moment.'

'Oh, I totally agree.' I nod enthusiastically, then suddenly a pang of guilt hits my stomach. We've just been geeking out about photography, and I've been ignoring Megan completely. She'll hate that. I look up and, with a sigh of relief, notice Megan deep in conversation with Callum's friend about a house party in building 4B. Megan's mum would be a frantic mess if she knew Megan was planning to join house parties with hot seventeen-year-old guys, but it doesn't surprise me at all.

Guilt appeased, I let myself relax back into the conversation with Callum. 'How would you describe this photo?' he asks, as he hands me a black-and-white image of an elderly lady holding her hand to her face. You can see the intricate detail of eight gold rings stacked on her fingers. Her eyes look sad, but her mouth is tilted upwards at the edges. Half her face is in darkness, and the other is burned with light.

'I think . . . she's saying, "I've lived a long life and I don't regret a single second of it."' I look at the haunting image then back up at Callum. Our eyes meet and the lines round his eyes are back as his smile creeps across his face.

'Ladies and gentlemen, can we have some applause for the cheesiest line ever?' He laughs and claps his hands.

'Hey, you asked!' I shrug my shoulders and return his smile.

'And that deep and meaningful analysis, my dear, is why I'm studying here and you aren't.' He winks at me in a playful manner and my mouth drops open in mock outrage.

'I might not write great captions, but talent can't be taught,' I shoot back, and I'm surprised by the words coming out of my mouth. I'm not normally this 'on fire' when it comes to banter. Who is this new Penny?

'Touché, Penny Porter,' he concedes. He shifts slightly and his leg falls against mine. We might have jeans on, but the small contact sends a current of electricity rushing through my body. I don't know if he senses it too, but pink spots rise in his cheeks even as he continues to look down at his photography. Maybe it's not just me . . .

Then a swell of anxiety follows the current like a tsunami. I can't even catch my breath, it comes over me so quickly. Everything that was fun and exciting turns terrifying. I can hear every slam of the ball from the table football. The a cappella singing is high and screechy in my ears. The air has become thick and warm, like breathing in honey.

My panicked eyes search for an exit route – and when I see a door I grab my bag and run. I don't think about Callum, his friend or Megan. I just run down the corridor, twisting round corners, through fire escape doors, until I'm outside and filling my lungs with fresh air.

After a couple of seconds Megan is by my side, her arm round my back. She's seen this before, and for all her faults I'm grateful she never makes a big deal about this. She's just there for me.

33

When my breathing has calmed down to normal levels, she ventures a question. 'What happened? Did Callum say something?' Her forehead scrunches into a frown.

'No, not at all. I think . . . I don't know. I suppose everything just got a bit much. I'll be fine.' I force a smile on to my face, and Megan squeezes my hand.

'It's OK, you know, to like someone else,' she says quietly.

My heart skips a beat as Megan manages to put into words the source of my anxiety. Because, deep down inside, another voice is telling me *I'm not so sure*.

Chapter Five

Megan leans against the side of the building, tapping away at her phone, while I perch on a wall and focus on my breathing. When I feel a measure of calm, I lift my eyes to watch people going about their day. *What are you up to?* I think, following the crowds. I pick out certain individuals. *Where are you going with that giant backpack – are you travelling the world? That couple holding hands – are they on a first date? Their third?*

Turning my focus outwards, concentrating on what might be happening in the lives of other people, is something my therapist told me to do when managing my anxiety. I only started seeing a therapist after coming back from the tour, and she has already helped my confidence massively. She's helped me learn that, while anxiety is part of my life, it doesn't have to define it. Little tricks, like people-watching, stop me focusing too much on my spiralling thoughts and the physical symptoms that dominate my body whenever I start to panic. Already I can feel my heart rate slowing down and the clamminess on my palms evaporating.

I look over my shoulder. 'Megan, I think I'll be OK now. If you don't mind, I just want a few minutes by myself to completely clear my head before going back inside.' I can tell I've caught her by surprise: she's smirking at a viral video of a puppy slipping on ice that she's had on a loop, but she turns off her phone and nods.

'Of course, Penny. I'll be in the common room. Think you can find your way back?'

'Yeah,' I reply.

'Cool. See you in a bit.' She walks back inside, leaving me sitting on the wall.

I continue to scan the scene in front of me, and my eye is caught by a young girl sitting on the bench opposite me, ending a call in a fury and wiping a tear away. I wonder who she's just argued with. A parent? A friend? Her partner? It's little things like this that remind me that absolutely everyone has their 'stuff' – stuff they struggle with or have to deal with on a regular basis.

To my alarm, the girl's single tear turns into uncontrolled sobbing into her hands. There's a battered rucksack between her black pumps on the grass by her bench and her glossy black hair is up in two neat buns, one on each side of her head. Suddenly she lifts her head and makes eye contact with me. I almost fall off the wall. Now she knows I'm just sitting watching her.

An awkward lump rises in my throat. She averts her eyes again and wipes her tears away, obviously aware I'm still watching her. I spot a Madame Laplage patch on her ruck-sack and realize she must be a student here. I slide off the wall. I can't just ignore her now that she knows I've been watching. There is a small possibility she'll tell me to clear off and yell at me for being so nosy, but it's a risk I'm willing to take. If she needs someone to talk to, sometimes a sympathetic stranger is as good as anyone.

She looks up when she hears the gravel crunching beneath my Converse. Despite the fact that her face is splotched red from crying, I'm struck by how pretty she is. Her delicate almond-shaped eyes are a beautiful dark brown and a small smile creeps over her face, displaying a dimple on one of her cheeks.

I take the smile as a promising indication that she doesn't mind me approaching. 'Sorry for intruding, but are you OK?' I slide on to the bench next to her. She's trembling slightly, reminding me of a delicate butterfly. She might fly away at any moment.

'I'm so embarrassed!' she says. She wipes her nose with the crumpled tissue in her hand. 'I hate crying in public. And I *especially* hate crying at school. I'm sure everyone's going to know now.'

'Do you want to go for a walk? Get away from here for a bit?' I say, and she nods.

We walk in silence away from the school, back towards the South Bank. There's always something soothing about water, I find. I prefer the sight of the sea off Brighton beach, but even the River Thames will do. The girl sniffs loudly. 'I . . . I don't recognize you from any of my classes, but please don't tell anyone at school about this.'

'Oh, I'm not at Madame Laplage,' I say.

'You're not?'

'No – I'm just here visiting a friend. Look, I'm Penny. I'm sorry for watching you, but you seem really upset. Have you had an argument with someone?'

She looks up at me, her eyes searching mine. I must pass her test because she nods again, slowly. 'I'm Posey,' she replies. 'Posey Chang. And yeah, an argument . . . You could say that! My mum is my best friend, but she doesn't half pile the pressure on. She just doesn't understand. I was trying to explain to her that I didn't want to play a certain role in the show because I can't bear the thought of being centre stage.' She blows her nose loudly and drops the tissue in a bin. When she speaks again, her voice is so quiet that I have to strain to hear her over the sound of the birds squawking and tourists chattering behind us. 'I know it's supposed to be an honour to receive such a big part. I'm studying theatre and music here after all, and it's something I've always loved to do, but I find it so difficult in front of an audience, and nobody really understands! Mum told me I was being ridiculous and that I needed to pull myself together and there was absolutely no way I was going to swap my role. I hate it because she's right. If I don't do this . . . I might not get my scholarship renewed. Then all the hard work to get in here will be wasted anyway.' She sniffs again and a single tear escapes down her cheek.

'What role do you have? My friend Megan is in the production too; it's *West Side Story*, isn't it?'

'Yeah, that's right! I'm playing Maria, the LEAD ROLE.'

A small tremble shakes her shoulders. 'Everyone *had* to audition and I hoped to get a small part, because it really helps your grades, but I certainly didn't think I'd get a lead. Now I'm desperate to switch it for a less daunting part.' She nervously bites down on her already non-existent nails.

'You must be really good to get the lead,' I say, trying to hide my confusion – her version doesn't fit with what I know from Megan, but I don't want to contradict her while she's so upset. 'And yet I also understand totally about being afraid.' (The closest I've come to stage fright was the time my knickers were exposed to the whole school, but I know it's not the same thing. That was about being frightened on a stage. Frightened of the gasps, the horror and the embarrassment of remembering I was wearing my oldest pair of frayed knickers.) Posey's stage fright sounds like it runs a lot deeper. To know that you have a duty to perform but to be terrified of the very platform you're supposed to love. 'The whole reason I came outside,' I tell her, 'is because I suffer from really bad panic attacks and anxiety.'

'Really? What helps you?' she asks, her big brown eyes open wide.

'Well, when I get anxious when I'm travelling, I wear my mum's old cardigan – it's like a security blanket. I guess you can't really take a security blanket on stage with you!'

To my relief she giggles. 'No, that probably wouldn't work – unless we switched plays to *Les Misérables* and I could pretend it was my rags.'

To my surprise, she closes her eyes and starts singing the opening lines to 'On My Own' from *Les Misérables*, her haunting voice drifting out across the water. She hits each note perfectly, but there's a delicate tremor in her voice that delivers the emotion of the song straight to my heart. I feel tears spring up in my eyes.

Her delivery builds and builds until she hits the crescendo, barely pausing for breath. I can hardly breathe myself, shocked that such a powerful voice can come from such a tiny body. When she finishes, the final note lingering in the air, I burst into applause. But I'm not the only one – behind us a small crowd has gathered and they clap wildly.

Posey spins round, her face beetroot red, but she gives a little curtsey and a small smile to the crowd. Gradually, they disperse and then we are alone again.

'Posey, that was amazing! I know you're not happy about it, but . . . I can see why they cast you as the lead.'

Her small smile droops. 'Thanks, Penny. I used to *love* singing to people – when it was just me, on my own, with a microphone and maybe a piano. That way, if I messed up, it was only me who suffered. But if I screw up in this show, it's not just about me. There are all the music students in the orchestra pit, the dance students in the chorus, the technical arts students doing the lighting and the sound work – not to mention all the other actors on stage. I'd be messing up for everyone. That's why I can't do it. So it's back to Manchester for me.'

'I know what you mean,' I say. 'I think that's why I like photography. Just me and the camera.'

She looks up and smiles at me. 'Thanks for understanding – it's been good to talk to someone who doesn't just think I should get over myself and do the role. You said you were just visiting someone. Is it someone in drama?'

I nod. 'Yeah . . . her name is Megan.'

'Megan Barker?'

I nod again.

Posey bites her bottom lip. 'I don't really know her that well, but she had a good audition. Did you know her from home?'

'Yeah, I'm from Brighton.'

Posey's eyes light up. 'Ooh, I've heard a lot about Brighton and I've always wanted to go there but never had the opportunity.'

'It's pretty far from Manchester,' I say with a laugh.

'True!' Posey looks down at her watch. 'I . . . I'd better be getting back. I should probably call my mum again. She's hard on me, but she'll be worried too.' She picks up her rucksack and turns away.

'Hang on, wait a second. Can we swap emails? Then if you ever need to talk to anyone again . . .'

She nods and takes her phone out of her pocket. 'That'd be great.' I type my email and number into her phone so she can WhatsApp me.

'Any time, OK?' I tell her.

Posey leaps forward and wraps me in a hug. I squeeze back, then together we walk back to Madame Laplage.

★ ⋆ Chapter Six ⋆ ★

When I head back to the common room, Megan is waiting for me just outside the door. She's looking down at her phone but her eyes are lit up like stars. If she's noticed that I've been gone for a while, she doesn't show it.

'Everything OK?' I ask, as I approach.

'Are you kidding me? Never better. That hot guy Luke asked for my number *and* he's just invited me to his flat party next weekend!' She turns her phone round to show me a Snap of Luke – topless – with his address and a time written across it.

'Wow,' I say, not entirely sure what my reaction should be.

'Right? He's so fit. All the girls in my class are going to be *so* jealous. Megan Barker's going to be back on top!' She links her arm through mine and lays her head on my shoulder as we walk back up towards her room. 'Penny, this has been the best day. Thank you.'

'Uh . . . you're welcome? Not sure what I did!'

She dances her fingers up my arm. 'I'm not the only one who got a bit lucky.'

'What do you mean?'

'Callum asked me for your number too! I hope you don't mind that I gave it to him.'

'What? Megan!'

She throws back her head and cackles, a wicked glint back in her eye. Now this is more like the Megan I know. 'Hey, he likes you and you obviously don't mind spending time with him. I heard you two yammering on about photography – lens this and angles that. What's the harm? If he calls you and asks you out, you can always say no.'

I bite my lip, but eventually I shrug. 'I suppose so.'

'Of course! But I wouldn't say no if I were you. I hear that Callum McCrae is not only a fox but a *super-rich* fox. His family own some giant estate up in Scotland. He's probably a *laird* or something.'

I grimace. 'Yeah right. And even if that is true, that's even more reason *not* to go out with him. He's probably really arrogant.'

'And betrothed to a countess,' says Megan, fluttering her hand in front of her like an old-fashioned fan. 'Ooh, maybe he knows the Royals? Sorry, Penny. He probably won't call. You're not quite on his *level.*' She pokes at me with her finger, but I feel the dig even deeper.

When we get back to her room, Megan bounces on her bed, still staring at the Snap of Luke. I perch on her office chair, staring around her room. I can't help but think about Posey. Not only about her beautiful haunting voice, but also about the role that she has in the show.

'Megan, can I ask you something?'

'Of course!' She sighs dreamily.

'Why has today been a good day? I mean, apart from being asked out by super-hunk Luke?'

She rolls over on to her stomach to face me, her legs kicking up behind her. She leans her chin in her hands and studies my face. 'I don't know. I guess . . . having you here has helped a lot. I haven't found it that easy.'

'What do you mean?' I ask gently. Megan is normally so hard to open up – she dances round issues as nimbly as a ballerina.

'Oh, you know, the girls here are such cows . . .'

'Megan . . .'

She swallows, then flips on to her back. Her toes creep up the wall, but her eyes flutter closed. 'I haven't really made any friends here. Not like back home, where I had tons of friends. And everyone's so freaking talented. Sometimes . . . sometimes I think I'm the least talented person here.'

I take a deep breath. 'Even though you've got this big role in *West Side Story*?'

She shakes her head. 'I don't really have a big role.' The words come out as barely a whisper, and I leave the chair to sit up on the bed next to her. 'I'm just in the singing chorus.'

'Why did you lie? You don't have anything to prove to us, you know. You're already at this hugely prestigious school. Everyone thinks you're amazing.'

44

'I know. I just didn't want people back home to see me as this big failure when I already felt like one.' Her eyes open and meet mine. 'Plus, I am the understudy for the big role – for Maria. The girl who got it is such a wuss anyway – she's bound to pull out – so I didn't think there was any harm in a little white lie.'

'A wuss?' I ask. The Posey I met didn't seem like a coward, just a bit lost.

'She's got severe stage fright or something – and she's here on a scholarship, so Madame Laplage will probably make her go home if she pulls out. But if you can't handle the pressure here then how can you possibly hope to survive in the outside world? That's *acting*, right?'

'But this is still school . . . Shouldn't someone be helping her through it?'

Megan frowns. 'Do you want me to get the part or not?'

'I don't think it's fair for someone to be punished for their anxieties.'

At that, Megan softens. 'I didn't mean it like that. Sorry, Penny.'

'So Madame Laplage is a real person?' I continue. 'Not just a name?'

'Oh, she's real all right. And she's *terrifying*. We don't see her around that much, but if you do, it either means someone's in big trouble or someone's about to be a big star. She's like *the* scout for young talent across a lot of industries.'

'Wow! Have you ever seen her?'

Megan shakes her head. 'First-year students almost never do. Besides, it's not just about who gets what role in the shows or plays. You remember those girls you met earlier?

They've all got these big blogs that everyone at school reads and they're so creative. So I started a blog too but almost no one reads mine. I don't know what I'm doing wrong.'

'Why don't you show me?' I ask. Megan's words about Posey were hardly nice, but I know she's going through a tough time.

'OK.' She turns on her computer and loads her blog. Just as I expected from Megan, it's really nicely designed and even the photos and fashions she's chosen to focus on are well put together.

'This looks really good!' I tell her honestly.

'Thanks . . . but hardly anyone visits.'

'Do you visit their blogs?'

'Yeah . . .'

'And do you leave any comments or anything?'

Her mouth drops open. 'Of course not! I don't want them to know I've been creeping on their blogs when they don't even bother to visit mine.'

'See, Megan? That's your whole problem right there. Maybe if you opened up a little, and let everyone see that you cared about them as much as you wish they cared about you, they might let you in. Blogging is all about community, and it seems to me like this whole school is like a little community too. You have to look out for each other. And you have to sometimes make the first move. If you like something they've blogged about, *tell them*. They might then come to yours to see what you've shared. Give and take, you know?'

'I bet you never comment on other people's blogs, now that you're big shot Girl Online.'

Now, it's my turn to look shocked. 'Are you kidding? Commenting on my friend's blogs is one of my favourite things! If nothing else, it shows that I appreciate how much time and effort they put into their posts – because I've taken the time to respond.'

'Hmm, I guess that makes sense,' Megan says.

'Try it. I bet you'll see more traffic on your blog. *And* maybe you'll make some friends in the process too.'

Megan smiles. 'Thanks for coming up here, Penny. I really mean it.'

'Any time.'

22 September

How to Get Your Blog Noticed

It's always a little disheartening when you've spent many hours slaving away over your laptop, trying to perfect a blog post, only to have no comments in response. We've all been there: nobody starts a blog with an audience ready and waiting, and actually it's all part of the fun. My friend recently decided to start her own blog and asked me for a few pointers, so I thought I'd sit down and write up a little list of the advice I gave her, in the hope it will help one of you reading this.

So, if you're looking for that little bit of guidance or reassurance, here's what I think:

1. Open up a discussion. End your blog with a question that ties in with what you've written and will encourage people reading to leave a response.

2. Get involved. Start up Twitter and get involved in blogging discussions using certain hashtags. Promote your blog to other bloggers and make

friends. You'll find that a lot of you will have something in common, so you will always have something to talk about.

3. Comment on other blogs that you love. Other people leaving comments will see yours and know you have a blog too. Plus, much like the point above, it's nice to get involved.

4. Promote your blog on social media. Use Instagram and link a photo back to your blog. There is a lot of traffic on Instagram, and if you use hashtags that people can search, there's a good chance they'll find your blog. Pinterest is also a great one!

5. Be natural. Don't spam people or tweet links 24/7. Nobody likes a try-hard – and it can be a little off-putting. Instead, you want to do what feels natural to you. Have fun and don't focus on the numbers! These things take time, but with a little bit of patience and some social media sharing, you'll have readers in no time!

Hope these few tips help you in some way. Numbers are numbers at the end of the day, and as long as you're enjoying writing for *you*, that's really all that matters. Even if my follower count dropped to five readers overnight, I'd still carry on writing here because I absolutely love it. It's my little escape and it makes me so happy! That's what's most important.

Have you started a blog recently? Are you going to take any of my tips on board? (See what I did there? See point 1 – ha ha!)

Girl Online, going offline xxx

Chapter Seven

The next morning, making our way to the Tube station, it's as if our entire conversation didn't happen. Megan is back to her normal self, flipping her hair and chatting away about her upcoming date with Luke. It's only when we come to a halt that she brings it up again.

'Please don't tell anyone at home that I've been . . . you know . . . struggling here. Don't want to ruin my reputation!'

'I won't, but – Megan – you don't have anything to be ashamed of. You're doing great. And you'll make so many more friends if you just be yourself.' I pause, then add, 'The nicest version of yourself.'

If Megan takes any offence at my little addition, she doesn't mention it. 'And you too. If Callum asks you on a date, you should go.'

'I'll think about it.'

'It's better than just worrying about the ghost of Noah Flynn jumping out at you all the time.' She wiggles her fingers mysteriously. Then she winks. 'I read *Girl Online* too, you know. And I'm going to follow all your blog tips.'

When we hug, I feel her squeeze my shoulders tightly. It's about as much affection as I've ever had from Megan, and I know it must mean she really misses me. 'I'll miss you too,' I say.

'I'll see you in November for the show, right?' she adds.

'Of course – I wouldn't miss it for the world.'

'And if you think of any more ways to make me Miss Popular again, let me know! Go on, you're going to miss your train.'

I look down at the time on my phone. Megan's right. After one more quick hug, I dash through the Oyster card barriers and throw myself on to the Tube before the doors can slam shut.

Once I've got myself settled on to my train back to Brighton, the south London suburbs whizzing past, I think about Megan and Posey – two totally different girls with similar dreams. One has all the confidence in the world, but needs to focus on her technical ability. The other has all the talent and technique, but none of the confidence.

Since going on the world tour with Noah, I've seen a lot of stars performing on stage – The Sketch, Leah Brown, and, of course, Noah himself. They all have different styles, but one thing they all have in common is that special magic – that charisma – that draws our eyes towards them and holds them there. Star power? X factor . . .?

Whatever it's called, I've seen it through my camera lens too. And it's nothing to do with just being famous: Elliot has it in spades, but neither Megan nor Posey is quite there yet.

My phone buzzes, letting me know I have a new email. To my surprise, it's from Posey. I open it.

Dear Penny,

I wanted to write to you to say thank you so much for being there yesterday. Sometimes I feel so alone in this place – but you've made me feel so much better. You understand that my stage fright isn't just something I can sweep under the rug and pretend isn't there. You're the first person who hasn't told me to 'just get on with it' and that means a lot.

I know we probably won't get a chance to meet again as I'll be going home, but I wanted to thank you anyway.

Posey xx

Reading her email makes me even more determined to help. The only person I know who's spent any time on a theatre stage is Mum. I remember Mum telling me that she suffered from stage fright (during what she refers to as her 'lost years' in Paris) and I'm sure she knows a few strategies to deal with it. It seems like the other students at Madame Laplage can be pretty ruthless when it comes to fears and anxieties. At least I know that Mum will give a sympathetic ear.

I hit reply and type up a quick email back to Posey.

Posey! So great to hear from you.

Are you free next weekend? My mum was an actress back in the 80s in Paris. Why don't you take the train to Brighton and you can meet her? Plus, it would be great to hang out. I can show you the sights, like the Pier, and we can go shopping in the Lanes.

Penny x

Now I can only wait and hope that she's able to come. I know that Mum would be able to help her, if only to reassure her that she's not alone.

That email sent, I lean my head against the train window. The London streets have disappeared, replaced by the rolling green hills of the English countryside. For once it's not even raining.

My mind drifts back to my own recent panic attack – and Callum, the common room and Megan's new way of life. Was it the attention I was receiving from Callum that made me feel so unsettled? I think it was the fact I felt OK with the attention from Callum. It felt new and exciting. I may have even been a bit flirty, and maybe it all got a bit too much to handle. Could this mean there is actually life beyond Noah? That is, if Callum isn't completely put off by the fact I've run home with no explanation?

He still asked for your number, a little voice reminds me.

I jump as my phone buzzes with a text. Could it be . . . but no, it's not Callum, it's Mum.

Are you on your way home yet? Big surprise waiting for you when you get back!! Xx

A big surprise . . . could that mean Noah?

I cringe as my treacherous heart leaps from one boy to the next.

Instead, I take out my camera and spend the rest of the journey flipping through the photos I've taken. There's more to life than just boys – and this camera is going to get me through.

Chapter Eight

As I walk up to our front door, I do a double take. Sitting in our front bay window is a small doll staring out on to the street as if she's waiting for someone to return home. She has wild strands of fiery red hair and her clothes have changed since I last saw her; now she's wearing a pink tutu and a bright yellow jumper – a far cry from the antique, Edwardian-style dress she'd worn when I first took her home. Still, the tutu and jumper are more appealing to her current five-year-old owner.

But if Princess Autumn is here . . .

I frown. *That can only mean . . .*

The door swings open and another familiar figure appears at the top of the stone steps. 'Penny!' she squeals with delight.

'Bella!'

Noah's pint-sized sister careers down the steps towards me, jumping into my arms. She wraps her legs round my waist and I hug her tight. 'It's so good to see you! But wow, how much you've grown in only a few months!'

'I've missed you, Princess Penny!'

'And I've missed you.' I kiss the top of her head as I place her back down on the floor.

She grabs my hand and begins to tug me towards the house. 'Hurry! Your daddy is making me pancakes with smiley faces!'

'Ooh, that's his speciality!' I say, unable to hide the huge grin on my face, even though my mind is *very* confused. I follow her up the steps and into the house.

Standing in the door to our living room is the elegant silhouette of Sadie Lee, Noah's grandmother. As she hears me approach, she turns round and beams with her warm smile. 'Penny! It's so good to see you, honey. You're looking well.' She embraces me with two kisses on the cheek. Her previously long grey hair has been cut into a chic bob. With her high cheekbones and sparkling eyes, she's the most sophisticated grandmother I've ever met.

'It's so good to see you too! Wow! Is . . .' The next words get stuck in my throat. *Is Noah here?* is what I want to ask, but I don't want to seem ungrateful about seeing her and Bella.

'Unfortunately, no,' says Sadie Lee, guessing my question and tilting her head in apology.

'Oh,' I say. I can't help the disappointment that settles on my shoulders.

'I take it you haven't heard from him either?'

I shake my head.

She sighs. 'That boy . . . He'll get in touch when he's ready.'

When I realize she means that they haven't heard from him either, fear grips my heart. 'Is he OK?' I ask.

She nods. 'He left a message with his new management giving an emergency contact number if anything really terrible happens, along with a request to respect his wish for a creative break. Noah's always been a free spirit, able to sort things out on his own, and he needs his privacy. I know him too well – if we go hunting for him, or keep checking up on him with messages and emails, he'll run further from the situation, whatever situation that may be. Giving him space is exactly what he needs, so we need to give it to him. Still . . . I'm glad that *we* get to see each other.'

'Me too.'

Mum waltzes in from the kitchen with an 'Oh good, you're back! Surprise, Penny darling!'

'It's the best surprise ever!'

Then Mum turns to Sadie Lee. 'Have you had a chance to tell her yet?'

'Tell me what?' I ask, instantly intrigued.

Sadie Lee laughs. 'Not yet! But there's no time like the present. Our visit isn't just a vacation to see you and your family, nice though that is. Your mom and I have decided to do another event together.'

'Oh really?' I clap my hands together in delight. 'Is it down here in Brighton?'

Mum shakes her head. 'Not this time. It's even better. Remember that wedding up in Scotland?'

'The one over half-term?' I ask. It's the biggest budget event that Mum has been asked to do so far this year – almost as big as the last-minute New York wedding at Christmas where I first met Noah. Because it's over half-term, Elliot, Alex and I are here to join in as helping hands. It's going to be my first time in Scotland, and already Elliot is picking out the perfect outfits for us to wear at the evening ball – with a touch of tartan, natch.

'Exactly. Sadie Lee has agreed to do the catering, so she and Bella are going to join us!'

My eyes dart from Mum to Sadie Lee. 'That's amazing news!' I say. Sadie Lee is a world-class caterer, who's made her name particularly with her incredible pastries. (But even her grilled-cheese sandwiches are the best – there's nothing she can't make super tasty.) Combined with Mum's awesome party-planning skills, the two of them together are a force to be reckoned with.

'But, we have a *lot* to prepare, so I'm going to be sweeping Sadie Lee off to the shop straight after breakfast. Can you look after Bella this afternoon?'

'Yay! Yay! Yay!' Bella jumps up and down, tugging on my dungarees in time to each word.

'Of course!' I say with a big smile. 'We'll have a great time, won't we, Bells?'

Dad's voice interrupts before Bella can answer. 'Who's ready for pancakes?'

'Me!' she squeals and rushes off towards the kitchen. It's only when Bella's left the room that it really hits me. They're actually *here*! My heart feels so full, it's about to explode. As if breaking up with Noah wasn't bad enough, it also hurt not to see his family either. I'd grown to love them too. Bella and Noah have the same warm, deep brown eyes, and having Bella here is a huge reminder that Noah isn't. Even though it makes my heart ache a little, I'm glad they still feel comfortable enough to remain friends with us.

Thinking of friends makes my mind jump suddenly to my bestie.

'Mum, do you mind if I go see Elliot? He'll have been cooped up with his parents while I've been away because Alex is out of town . . .' *And I have to fill him in on my crazy Saturday.* He will absolutely fall to pieces when he finds out about Callum. I hope he will be proud of me for taking a step in the direction away from Brooklyn Boy.

'Have you eaten already?'

'Yup! I had a sandwich on the train.'

'Then sure! Just be back before eleven. Your dad can look after Bella until then.'

I give her a kiss on the cheek and then hug Sadie Lee tightly. I head back out of the front door and jump across the steps to the front of Elliot's house.

'. . . *Maybe* if you listened a bit more!'

'*Me?* Listen? *You* don't even let me get a word in EDGEWAYS!'

My finger hovers over the bell as the angry words drift through the door towards me. I cringe. Elliot's mum and dad are fighting again. I take a step back and look up at the highest window to see if I can signal to Elliot somehow, without interrupting his parents.

It turns out I don't have to. The door swings open and a red-faced Elliot barrels out, almost knocking me back. 'Elliot!' I cry. His head shoots up, then – when he sees it's me – he throws his arms round me.

'Get me out of here?' he whispers in my ear.

I grab his hand and together we hurry down the steps. I know exactly where to go.

Chapter Nine

Inside Starbucks, hands wrapped round a pumpkin spice latte, Elliot is a torrent of emotion. Tears flood his cheeks and the poor barista who serves us gives him a free extra shot of syrup to help cheer him up.

'I just can't take it any more, Pen. They've been fighting from Friday night, all yesterday and they've started up again this morning. And do you know what they started fighting about?'

I don't even want to ask, but he goes ahead and tells me anyway.

'The colour of Dad's tie. Apparently he went to work wearing one tie and came back wearing another. Mum wanted to know why. Dad gave some lame excuse about spilling soup down it at lunch or something.'

'Well . . . that could've happened.'

'It *could* have. But it doesn't matter because Mum doesn't believe him. So they just shout and shout until I make the mistake of coming downstairs to make myself avocado on toast before I starve to death. Mum corners me and asks me what *I* think.' He takes an extra-large gulp of his coffee.

'Oh man, what did you say?' I ask.

'I didn't have to say anything! Dad screamed something about "Why ask *him* for relationship advice when his relationship is not welcome in this house?" and then Mum screamed at him not to be so homophobic, then she switched tactics and asked me what colour his tie was on Friday morning and I said I didn't know because I was at Alex's. Then Mum burst into tears and said I cared more about Alex than about them and I wasn't allowed to spend any more nights there. At which point, I stormed out and – here we are.'

'Oh, Elliot. I'm so sorry.'

'It's just so frustrating. It went from, like, my parents being the ultimate stoic, silent, bottle-your-feelings-up-until-you-explode couple to them constantly letting rip in these epic fighting matches. It's like twenty years of pent-up anger blowing its top. I can't handle it. The tension in the air is so thick, I feel like I need to shower every time I walk inside.' He shivers. 'Alex is my only escape so there's *no way* I'm giving up nights there – even if I can't go back home ever again.'

'You don't mean that,' I say.

His blue eyes glisten with tears behind his bottle-green glasses. 'Maybe not. Maybe I do. My Great Escape Card is getting topped up every time Mum feels guilty and gives me money for fighting all the time. You don't understand what it's like there any more. It's hell on earth.'

I know it must be serious if he's talking about his Great Escape Card. Elliot's always full of wild plans, often starting with 'Let's run away to . . .' and ending with some glamorous place like 'Paris!' or 'LA!' or once even 'the circus!' ('but not any old circus – it'd have to be Cirque du Soleil'). Even me pointing out that I couldn't do so much as a cartwheel didn't deter him. At some point he realized he'd need money if he was ever going to make any of those plans a reality, hence the card – a debit card for his 'just in case' savings. Something I've always been wildly jealous of, but never quite been sensible enough with my own money to create. I reach out and grab his hand, squeezing it tightly. He squeezes back, giving me a small smile.

'So, distract me,' he says. 'Tell me about your day with Mega-Nasty.'

'Aw, she's not that bad, Wiki. Her school is really cool. I've honestly never seen anything like it . . . it's like something out of a TV show. Still . . .' Elliot leans forward, sensing the juicy gossip. I don't want to break my promise to Megan and tell him how bad she's found it, but I also need Elliot's advice on Posey. I take a deep breath and continue. 'I had a little panic attack and had to go outside, where I met this girl who's also in Megan's class. She's this *amazing* singer, but she has really terrible stage fright and she's just been cast in the lead role of *West Side Story*.'

'Wait, but I thought Megan had the lead role?'

I shake my head. 'She's the understudy.'

'What? So she's lying on Facebook?'

'Well . . . if this girl can't perform, then Megan does get

63

the lead role. So now I feel torn – I really want to help this girl, but if Megan finds out, she's going to kill me.'

'Well, well, well,' says Elliot, rocking back in his chair. 'The Mega-star is a Mega-fake.'

'Elliot . . .'

He laughs. 'Don't worry, I won't say anything.'

'There is something else too, that might change your mind about her. It's something you guys actually agree on.'

'I doubt it, but do tell.'

'Well, in the common room there was this guy and she gave him my number.'

Now Elliot leans forward again, his palms flat on the table. 'STOP! I need details. How tall? Eye colour? Hot? Name? Occupation? Spill *everything*, Penny Porter.'

I laugh. 'His name's Callum and he's Scottish.'

'I love him already,' says Elliot, faking a swoon.

'He's a photography student at Madame Laplage and he's super tall with these amazing green eyes and short, wavy blond hair . . . I guess he's a little bit gorgeous!'

'A smoking-hot photography geek? Are you sure you didn't just dream this guy up?'

I feel a blush rising in my cheeks as I talk about Callum. 'No, but it was weird meeting someone I had so much in common with. At least, on the surface anyway.'

'That's why you *have* to go on a date with him, Penny. To find out if there's anything more than skin deep!' He winks. 'And I take it he has a hot Scottish b*rrrrr*ogue?'

'A what-now?'

'An accent. *Och aye the noo, lassie*, "Auld Lang Syne" and all that?'

I grimace at his terrible Scottish impersonation. 'Not like *that*, but yes, sometimes I had to listen a few times before I understood what he was saying! It sounds like he's speaking another language sometimes, but I like it.'

'Oh, it's so romantic!'

'Don't jump the gun – he hasn't actually called or messaged me yet.'

'He will.'

'How do you know?'

'I just have this gut feeling. Aw, Pen, I'm super happy for you.'

I nod. 'Don't talk about it once we get back to my house, though.'

'Why not? I bet your mum and dad would be happy too that you've met someone else and won't be moping around any more.'

'OK, one – this is hardly a relationship – he just asked for my number! And two – Sadie Lee and Bella are at my house.'

'What? Why? Is –'

'He's not back,' I say quickly. 'Sadie Lee's going to be doing the catering for the Scottish wedding in a couple of weeks.'

'And are you happy with that?' he asks, immediately able to read me like an open book.

'Of course I am! I love Sadie Lee and Bella!'

'But . . .'

I sigh. 'But . . . it just makes me think of him even more. And worry about him. And wonder what he's up to . . .'

'I know. But now you have Project Callum and Project Drama Student to keep you focused.'

'I can only hope. When is Alex back?'

'Should be later this morning, thank goodness!'

'Want to invite him over? You guys can help me babysit Bella.'

'Sounds good. Although we'll probably hear my parents' screaming match through your walls. Might have to blare out that cheesy nineties album you keep next to your bed.'

'Hey, nobody can resist a bit of Spice Girls on a dreary autumn evening. Don't worry, I have an idea for something we can do later that'll get us out of the house again.'

Elliot nods, but suddenly he looks so miserable again. I bite my bottom lip. 'Oh, Elliot, what are you going to do?'

He shrugs. 'It's not up to me. It's up to them. I'm just on a countdown until I can get out of there for real.'

We end up back at the house just before eleven, where we're in time for Elliot to have his own reunion with Sadie Lee.

'Oh, honey, we'll have to have a proper catch-up soon – you need to tell me all about your internship. Maybe one day you can come out to New York? You'll always have a room at my house.'

Elliot's eyes sparkle – but this time with tears of joy rather than sorrow. 'Really? New York is, like, the DREAM. I'll be like Heidi Klum on *Project Runway* – *auf wiedersehen*!'

'Perfect! Now, we've got to fly. Ready, Rob? OK, Dahlia?'

she asks my mum and dad. 'It's down to business for Dahlia and me, but we'll have lots of time very soon.' Mum and Sadie Lee leave in a whirlwind of kisses and hugs, Dad lugging his golf clubs in tow for his weekend game.

When everyone has gone, I lean down on my knees. 'So, Bella, do you want to see where dragons live in Brighton?'

Chapter Ten

'I can't believe I've lived in Brighton all my life and never been here!' exclaims Elliot, his neck tilted up to the ceiling.

We've come to the Brighton Pavilion, a beautiful – but strange – former royal residence in the heart of Brighton and one of the most interesting buildings in the entire city. I remember visiting with my parents when I was a child, so I thought it would be the perfect place to take Bella, but I'd forgotten *just* how awe-inspiring it was. I used to call it the Mr Whippy palace, because its white domes reminded me of ice cream.

It's so strange how you can become oblivious to the amazing places that exist in your own backyard. Brighton has always been my home and there is so much about it that I take for granted. I make a silent vow to appreciate my home town more often.

'Did you know this used to be a military hospital in the First World War for Indian soldiers?' says Elliot.

Alex throws his arm round Elliot's neck and kisses him on the cheek. 'My little nerd! Such a know-it-all,' he announces.

'Yeah, but you love it,' Elliot throws back.

'You know it's true, though,' Alex says with a wink.

I grin at the two of them. 'At least *someone* now appreciates all of Elliot's knowledge.'

'*And* did you know that Queen Victoria sold this place to the town for the measly sum of about fifty thousand pounds because she didn't like Brighton? I don't know what her problem was . . .'

Elliot and Alex walk on ahead, hand in hand, following the chain of velvet ropes that line the visitors' route through the Pavilion. I'm so glad Elliot decided to forgive Alex for being indecisive last year – and that Alex chose to step up to the plate. With all the turmoil and upheaval that is going on in Elliot's life right now, he needs Alex's constant, reassuring love. All of the tension that had been gathering in Elliot's shoulders disappeared the moment we saw Alex. Even I don't have that effect on him any more. If there's ever a couple that is in it for the long haul, it's Alexiot.

We move through the different rooms and into the kitchen, where huge great copper pots hang on the wall. I can't help but think of all the wonders Sadie Lee could pull off in a kitchen like this.

Then, as we step into the Banqueting Hall, I can only dream of the events Sadie Lee and Mum could host here together if they ever got the opportunity. Maybe I should suggest it to them . . .

'Penny, look!' Bella grabs the edge of my cardigan and

tugs. I follow the line of her chubby finger, which is pointing up at a stunning gold chandelier with a serpentine Chinese dragon twisting round the chain.

I grin widely. 'See, I told you there were dragons in Brighton!'

'Wow . . .' she whispers, and steps closer to my leg.

I give her a tight squeeze. 'Don't worry, they're only for decoration.' I'm itching to take photos, but I'm not allowed to in here. My camera stays buried in the bag at my side.

Alex is staring at the beautifully laid-out banquet table, where not a single fork is out of place. 'This guy – who was he again?'

'Prince George, before he became George IV,' replies Elliot, fount of all knowledge.

'He had interesting taste, that's for sure,' Alex finishes.

'I think he's my hero,' Elliot says, almost breathless with awe. 'It's so over-the-top . . . If I could, I'd move in here tomorrow.'

By the time we finish touring the Pavilion, we end up in the Tearoom. Bella is exhausted from the tour and her jet lag, and after she finishes her carton of apple juice she crawls up on to my lap for a nap. Elliot, Alex and I have all ordered tea, and we giggle as we take sips.

Elliot leans forward over his chai tea. 'I think we're the only people under twenty in this whole room.'

I quickly glance around me, and he's not wrong: most of the people sitting in here are much older. Still, the Tearoom serves amazing scones, so we aren't going to complain.

'Want to check out a film tonight?' Alex asks us.

'I'd love that!' I say. 'But I'll have to check with Mum first if Sadie Lee is staying for dinner.'

Elliot grins. 'Oh, a film sounds great. There's this new subtitled film from Sweden –'

'No!' say both Alex and I in unison. Elliot pouts, but he's not going to win this one.

'I want to see the new Avengers movie,' says Alex.

'Veto!' says Elliot. 'No way am I watching another over-CGI-ed, eardrum-exploding Hollywood comic book spin-off.'

Movies might be the *only* thing that Elliot and Alex disagree on, even if they both love watching them.

I hold up my hands between them, before it turns into a full-blown world cinema versus commercial film debate. 'How about *I* check what's on before we start World War Three?' I say.

Moving slowly so that I don't disturb Bella, I fish my phone out of my bag. Habit means that rather than open my browser I click straight away on the email icon, which is showing two new messages.

My hand flies to my mouth. 'Yay!' I cry out, when I read the first message.

'What is it?' Elliot leans towards me and Alex raises an eyebrow.

'Posey's going to come down next weekend! She can make it after all!'

'That's great! That means Project Drama Student is on!'

I nudge Elliot in the shoulder. 'She's not a project; she's a new friend. And I bet you'll really like her. She'll kick your butt at SingStar and everything.'

Elliot looks affronted. '*Nobody* kicks my butt at SingStar!'

Alex laughs. 'That's because we're not brave enough to listen to you!' He turns to me. 'Tell me – who's Posey?'

I fill Alex in on my trip to see Megan and on Posey's stage fright.

'Wow, which one is Megan again?' asks Alex.

'The one who's always using Penny for her friendship,' snaps Elliot.

I grimace. 'She's not that bad . . . you just have to get past the front she puts on. Deep down, she's a really nice person.'

'For sure . . . Grand Canyon deep,' mumbles Elliot.

If I didn't have a sleeping five-year-old on my lap, I would kick him under the table.

'*Actually*, did you know that the Colca Canyon in Peru is more than twice as deep as the Grand Canyon?' says Alex, a teasing gleam in his eye.

'Well, see?' says Elliot, laughing. 'I wouldn't say she's as bad as that! But *now* who's the know-it-all!'

As they talk, I type a rapid reply to Posey.

That's the best news!

I'll wait for you in the station at 11 on Saturday. I'll be standing next to the free piano. (But definitely not playing! No skills there I'm afraid.) x

Now that there's a plan in place to see Posey, I feel much happier. There's just a tiny niggle at the back of my brain, which is me wondering whether I should tell Megan. But Megan doesn't police who I'm friends with. 'Shall we go?' I say. 'Oh, I forgot to look up movie times!'

'Don't worry, we did it,' says Alex with a grin. 'And we've decided on the newest Disney film. Are you in?'

'Yes! I'll check with Mum.'

On my lap, Bella wriggles awake and yawns widely.

'Are you ready to go home?' I ask, brushing a few loose strands of hair from her face. She smiles and a dimple appears in her upturned cheek. Suddenly I'm struck by just how much she looks like Noah. But it's time to stop seeing his ghost everywhere, and time to step out into the light. I have friends who love me, and new friends who I'm growing to love.

And *that* takes precedence over a guy any day.

Chapter Eleven

The next day at school, I wash the last of the chemicals off my black-and-white prints and hang them up to dry on the line in my school's darkroom. I'd taken shots of Bella playing with Princess Autumn, but they just haven't turned out the way I wanted them to and I thank my subconscious brain for making me take some on my DSLR too. Normally, the darkroom is one of my happy places (even if it does leave me with brown fingernails when I forget to wear gloves). But today it's just not working for me.

Ever since I saw all the work Callum put into his portfolio I know I need to up my game. I can't help the niggling feeling I'm just not putting enough time and effort into my craft – not if I really want to make it as a professional. I've had a few lucky breaks, but I don't want to get by on luck alone. Plus, the words 'uniquely Penny' keep ringing in my brain. These shots don't even come close. I have half an urge to just turn on my iPhone and use the light to ruin them all.

Unfortunately, I need to share the darkroom with my class-mates, so I just grit my teeth and leave the prints to dry.

Miss Mills is sitting in the classroom outside and she looks up as I slam the door to the darkroom, my frustration getting the better of me. Her eyes open a little wider. 'Everything OK, Penny?'

'Oh, sorry, miss – yeah, I'm OK.' She waits a few moments until I cave in. 'It's just I can't seem to get things right with the film camera lately. Everything I try is just . . . off. I don't know what to do or how to change it. I don't want to rely only on digital shots and Photoshop for this project.'

She gestures to the chair opposite her for me to sit down and I sink into it, dropping my bag at my feet. 'You have been putting an awful lot of pressure on yourself, Penny. You're doing fantastically well in your coursework and you need to keep things in perspective. Not every photo you take is going to be album-cover worthy,' she says with a wink.

'I know that, I do . . .'

'But?'

I grin. Miss Mills knows me so well. She's been a rock for me since the events of last Christmas turned my life upside down, and she supported me all through the craziness of the tour with Noah – even though it was the summer holidays. She's also one of the few people who read *Girl Online* when it was private. I trust her implicitly. 'But I want to get better. I want to have a *style* that's mine. I want someone to look at one of my photos and say, "Oh! That's Penny Porter!"'

She leans forward across the table, resting her chin in her hands. 'A style is something you develop over time, and you often have to try lots of different things until you find some-thing that's yours. I think what you need is a change of scene. Many of your pictures are of places round here in Brighton, but some of your best work has been when you've pushed out of your comfort zone a little.'

'Hmm, that's true, I guess.' My mind starts to whirl, think-ing of where I could go to take different photos, then: 'Oh! I'm going to Scotland for half-term. Maybe I can take pic-tures there.'

'That's great! But remember to look *beyond* the ordinary. You're good at that, but I think that's why you're feeling a little lost right now – you've only been looking at what's right in front of you. You just need to refocus and open your eyes again.' She sits back in her chair. 'I'm not worried, Penny. You always find your way.'

'Thanks, miss. Are you doing anything nice for half-term?'

'I wish! It's all marking, marking, marking for me . . . Good thing I love what I do.'

'Aw . . . well, I hope you get a bit of a break.'

'Me too, Penny!'

I grab my bag off the floor and head out of the door. As I walk towards my locker, I can see Kira and Amara waiting for me.

'Hey, guys!' I wave and run up to them.

'Penny! How was Megan's fancy-pants new school?' Kira's eyes sparkle.

'Honestly, it was like something out of *Glee*! It's very cool. It suits her a lot.'

'That's good. Maybe we should go visit her too,' Amara suggests, perking up.

'When? I have so much studying to do!' Kira moans. She is definitely the most worried out of all of us about her marks. I put my hand on her arm and give her a quick squeeze.

My phone buzzes and I fish it out of my bag. I bite my bottom lip as I open the text message –

I can't believe it's actually happened.

'Penny? What is it?'

I look up at Kira. 'What do you mean?'

'You've gone as red as a tomato!'

'Well, when I was at Megan's, I met this guy . . .'

Amara and Kira let out a synchronized squeal that I'm sure only twins can pull off.

'What? Spill!' says Kira.

'His name is Callum, and he's a photography student at the Madame Laplage school.'

'Is he cute?' Amara asks.

'*So* cute,' I reply, and now I can really feel the blush building. 'And Megan gave him my number.'

'And he texted?' asks Kira. 'That's awesome! Are you going to meet up with him?'

'What about Noah?' Amara asks.

Kira punches her sister in the upper arm. 'What did you bring him up for? Penny doesn't need to be thinking about that right now.'

'I know, but I *love* Pennoah. I always thought you two would get over this and be together forever,' Amara says with an apologetic shrug.

'Pennoah? When did we ever get called that?' I ask, completely baffled. I mock-retch at how sickeningly sweet it is.

Amara laughs. 'Oh, it's just something we saw online one time and thought it was so funny we had to adopt it.'

'Thank *god* that didn't catch on!' I say, wincing. 'And it's OK. Noah and I will always be friends . . . if I ever hear from him again, that is. And Callum was really nice, but I don't really know him yet.'

'Ignore my stupid sister,' says Kira. 'This is a really good thing. You have to go for it, and then make sure you come back and tell us all about it.'

'OK, OK. Let me reply.'

I read his message one more time.

> Hey Penny, this is Callum – we met at MLP? I'd love to meet up again sometime to chat more photography stuff. When are you free?

I take a deep breath, then type back a quick reply.

> Hi! Nice to hear from you. I'm not free this weekend, but maybe the weekend after?

I hit send, and I'm surprised myself at how little I care about the wording of my text – especially compared to how much I agonized over my first message to Noah. I hope this is part of growing up and not because I don't seem to be having those same spiralling, fizzy feelings I did when I was texting Noah.

My phone buzzes again. Kira raises a threaded eyebrow. 'Wow, he must be really keen if he's replying straight away! James takes ages to reply.' James is a rugby-playing pretty boy from another school and Kira's current love interest.

'That's good. It means he's not playing some weird guy game,' says Amara. 'What does he say?'

I read the text out loud:

> Sounds good! Gives me time to plan something a little more exciting. I'll send you another text when I figure out where to meet x

Kira clutches her hands together. 'Oh my god. He's going full-on date-mode. I wonder where he'll take you.'

'I have *no* idea,' I say. *But wherever it is, it won't be as good as my first date with Noah,* I think. Then I curse my treacherous mind.

My phone buzzes once more.

> Bring your camera. I want to see the great Penny Porter in action x

Reading his final message releases a tiny flutter of butterflies in my stomach. He's not Noah, but maybe this will turn out to be something, after all.

★ ★ Chapter Twelve ★

I spot Posey's bright green beret coming down the platform and I wave wildly. I've felt a surge of nervousness leading all the way up to this weekend, wondering if maybe she was going to bail on me. It's a pretty big deal to come all the way down on your own to meet someone you've only met once. I give myself a shake. It will be fine. We've exchanged about a hundred messages on WhatsApp, chatting like we've known each other our whole lives.

I'm standing just where I told her I'd be – by the piano in the middle of the station, which is there so that anyone who wants to can play for free. When she passes through the ticket barrier and walks over to meet me she's smiling shyly. She stops a few feet away.

'Hey, Penny,' she says.

'Hi! Was your journey OK?'

'Not too bad.' Her eyes flit around the station, taking in the flower stall and numerous pasty stands and coffee shops. She seems to want to look anywhere but at me. She must be feeling as nervous as I've been feeling, but I'm determined not to make it awkward.

'Anywhere you want to go first?' I offer. 'The Pier? The Lanes?'

She gives me a small shrug.

I keep talking as we start to walk down the street leading away from the station. 'Well, of course you wouldn't know where – you've never been here before!' When she doesn't reply, I wish I'd invited Elliot along. He knows how to break anyone's barriers down.

'Is that the sea?' she asks, her eyes widening. We've come to the top of Queen's Road, a long hill that leads all the way down to Brighton beach. I'm glad that it's a sunny September day, because Brighton is showing itself at its best. It's hard not to be enchanted by the city when it's sparkling in the sunshine.

'Yeah. Want to go down there first?'

She nods, biting her lip. 'I love the ocean.'

'Me too!' I link my arm through hers, and the mood lifts. From then on our conversation flows easily, like the awkwardness was a dam we managed to break through.

'I heard from Callum,' I say. 'He asked me out.' I'd filled Posey in on all the Callum-and-Noah drama.

'Are you happy about that?' she asks.

'To be honest, I don't know . . . It still feels strange.'

'I think that's normal. He seems like a nice guy – you should give him a chance at least. What's the worst that can happen?'

It's refreshing to talk to someone who doesn't just know

me as Noah's girlfriend. She doesn't make me feel like I'm betraying him by considering going out with another person.

We breathe in the salty air down by the seafront, and Posey squeals at the sight of the pebbly beach. 'Is it comfortable?' she asks. 'I always see these photos of people cramming on to the beach in the summertime, but I didn't realize there were so many stones!'

'You get used to it,' I say. 'It's like the Brighton hot stone massage – trying to find the right position to sunbathe!'

On the Pier, we get a tall, fluffy stick of candyfloss and laugh as the colour turns our tongues blue. We get a few tokens and ride the bumper cars, and I remember how much fun it is just hanging out with a girlfriend.

Once we've worn out the fun on the Pier, we stop at my favourite ice-cream shop – Boho Gelato – where we both get cones of the best flavour: carrot cake. It's so soft and buttery, it's like a piece of cake melting in my mouth.

We make our way over to the Pavilion Gardens with our ice creams, and laugh until our sides hurt at the pigeons mating and squirrels stealing food from the school party of German kids trying to eat their lunch.

We then wander up through the Lanes, and I point out the antique jewellers, ogling at the 1930s Art Deco rings and the pearls and diamond necklaces from the 1950s. We pick out our engagement rings (even though we're years away from that) and when we get bored we go to the candy store and both get jelly rings to wear.

'My mum's shop is just round the corner,' I say. 'She's

dying to meet you. I apologize in advance if she's a bit . . .
full-on.'

Posey laughs. 'I get full-on mothers, trust me!'

When we reach To Have and to Hold, Posey gasps at the
window display. This week, the theme is Harvest Bounty,
and everything is shades of bronze, red and gold, just like
autumn leaves. The dress in the window is made of crimson
silk, and has long sleeves that fall to a point, like something
Maid Marian would have worn in the Middle Ages. At her
feet is a basket with dozens of apples tumbling from it, and
a reed-woven cornucopia full of autumnal delights: conkers
shiny and brown, oak leaves already crisp and orange, and all
sorts of pumpkins and gourds.

'This is your mum's shop? It looks amazing!'

'Why thank you! You must be Posey!' says Mum, who just
then opens the door to see a client out and welcome us in.
'See you later, Chantal!' she waves to the woman leaving.
'Come on in, girls,' she adds, returning her attention to us.

I always love coming to Mum's store. It's a cornucopia in
itself, stuffed to the brim with goodies and shiny things.
Posey and I walk around first, Mum pointing out to us some
of the store's interesting props and telling us the stories
behind them. 'Ah,' she says, coming across a huge headdress
adorned with black and red feathers. 'I wore this when I was
in Paris. Whenever anyone wants a Moulin Rouge theme,
this is what I pull out . . .'

'Penny tells me you used to act in Paris in the eighties?
What was that like?' asks Posey.

'Ah, Montmartre . . . those were the days,' she says

dreamily. 'It was a different Paris then, and I felt so bohemian. We didn't call ourselves actors; we were troubadours, and we were as comfortable performing in the street as we were on stage.'

'Sounds like a dream,' Posey says.

'Posey's a music and drama student at Madame Laplage, just like Megan,' I say. 'She's the lead in their production of *West Side Story*.'

Mum clasps her hands together. 'That's wonderful! Tell me all about the production. Are you performing the classic version of the show?'

'It's the classic version, but it's abridged – unfortunately.'

Mum's hand flies to her forehead in a dramatic swoon. 'Abridged! A writer's worst nightmare!'

'I know,' says Posey ruefully. 'But it's still a good show. Or, it will be, once Megan takes the lead.'

'I'm sorry?' Mum asks.

Posey turns her eyes to the ground and I put my hand on her shoulder. 'Posey has really bad stage fright,' I say, 'and I thought maybe it would help if you could talk to her?'

'Oh my, yes. I used to get so nervous that I would throw up before a performance. I can show you some breathing tricks if you want. Eventually I gave up performing,' says Mum a little wistfully. I can see it's not helping Posey, though, so I give her a pleading look. She nods. 'But, honey, *lots* of actors suffer from it, and they keep on performing! In France it's called *avoir le trac*. I remember one of my best friends from that time, Éloïse, she used to have *le trac* until she learnt to picture the audience naked . . .'

Posey shudders. 'Somehow, I don't think I want to be picturing all the kids in our class naked. That just seems wrong.'

'Hmm, yes . . . that probably wouldn't be the right way forward. Tell you what, I really should get in touch with Éloïse again. Maybe I'll write to her and see if she has any tips for you?'

'Thank you, Mrs Porter,' Posey says politely. I can tell that any hope she might have had of my mum being able to help has disappeared. Posey needs to speak to someone who's overcome it and kept going.

'Yeah, thanks, Mum. I'm going to take Posey back home now. See you for dinner?'

'Sounds good,' Mum says with a smile. 'I hope you like spaghetti bolognese?'

'I love it,' says Posey.

We take one last trip through the Lanes before hopping on a bus back to my house. 'I'm sorry that talking to my mum wasn't that helpful,' I say.

Posey smiles. 'This is something I've been dealing with for so long now that I don't expect an easy fix. Don't worry, Penny, I didn't come down here only because of that. I'm having a lot of fun.'

'Me too,' I say, matching her grin. But I'm determined not to give up. 'I do have another idea, though. I have this blog online that I've had for a while. Whenever I have a problem, I always post on there and I always get really good advice back. Do you mind if I ask my readers for help?'

She shrugs. 'That might work. But, honestly, there probably isn't a "cure" or "method" that I haven't already googled.'

'I know, but it might be worth a try, right?'

'Sounds good. What's your blog?'

'It's called *Girl Online*. It used to be anonymous, but then when all the stuff with Noah happened it kind of gave away who I am. Still, I'm glad. Some of the people I know through my blog have become some of my best friends – even though we haven't met!'

'Oh, you're so brave having a blog. Lots of people at school have them too, but I just can't get my head round it. I just don't think I'm the writing type.'

'No, you're more the singing type!' I say with a laugh, and we jump off the bus, walk to my house and head upstairs.

'Wow, your room is awesome!' Posey gasps, as she takes in my cosy space in the attic.

'Thanks! I love it. It's sort of like a Tardis.'

'What do you mean?'

'Well, there's all these nooks and crannies and hidden spaces behind the panelling, and my best friend lives in the room that's just the other side of this wall. So, even though it feels small, there's more space here than you think.'

'You're so lucky. I had to share a room with my sister until I got in to Madame Laplage. I really don't want to leave there,' she says quietly.

I'm about to say something further, when Posey squeals. 'Oh my god! Have you met Leah Brown?'

She's staring at my mirror, where I have Leah's album cover with my photo on it. She's signed it too.

To Penny, who saw the real me. Big love, Leah.

'Yeah,' I say with a sheepish grin. 'That photo is one I took of her in Rome.'

'You're kidding! Isn't this her new album? *You took this?*' Posey says breathlessly. 'Wow, you're so lucky. She's, like, one of my idols.'

'She's pretty great,' I say with a laugh. 'And yes, weirdly that somehow happened!'

The rest of the evening passes in a whirl of laughter and stories. Mum grills Posey about the current theatre scene and regales us with stories from her Paris days. I learn more about eighteen-year-old Mum in one evening than I've known my whole life – and I'm not sure I was quite prepared for it.

After we drop Posey back off at the station and wave goodbye, we all wish she could have stayed longer. I turn to Mum. 'Do you think she's going to be OK?'

'I genuinely don't know,' says Mum with a sigh. 'I've known a few actresses who let stage fright ruin their careers. Éloïse managed to overcome it, but I don't know how. It has to come from deep down inside, I think. There's no easy fix.'

When I'm back in my room, I type up my post to *Girl Online*.

26 September

Girl Online Asks For Help: Stage Fright?

You know when people say 'I'm asking for a friend', but really they mean themselves? This isn't one of those occasions for once. I really, genuinely am asking for a friend. A new friend actually, who has brought a lot of positivity to my week. Don't you just love it when you meet someone and you instantly click? I love spending those first few weeks messaging back and forth, learning the ins and outs of someone and building a friendship that you know is going to be so solid. It's like your lives just piece together and you wonder how you lived before without them in it. Like they've always been a member of your girl gang but you didn't know it yet. That's the feeling I've been having when I met Musical Genius.

Now here's the thing about MG. She's landed a lead role in her school production (claps all round) but she suffers from stage fright. Although I have anxiety, stage fright isn't something I can fully relate to. Unless of course you count the last time I was on stage and managed to flash my frayed knickers at the entire audience – let's be honest, that's enough to leave *anyone* frightened. I want to give her the advice she needs in order to feel a little better about it, but I'm struggling. I don't know what it must be like to love doing something so much but feel like, no matter how hard you try, you can't give it your all. She describes it to me like she's standing on the stage, looking out into the audience ready to sing, but her tongue has disappeared from inside her mouth. Then the panic rises as she realizes nothing is coming out and suddenly she's frozen to the spot and the audience are a pack of lions, baring their sharp teeth in slow motion.

I'd love to know if any of you suffer from stage fright and, if you do or if you've overcome it, please leave me any tips that I can pass on to my friend. I also think it would really help other readers too. I can't let MG pass up on something I know is a huge dream of hers just because her mind won't cooperate at that very moment she needs it to most.

Girl Online, going offline xxx

Almost instantly, I get a direct message on Twitter from Pegasus Girl.

Hey Penny! I just read your latest post in my BlogLovin' feed . . . Have you spoken to Leah Brown about how she overcame her stage fright? xx

I raise my eyebrows in surprise. Leah?

No? I didn't even know she had stage fright!

Oh yeah! I read about it in an interview with her in *Teen Vogue*. She didn't go into a lot of detail, but you could tell just from the short snippet that it was a big deal for her.

I think of how Posey's face lit up when she saw Leah Brown's album cover in my room and found out I knew her. And if she – only *the* biggest female pop star of the moment – once struggled with stage fright too, then maybe there *is* something I can do to help.

My fingers itching with excitement, I open a new window to compose an email. I write to Leah.

From: Penny Porter
To: Leah Brown

Leah!!

Hope you're well. I saw your pics on Instagram of your Australia holiday – it looked amazing. Jealous much?!

Things are pretty same old, same old (still no news from Noah – don't suppose you've heard anything?) but I do have a favour to ask . . . I've met a friend here who's studying to do musical theatre. She has an *amazing* voice but also suffers from terrible stage fright. I heard you went through something similar . . .
Is there any way you can give me some tips to pass on?

Love and huge hugs,

Pen xxx

Chapter Thirteen

When I wake up in the morning, I roll over on to my tummy and grab my phone from where it's been charging on my bedside table. It looks like it's been busy overnight. There's a message from Megan that just says 'Call me', a ton of notifications letting me know there are comments on *Girl Online*, and also an email reply from Leah. She's several hours behind in Los Angeles, so she must've had time to reply overnight. I open that first.

From: Leah Brown
To: Penny Porter

Hey!! So great to hear from you! No news from N I'm afraid ☺

Actually, I can do you one better than just tips. I'm gonna be in London on Saturday, recording with one of my favorite producers. Why don't you and your friend drop by? I'd love to see you and help if I can.

L xxx

It's even better than I could've hoped. I roll over to the other side of the bed and knock five times on the adjoining wall between my bedroom and Elliot's, part of our code for when we want to get each other's attention – it's even better than a text message. When he doesn't reply right away I knock again, even firmer this time. Finally, I hear two lazy knocks back. I check the time. It's 10 a.m. It's not *too* early to be waking Elliot, but I know he still might be a bit grumpy when he comes round.

I throw on my comfy towelled dressing gown, clip up my knotted bed hair, then write her a reply.

From: Penny Porter
To: Leah Brown

Yesss!! Can't wait to see you. And thank you so, so much for this. On such short notice too. Did I ever tell you that you're the best?

P x

Then, I have someone else to tell. I check my WhatsApp and see that she's online, so I send her a message.

Posey, hey!

Hey Penny! That's so weird . . . I was just thinking about you

SNAP! In fact, I have something to ask you. Are you free next Saturday morning, 10ish?

Uh . . . you have me worried now! But yes, I think so! I have rehearsals in the afternoon, but before that is fine. Why?!?

You may think I'm kind of crazy but I want it to be a surprise. I think I might
really have found someone to help you with your stage fright. Meet me
outside Victoria Station at 10 next Saturday?

Penny . . . it's really nice of you to want to help me, but I've tried what
feels like everything to get over this. It might just be better for me to
accept that this is my reality. I can't do it, and I won't ever be able to

I pause for a moment, not sure how to respond. I can recognize in her words all the familiar feelings I get when I am overwhelmed by anxiety – the idea that nothing will ever change, and that I will never be able to live a normal life because of it. For Posey, I know it must be even worse, because the thing she loves doing most is also the source of her biggest anxiety. But if my therapist has taught me anything, it's that it's always worth trying.

You could be right. But if you're still willing to try, will you meet me?

There's a long pause from her this time, and I stare at the word '*typing* . . .' that's appeared underneath her name, waiting for the reply to come.

OK, let's do this. It can't get any worse, right?

:D Yay! I'll see you then

'What's the big news?' It's Elliot, framed in the doorway of my bedroom. He's also wearing a dressing gown and slippers, bleary-eyed and with his hair sticking out all over the

93

place. He very rarely lets anyone see him like this, but he looks so adorable. He bounces down on to the bottom of my bed.

'Leah's coming to town next week! Pegasus Girl told me that Leah had stage fright once, so I'm going to take Posey to meet her.'

'Only *you* have a world-famous pop star willing to help you out at the drop of a hat,' he says with a wink. 'What does Megan think about all this?'

I frown. 'What do you mean?'

'Well, she's going to kill you if she finds out you've arranged for someone else to meet Leah Brown before her.'

I raise my eyebrows. 'Oh yeah . . .' I think about her blunt message: 'Call me'. But there's no way she'd know that I've arranged to meet Leah already. It must be about something else. 'What if I invite her along? Then she won't hate me.'

Elliot wrinkles his nose. 'True. Megan's far from my favourite person –'

'*That's* an understatement.'

'– but she's not stupid. She'll be so thrilled to meet LB she'll forgive you anything. I mean, knowing her, we can expect her to turn this whole thing into *her* charity project, but who cares.'

'Phew, OK. I feel better now.'

'You better tell her before she finds out through the grapevine, though. I'm going downstairs to see if your dad will make us Sunday pancakes. I'm like Linda Evangelista – it's just *not* worth getting out of bed for anything less than five pancakes stacked with maple syrup. Plus, I haven't done my hair and feel a mess. Only pancakes will make it worthwhile.'

'I think for the supermodels in the nineties it was ten thousand dollars . . .'

'When it comes to your dad's pancakes, same difference.' Elliot jumps back off the bed and heads downstairs.

I have a bad feeling about Megan's message, but I try not to assume too much before I've spoken to her. I hit the Face-Time button under her contact page on my phone.

Within a few rings, she's answered. She's already in full make-up, her hair artfully sculpted into glossy waves round her face. Compared to me – no make-up and bed-head hair – she's distinctly glamorous for a Sunday morning. The only thing marring her appearance is the grumpy look on her face. My stomach does a flip. Maybe my instincts weren't too far off after all.

'Penny,' she says, her mouth a firm line.

'Hey, Megan,' I say, trying to keep my tone light. 'What's up? I got your message.'

'Yeah. So, what was your blog about?'

'My blog?'

'You know, the one about stage fright? What's going on?'

'Oh.' I pause for a second. I hadn't technically told Megan about meeting Posey – there hadn't been a good moment. I didn't mean to hide it from her, but also I hadn't been in a rush to tell her. 'When I was up visiting you, I met this girl, Posey . . .'

'You mean Posey Chang, the girl who's playing the lead role.'

'Yeah . . . She was really upset and we bonded over anxiety, so I thought I'd try to help her out.'

'What, so are you, like, *trying* to ruin my life?'

I frown. 'No. I'm just –'

'Just trying to make sure the person *I'm* the understudy for doesn't drop out of the role that's rightfully mine?'

'Well, it's not rightfully yours if –'

Megan steamrollers right over me. 'What are you thinking? I thought you were supposed to be my friend?'

'I *am* your friend, Megan, but I'm also now Posey's friend. And anyway, I had something I wanted to ask you.'

'Whatever,' she says, rolling her eyes.

'It's about Leah Brown. She's coming to town next Saturday and wants to meet up at her studio. She said I could bring friends, so . . .'

Like a dark grey cloud splitting apart to reveal bright sunshine, a huge smile appears on Megan's face. 'Can I come? Seriously?'

I can't help laughing at her change in demeanour. 'I mean, if you aren't ignoring me that is.'

'Oh my god, Penny, all is forgiven! I promise!'

'Well, don't promise yet. I'm also inviting Posey along. Do you think you can be OK with that?'

The cloud passes over Megan's face once again, anger like a flash of lightning in her eyes, but then it goes. By the time I've blinked, she looks serene again. 'You're just too nice,' she says, her voice all sugar. 'But wait, isn't Saturday your date with Callum?'

'I don't think it's technically a date . . . but yeah,' I say, a

96

blush rising in my cheeks. I'd kind of put that to the back of my mind. 'But that's in the afternoon. I have the morning free. I was going to meet Posey at ten.'

'It's definitely a date with Callum, Penny. Why don't you text me the address of Leah's studio and I can bring Posey, then we can just meet you there?'

'OK,' I say. 'Just remember – it's a surprise for Posey so don't tell her where we're going.'

'Brilliant! Can't wait till Saturday. Oh my god, what do you wear when you're about to meet your idol? I need to go shopping. You rock, Miss P.' She hangs up the phone.

I head downstairs, still feeling in a daze.

'How'd it go?' asks Elliot, already with a mouthful of pancake.

I blink several times. 'I actually have no idea. But I think I managed to make everyone happy.'

Elliot fixes me with his most grown-up stare from beneath his tortoiseshell-rimmed glasses. 'Penny, you know that's impossible.'

'I know. But I still have to try. I just can't help myself.'

Chapter Fourteen

The days disappear in a blink, a whirlwind of schoolwork, chats with Posey, and dinners with Sadie Lee and Bella. Since starting sixth form, my workload seems to have increased immensely – even the stress of GCSEs doesn't compare to the looming pressure of A levels. I welcome the distraction, though. If I wasn't nervous when I texted Callum, the thought of going on a real, actual date has sent my nerves into overdrive. Plus, I want everything to go well with Leah Brown, Posey and Megan.

After much debate with Elliot about what to wear up to London, I decide on a black-and-white stripey top with my black denim dungarees, and my mum's old battered leather jacket. I leave my long auburn hair loose round my shoulders, only twisting and pinning a few strands of my fringe off my face so I don't get annoyed. I've kept my make-up to a minimum but used a matte red lipstick to add a bit of low-key glam – 'It's only an afternoon date, my love, not a night on the razzle-dazzle,' says Elliot, shimmying towards me with jazz hands – and I've painted my nails a coral pink. I wish I hadn't though as by the end of the train journey I've almost picked it all off.

I keep checking my phone in the taxi, scrolling through the running WhatsApp chat I'm having with Posey, who keeps trying to figure out what I'm up too.

> PENNY!! I just googled the place we're going to and it's a recording studio?! What am I going to do there?

> Wait, how did you find out?

> I saw the address on Megan's phone. Argh, I don't know if I can do this!

> Of course you can!

> Well, I don't have much choice – we're almost there. See you soon?

> See you!

I breathe a sigh of relief that Posey is not bailing on me.

'Here you are, love,' says the Uber driver. My mum had linked her debit card to the app on my phone because she didn't want me to get lost in the London streets. I thank the driver and step out on to a tree-lined road. It's eerily quiet and leafy, tucked away from the main London thoroughfares, and the only thing out of place is a long black stretch limousine parked a little bit further down the road. Most likely Leah's ride. Who even drives around in limousines any more? I guess if anyone does it's Leah.

I glance up and down the street but there's no sign of Megan and Posey just yet. I lean up against a low stone wall, enjoying the warm autumn sunshine on my face.

'Penny! There you are!' Megan appears from round the corner, Posey in tow. Posey is wearing dark sunglasses and a cute panama hat pulled down low over her face. Megan is dressed to the absolute nines in a tight minidress and high-heeled boots. It looks more like she's ready to go clubbing than hang out in a studio.

'Hey, guys!' I say with a wave. Once they're close enough I give them each a big hug. 'Are you ready?' I ask.

Posey lifts her sunglasses up. 'I don't know! We'll see,' she says. She stares over my shoulder at the door to the studio and I turn to face it as well. In fact, it looks just like an ordinary London house – or rather, a London mansion: a tall, three-storey, white-painted town house standing behind a black cast-iron gate with elegant gold finials. The only indication that it's a world-class recording studio is the small glass plate inscribed OCTAVE STUDIOS above the push-button bell on one of the gateposts.

I press the button and give my name to the crackly voice that answers: 'Penny Porter and friends here. We have an appointment?'

The gate swings open and we walk through and up the steps to the main entrance. The front door opens, and we're greeted by a girl who doesn't look much older than us – although she looks *much* cooler in her worn leather jacket, black vest top and studded jeans. Megan tugs nervously at her hemline.

'Hi, are you Penny?' the girl asks me. I nod. 'Great. I'm

Alice. I work at the front desk here at Octave. She's expecting you, but she's in the studio already, checking the set-up. You can go right on through – it's just down the stairs and follow the corridor. You can't miss it.'

'Thanks,' I say with a smile, which I hope makes me look more confident than I feel.

'Wait, are we meeting someone here?' asks Posey. Excitement laces her every word.

'Maybe.' I can't help the small grin that appears on my face. Once upon a time, the thought of meeting Leah Brown in person would have had me quaking in my boots, but now I just want to jump for joy. Even though she's always mega-busy, she's become a great friend since the tour. She lives in another world, but she's never too high and mighty to come back down to earth once in a while.

The stairs down to the main part of the studio are lined with famous faces – including a stunning black-and-white portrait of Leah. I try not to linger on it in case I give everything away.

When we reach the bottom, I recognize Leah's personal assistant, Talia, who gives me two kisses on the cheek. 'Hello, lovely!' she says. I'd briefed her that it was a surprise, so she winks at me. 'This way.'

I grab Posey's hand so that she will be the first person to see it all.

We push through into the studio, and there, behind the glass, singing her heart out, is Leah Brown.

'No. Way,' whispers Posey beside me. Her hand suddenly grips mine so tight I start to lose feeling in my fingers.

Leah, as always, looks amazing. She's made almost no effort with her appearance (because on recording days there's no need for her to care about it, only her music) – just thrown her long blonde hair up into a messy bun that still manages to look Instagram-worthy.

As soon as Megan sees, there's an ear-piercing squeal and she throws her arms round my neck. 'This is amazing! Is this really happening? Leah Brown!'

'That's her!' I say with a laugh. Megan and Posey jump up and down, and I collapse into a fit of giggles.

The commotion attracts Leah's eye as she finishes her warm-up, and she waves to us. Then she detaches herself from her headphones and makes her way through the sound-proof doors towards us.

'Oh my god, can I Snapchat this?' Megan asks me.

Before I can answer, Talia pipes up. 'No social media inside the studio. In fact, no photos or recording of any kind. Normally we'd collect your phones but . . .'

'No need for that; we're all friends, right?' says Leah as she walks up to us. 'Any friend of Penny's is a friend of mine.'

'Leah! So good to see you!'

'And you too, Penny!' We give each other a huge hug.

'This is Posey and Megan, my two friends who are study-ing at the Madame Laplage School for the Arts.'

'So nice to meet you both!' She reaches out and gives them both hugs too, even though they are frozen stock-still like statues. Leah's used to having that effect on people. 'Wow, Madame Laplage – I know a few other singers who went there. What an awesome opportunity.'

'Oh, it's amazing,' says Megan, recovering from the hug faster than Posey. She flips her chestnut hair, sending it cascading across her shoulders. 'We get *real* vocal training there, which will set us up for the rest of our careers.'

A small frown flits across Leah's face. My jaw almost falls to the floor at Megan's rudeness. Was she making a dig at Leah's singing – within two seconds of meeting her?

But the frown disappears before Megan can register it, and Leah's smooth smile is back again. She turns it on Posey next, who is shaking like a leaf. Leah reaches out, takes Posey's hand and leads her over to one of the sofas. Leah hops on to the cushions, crossing her legs underneath her. Posey follows her obediently, and I can see the tension relax from her shoulders. I marvel at Leah's ability to make someone feel at ease without even having to say a word.

'So, Posey, I hear you have some trouble with stage fright?' says Leah, getting straight to the point.

Posey looks up at me with alarm in her eyes. 'You told *Leah Brown* about my stage fright?'

I nod. 'I –'

'She told me,' says Leah before I can say anything else, 'because she knows I can help. I went through it too.'

Posey blinks. 'You did?'

Leah nods. 'I did. But before we get into that, I'd love to be able to hear you sing? Please?'

'Oh no . . . I couldn't. I can't! I'm such a huge fan of yours . . .'

Leah waves her hand dismissively in front of her face. 'No, no, none of that. Does it trigger your fright to sing for a small group?'

Posey wrings her hands, the bracelets on her wrist clinking together. 'Not normally. It's really only a stage and large audience thing . . .'

Leah nods sagely. 'I get that. The recording booth is so dark you can forget you're even there. The glass can be tinted so it's only one way. Will you sing for me?'

Posey thinks about it for a moment, then nods. 'OK.'

Leah claps her hands together. 'Great! Have you been in a live room before?'

Posey shakes her head.

'Oh, don't worry, it's easy. Just head through the door, make yourself comfortable in front of the mic – sit on the stool or stand, whichever you want – then put on the headphones. Then there's a button on the side that you can use to communicate with us in the control room, and vice versa. You can just start when you're ready.'

'OK,' Posey says, before biting her bottom lip. She stands up slowly, then walks a little shakily through into the other half of the studio. My eyes follow her. She reaches the stool and moves it aside. When she sees the microphone, though, her eyes light up.

'She looks like a natural in there,' says Leah. 'Here, pull up a chair to the mixing console, you two.'

Megan and I drag a couple of ergonomic rolling chairs from the corner of the room and slide them over to the huge mixing console – a table on a slight tilt with what seems like a million buttons on it. I'm grateful suddenly that my camera only has a few as even those are tricky enough.

'Impressive, right?' says Leah, as I stare at the rows and rows of controls.

'You're telling me!'

'We have three of these in the basement at Madame Laplage,' says Megan. 'They're *top* of the line and donated by a former student.'

'Well, you're really lucky. I didn't get into one of these babies until I was signed up by Sony! Before that I was just recording in my bedroom . . . Trust me, when you have three younger brothers, no room in the house is soundproof.'

There's a short beep and then a barely audible voice comes through the speakers. 'I think I'm ready,' says Posey.

Leah presses one of the buttons on the mixing table. 'Great!'

We all stare through the glass at Posey, but she's not looking at us. In fact, her eyes are closed and she's nodding her head to hidden music. Then, almost without warning, she breaks into Maria's section of 'Tonight' from *West Side Story*.

As her incredible soprano voice fills the room, the three of us lean back in our chairs, blown away by her talent and tingling all over with goosebumps.

And, when the song finishes, Leah Brown leaps from her chair and gives Posey a standing ovation.

Chapter Fifteen

When Posey comes back into the control room, her cheeks are glowing with the flush of singing such a demanding piece. 'Thanks, guys,' she says, as we continue applauding. Even Megan joins in, unable to hold back her appreciation.

'That was really amazing!' Leah says. '*Gurl*, you have real talent.'

'Thanks,' Posey says again. But then she hangs her head. 'It's still not going to do me any good, though. There, in that room, with only you guys watching . . . I'm not afraid of that. But put me on stage and it's a whole other story.'

'Good luck *actually* performing then,' Megan mumbles under her breath, but I hear her and shoot her a sharp look. Megan rolls her eyes and folds her arms across her chest – she's been bitten hard by the green-eyed monster.

'Tell me what happens,' continues Leah, her voice soothing. Thankfully, I don't think she heard Megan.

Posey sits down on the sofa, crossing her ankles. I've never met someone who sits and stands with such incredible posture, so ram-rod straight. But then, that control is also evident in her singing. Even I, with my untrained ear, can tell she hits every note with ease and precision.

'It's like . . . when I leave the safety of the curtains, I'm not going out on stage towards the audience. I'm on a narrow plank over shark-infested waters. With each step I take, all my muscles seem to weaken until I can barely stand up. My fingers tingle, my mouth goes dry – no matter how much water I've had backstage. And then the worst thing is – my mind goes blank. All the practice I've put in, all the hours of memorizing every word and note and beat and movement . . . gone. In a snap.' She snaps her fingers to emphasize the point. 'Once that happens, I can't recover from it.'

Leah nods her head all through Posey's description. 'Check, check, check. I've experienced all that.'

'There's a bit more, though,' Posey whispers, in a voice so quiet I have to lean in to hear her. 'At the beginning of the summer I was playing Sandy in our school's production of *Grease*. But on opening night I couldn't do it. I just froze – in front of *everyone*. The worst part was, my legs were so heavy I couldn't even move them and someone had to come and basically drag me off the stage and send in my understudy. And they were already in costume as one of the Pink Ladies. It was an awful, awful mess and I ruined everything.' Tears well up in her eyes as she talks and I can't help it – I feel my eyes begin to prick as well. 'I should have just given up then and there and refused my place at Madame Laplage.'

'You know, I pulled out of a Broadway role once, for the

same reasons. It went on to win a Tony – it would've been an amazing experience and I regret that decision every day. So I know how you feel, honestly,' says Leah.

'But you get up on stage and sing to thousands of people all the time! You're carrying your own tour! I bet you don't get stage fright now.'

'Unfortunately, that's not true. Every time, I have to compose myself. Every time, I have to remind myself that *I* am in control – not my fear. And, Posey?'

'Yes?'

'You were born to do this. I know there's a passion inside you, burning just as strong as your fear. Maybe even stronger – otherwise you wouldn't have auditioned for Madame Laplage in the first place. You *can* do this. You *need* to do this – for your own sanity. You might think that going on stage is insane. But it's not. You *not* being on stage, you *not* performing – *that's* insanity. Find that kernel of confidence, cling on to it for dear life, and eventually that seed will grow into a shoot, and the shoot into a sapling, and the sapling into a massive great oak of confidence, with roots that reach every part of your body. I'm not saying your stage fright will completely go away. But under that tree you will have sanctuary from the storm.'

'Are you sure?' says Posey breathlessly.

'Absolutely.'

'I can't believe even the incredible Leah Brown gets stage fright,' says Posey, smiling for the first time since she finished singing.

'Oh, you'd be surprised! When I first spoke about it in

public, I got loads of messages from performers you wouldn't dream have stage fright. Some of the most famous singers and actors in the world. In our case – and I know this maybe isn't the case with other anxieties – the only way out is through. You can't remove it, but you *can* control it; you *have to* embrace it. Use it. You *can* do this. I promise you.'

Posey nods, but I can see she's not quite convinced. I feel for her. I'd hate to be in her position, as I know there's absolutely no way I could push through my anxiety. When it wells up, I just have to ride the wave – and (normally) I can escape from any audience I may have. For Posey, there's no escape. But there *is* her talent. I only hope she can grow that tree of confidence quickly, or else I know she will let it wither and die without a chance.

'Do you want to sing some more?' Leah asks Posey.

Posey's eyes instantly light up. 'Yeah, I'd love that!'

'Great! We can duet. Do you know "For Good" from *Wicked*?'

'Of course!' Posey leaps from the sofa. 'I just *love* that musical.'

'Ace, me too! Then, if you guys are up for it, I'd love to play you some of my new album. *Top secret* of course.' Leah winks.

'Oh, we'd love that!' I say. 'Would you mind if I set up to take some pictures of you guys?'

'No problem.'

When the two others are in the studio, Megan spins round her chair to look at me. 'Do you really think it's going to be that easy for Posey?'

'What do you mean?'

'One session with the great Leah Brown and she'll be –' Megan mimes air quotes with her fingers as she says the next word – 'cured?'

I shake my head. 'I don't think that at all. But I do think Posey has something special she wants to share with the world – and stage fright isn't going to stop her. Whether it's this performance or another one – she'll do it. I only think that she shouldn't give up hope.'

Megan snorts. 'Maybe.'

'Hey, why are you being so sour about this? I thought you said you wanted to help?'

Megan shrugs. 'You can't help a lost cause.'

I grit my teeth. 'OK, well, I'm going to step outside as I think the lighting will be better out there for a photo. Let me know when Leah starts singing her new stuff?'

'Sure.'

Once I leave the control room, I breathe a sigh of relief. Sometimes being cooped up with a grumpy Megan is like torture. I head up the stairs again, towards the bright entrance hall I saw when we first walked in. Alice is nowhere to be seen, but I'm glad – it gives me a moment to look around properly.

The aspect I'm most instantly drawn to is the huge skylights – they flood the room with light, making the space feel incredibly airy. The white walls – which could look a bit clinical – are warmed up with lots of hanging ferns, their long, pointed leaves draping over large, burnished copper pots.

I set up my tripod in the middle of the room, facing two low white sofas. There's a patch of sunlight on the ground in the perfect shape of a parallelogram on the floor in front of them. I bite my bottom lip. I'm not sure whether the lighting is going to work – it might be a bit too harsh on Leah and Posey's skin with so many reflective surfaces.

I need a test model.

'Uh, Alice?' I walk back to the front desk, but Alice is nowhere to be seen – and neither is Talia. I debate going back to ask Megan to pose for me, but I want a break from her.

There's only one option: I'm going to have to do it myself.

The thought makes me shiver. I don't like being in front of the camera – I like being *behind* it. But this is just a test shot, I tell myself. I can always delete it straight away.

With a few button clicks, I set the self-timer on my DSLR. Then, I grab my laptop out of my bag – if there's one thing I hate even more than being on camera, it's having to look at the camera – and jump up on the sofa. I open up my laptop and pretend to be working until I hear the beep signalling that the photo has been taken.

Of course, in 'pretending' to work, I actually do open up my browser and check on the comments for *Girl Online*. I have a post brewing in my mind for later tonight, but I still have to see how the rest of the session goes with Leah. I haven't written about Callum yet – I don't want to jinx anything – and it's more difficult now that people I know (including Callum himself) will be reading and analysing every word. Before I know it, I'm sucked into the comments section – which, luckily, on my blog is really supportive and lovely. I've worked really hard to maintain that atmosphere and keep *Girl Online* a safe space for my readers.

My blog once was a source of such anxiety for me, I wanted to shut it down for good. But now I know that it can be a force for good. I hope Posey realizes that too, eventually, about her stage fright.

When I'm finished with the comments, I've been sitting there for much longer than I intended. I rush back to the screen to see how the photo turned out. And, in fact, I'm pleasantly surprised. There's a weird effect in the photo – because of the way I held my laptop, it looks like the parallelogram on the floor is a shadow of it – or rather, a *reverse* shadow, as if the laptop itself is casting light. I was right, the lighting is a little harsh on my face – but contrasted against the white wall it looks kind of edgy. My eyes are glued to the computer screen, and if I zoom in close enough there's even a little reflection of the laptop in my pupils. It looks . . . unique.

Uniquely Penny. A shot of me, doing something *else* I love.

A tingly feeling runs through the palms of my hands, all the way up to my heart. I think I might be on to something there.

Chapter Sixteen

'Hey, what are you doing?'

The voice startles me, and I look up to see Megan standing at the top of the stairs.

'Oh, I was just checking a test photo for later. All looking good!' and I give her a thumbs up.

'Do you know where the bathrooms are?' she asks.

'Just over there, I think.'

'Cool.'

I leave the camera in place but head back down the stairs. When I reach the studio I'm surprised to hear Leah finishing up a song that I haven't heard before and I feel disappointed that I've missed listening to her new music. A few moments later, Megan walks back in. 'You just missed Leah singing her new stuff!' I say.

'Oh darn,' she says, but she doesn't seem that disappointed herself. She sits down, picks up her phone and starts playing *Candy Crush Saga*.

I sigh, spinning round until I'm facing Leah and Posey in the live room again. I wish I hadn't invited Megan. She's been nothing but bad news ever since she arrived at the studio.

'I can't wait to be doing this one day,' Megan says, oblivious to my annoyance. 'Can you ask Leah if she'll listen to me sing too? Maybe she can introduce me to her manager.'

'Ask her yourself,' I say, then close my eyes and listen to another of Leah's new songs. It's different to her previous stuff – less 'poppy', with a darker sound – but still catchy as ever. When the chorus comes again, I can already feel my brain latching on to the lyrics. Leah knows *exactly* what makes great music.

When she and Posey return to the control room, Megan and I clap wildly again. 'That was so great!' I say to Leah. 'Did you write that last one?'

To my surprise, Leah cringes. 'Yeah – is it OK? I wrote these myself. I'm trying to do more and more songwriting on my albums.'

'It's brilliant,' I say with a smile.

'Phew. I have Carmen Delaware coming in tomorrow to sing with me and I want it to be good.'

Megan looks up from her phone sharply. 'Carmen Delaware? But isn't she, like . . . your sworn enemy?' Carmen is another pop star but from the UK, not America, who emerged on the scene about the same time as Leah.

Leah throws her head back and laughs. 'Are you kidding? Carmen and I go *waaay* back – it's only the media that likes to pit us against each other. I could not have gotten where I am today without her. I'm pretty sure it was she who gave me the tree speech before I gave it to you.'

'What about when she won Best Song at the BBMAs before you? Didn't you hate that?' Megan asks, referring to one of the most recent media headlines about Leah. 'And that song of hers, "Knock You Down", isn't that about you?'

'Geez, I hope not! It was written about her accountant who embezzled funds from her music sales. But I can see that it's more fun to think that it was about me.'

I spot a dangerous wrinkle in Megan's nose – meaning she's still sceptical – but I interrupt before it can turn even more heated. 'Want to follow me upstairs, guys? I've set up the tripod so we can get some really nice pictures.'

'Awesome! Let's do it!'

But as we walk up the stairs together, Megan still can't drop it. 'I just can't believe it about you and Carmen. How can you like her when she has everything you want, always one step ahead of you? She soloed her first tour before you, went platinum before you, won that award . . .'

'Wow, you sure do know a lot about me and Carmen.'

'I watch a lot of TMZ,' Megan says with a shrug.

Leah doesn't say anything until we reach the white sofas, then she positions herself in front of my camera. Then, her steel-blue eyes meet Megan's, and I know that look all too well. You do *not* want to be its recipient. 'Look, I think you have an important lesson to learn. You have to stop looking sideways all the time – at Penny, at Posey – and start focusing on your own lane. Carmen's success does *not* impact me or detract from what I've achieved. I love that she's done so well, and hope that she continues to hit those milestones! I know that I'll get there one day too. She's paving the way for me, not building a wall I can't climb. This is still a tough industry. We girls have to look out for one another. Whether it's in the Top Forty charts, in the blogging world, or . . . in a drama school show. Right, Penny?'

'Right,' I say firmly. Thank goodness Leah is able to put Megan in her place.

Megan clenches her fingers and I swear I can hear her mind whirring away like an overheating hard drive. 'I know that!' she says. 'But it's not my fault if she's a hopeless case.'

'I'm not sure you know anything,' says Leah, a sad smile on her face. 'But you'll learn. Without support from your peers and you supporting them in turn, you won't get very far in this industry. Trust me. And if you're not willing to support your classmate then I think you should leave my studio now.'

Megan's jaw drops and bright red spots appear on her cheeks. 'Fine. Some of us don't *need* to ride on other people's coat-tails to get to the top.' She gets up, spins on her heels and flounces out.

Even though I don't agree with what she said, I want to run after her to make sure she's OK, but Leah puts her hand on my arm. 'She's a big girl and she'll be OK. Talia will put her safely in a taxi, so you don't need to worry about her getting home.' She turns to Posey. 'Ready for our close-up with the best photographer in the biz, hon?'

Taking pictures of Leah and Posey is great, and they seem to really get on well. As they chat, I pull out my laptop again. Leah's speech has really inspired me, and I know that it would make a great short but sweet blog post. I'm itching to send out her message to my *Girl Online* readers.

3 October

Someone Else's Success Is NOT Your Failure

Have you ever aced an exam with flying colours, but the girl who sits opposite you gets a *higher* mark? And even though you feel you put in more effort, it didn't pay off?

Have you ever worked hard for a job, working your fingers to the bone, but someone *else* gets the pay rise you think you deserved?

Have you ever stayed up all night creating something you're so proud of, but someone *else* comes along with something even better, claiming to have spent no time on it at all?

It happens sometimes, and let's be honest – we all go green-eyed monster and wish we had someone else's luck or talent or drive. When you work in the same industry as someone, doing the same things, full of the same passions, their success can really knock you back if you feel you aren't quite in the same lane and going at the same speed.

What if, whenever I read someone else's blog and it's good, I say, 'Hey, mine isn't as good as that, so I hate this other blog because it's getting more hits than mine'? What exactly would that achieve? There's enough room for *everyone* to do the thing they're good at. There'll always be someone who is more successful than you, but always someone who wishes they were as successful as you too. Everybody wants to succeed, but we don't need to isolate ourselves with jealousy in the process. One thing I've learnt recently is that blowing out someone else's candle doesn't make yours shine any brighter.

As a very wise friend of mine would say: focus on your own lane, go at your own pace, don't look sideways. Someone else's success does not have to impact you or detract from what *YOU* achieve.

A little Saturday thought for you.

Girl Online, going offline xxx

When we leave the studio, Posey gives me a giant hug. 'Thank you for this. It was really special. And . . . I promise not to give up. Even if it's not this show, not this role, I'll keep trying.'

I grin. 'I think that's all I can ask for!' I look down at the time – it's almost 1 p.m., the time when I agreed to meet Callum.

'You OK, Penny? You look like you've seen a ghost!'

'It's not that, but I think I have . . . a date to go to!'

Chapter Seventeen

Standing outside St James's Park station, I fidget with the straps on my dungarees. I kind of wish I'd worn something a bit more fitting so I didn't look three sizes bigger than I actually am. I keep looking over my shoulder, wondering if it would be too rude to bail. Memories of every terrible date I've ever had come rushing back – and how awkward I was with Oli when I had a crush on him. That was the period of my life I'd designated BN – *Before Noah*. Penny BN was *not* a cool cucumber. She lacked knowledge of guys and relation-ships, she'd never been kissed properly, and she cowered away in the corner when Robbie Williams's 'Angels' came on at the end of the awful school discos Megan dragged her along to.

A hand taps me on the shoulder before I can make any sort of decision. I look up and a goofy grin appears on my face. Callum's *just* as cute as I remember, and he really seems to have made an effort for today. He's got a preppy blazer on over a patterned shirt, and khaki slacks. The only thing that's out of place is a heavy backpack, which I recognize as a Lowepro brand camera bag. Swanky.

'Hey, Penny!' He reaches over and gives me a kiss on the cheek, which I am *not* prepared for.

'Callum, hi!' I take a step back and my foot catches on my loose shoelace. I lose my balance, limbs flailing, but Callum reaches out and grabs my upper arm to steady me.

'Don't fall head over heels for me *right* away. Give it until the end of the date at least,' he says with a laugh.

'You'll learn that, for me, sometimes standing still isn't the easiest thing.'

'I want to learn everything about you,' he says with a dreamy smile.

I don't really know what to say to this, so I leave the uncomfortable silence hanging for a moment before recovering myself. 'So . . . where are we off to?'

From behind his back, Callum produces a beautiful dove-grey hamper. 'I thought, since it's a nice day, maybe we head to the park for a picnic?'

I release a breath I didn't even realize I've been holding. For some reason, I'd been waiting to be disappointed by his choice of date. But there's no disappointment. A picnic is the perfect low-key first date. 'That sounds amazing!' I say.

'Great!' He holds out his hand, and I take it.

The park is beautiful at this time of year, with the leaves only just beginning to change colour, but the air is still plenty warm enough to sit outside without worrying.

'Did you have a good morning?' Callum asks, oddly

formal in his chat. His accent still makes me smile. I also get the sense that the picnic basket is rather heavy, as he's walking with a slight tilt to one side.

'Oh yes, thank you.' For some reason, I feel like I need to be formal back. I wish we could just skip to the part where we're comfortable with each other, but I know it doesn't work that way. *Except with Noah*, an annoying part of my brain says. 'I went to see my friend, who's a singer. Leah Brown?'

Callum laughs. 'Oh, just casually throw in a name-drop, why don't you! I saw a friend too, but unfortunately it was just my flatmate in his pants.'

I wrinkle my nose. 'Haven't you guys ever heard of clothes?'

'Not on weekends! Unless we have a date with a hottie, of course. Want to take a walk round the lake before we eat?'

I'm about to answer when my stomach lets out an enormous, very *un*-'hottie'-like grumble. I'd forgotten that I hadn't really eaten anything since a very quick cereal bar this morning.

'I'll take that as a no then!' Callum says with a laugh.

Inside, I cringe. Why can't my body just behave normally in a date-like situation?! 'Do you mind?' I ask in a small voice.

He releases my hand and instead throws his arm round my shoulder, pulling me in close to him. 'Don't you worry, Penny. How about that spot over there?'

I follow the line of his finger to a patch of grass beneath an oak tree, already strewn with orangey-red fallen leaves. It looks perfect and really romantic. In fact, not too far away, I spot a couple having what looks like an engagement shoot. They're sitting on the grass, back to back, two hands posed together in the shape of a heart. It looks cute, but it wouldn't be my style of photography. I prefer capturing more candid moments, natural shots that really show how a couple are together.

Seeing the photographer at work, though, inspires me. 'Hang on a second,' I say. I take my camera out of my bag and take a snap of the tree and the couple. From this angle, I can't see their cheesy pose – they just look relaxed.

'Of course! I should have known you would want to pre-serve this moment.'

'I'll put it away soon.'

'No, don't! I like seeing you take photos. What lens do you have?' Callum places the hamper down on the ground and I pass him my camera. He turns it round in his hands, examin-ing my lenses, then looks through the viewfinder.

'Oh, this is a *nice* piece of kit. But have you thought about upgrading to the 5D mark 3 model?' he asks.

I smile. 'Well, I would, but that's *way* out of my budget. I'd love to get the wide-angle 16–35mm, but that would be, like, three Christmas presents and a birthday.'

He nods, then passes the camera back to me. It's fun hav-ing someone to geek out with about photography. Callum's so different to Noah, who wouldn't know a macro from a zoom lens. Callum spreads the picnic blanket over the bed of leaves. I sit down on the edge and watch as he carefully sets out a delicious array of sandwiches.

'Wow, this all looks amazing! And are those scones?'

'You better believe it.'

'Where does a seventeen-year-old Scotsman find scones nowadays, anyway?'

Callum winks. 'Let a man have his tricks.' After the scones, he pulls out what looks like a half-sized bottle of cava.

'Oh, I'm sorry – I don't drink,' I say quickly, cringing inside at how young I must sound. 'It doesn't go down too well with my anxiety stuff,' I say, rushing into my excuses even before he's asked for one.

'Really?'

'Yeah . . .'

'Not even if I mix it with some orange juice?'

'I'd rather not, if that's OK.' I feel goosebumps begin to prickle along my arm – I wish he would just drop it already.

Thankfully, he shrugs, and puts the bottle back in the hamper. Lastly, he's even remembered to pack paper plates and cutlery. He sets out a plate for me, positioning each item of food perfectly.

'So, you were in Rome over the summer, eh? I love it there.' He passes me my plate. The sandwiches look almost too pretty to eat. Then I remember my rumbling stomach. *Almost.* I pop one in my mouth practically whole, then I have to chew awkwardly until I'm ready to talk.

'Oh yeah, it was great. The ice cream especially was *whoa.*'

'Do you like to travel then?'

'I like travel, but not *travelling*, if that makes sense. I want to see all the amazing places in the world, but getting on a plane is . . .' I shiver even though it's not cold.

'Don't you wish you could just click your fingers and be there?'

'That's exactly right!' I say with a smile.

'I feel that about the long journey back home. I wish Scotland wasn't so far away. Have you ever been?'

'No, but I'm going during half-term actually!'

Callum's eyebrows rise towards his hairline. 'You are? What part? Edinburgh?'

I shake my head. 'No, somewhere in the Highlands – Castle Lochland. Have you heard of it? My mum is an event planner and runs her own wedding shop down in Brighton. She's doing a big wedding up there and I'm going to go help her out.'

'You're joking,' Callum says, his mouth dropping open. There's a piece of chewed-up sandwich inside that I can't stop staring at – *ew*.

I frown. 'What? No . . . she really is a wedding planner.'

'No, no, not that. It's just, my cousin is getting married at Castle Lochland over half-term. Jane Kemp?'

The name does ring a bell. 'I think it is the Kemp–Smithson wedding,' I agree. Normally, I wouldn't remember details like that, but this is an exception as it's such a big deal for my mum.

'Smithson! That's it. I always forget the guy's name. What a coincidence! In fact, I think it must be fate.' He leans towards me, his hand casually falling on top of mine. I feel as if he's leaning in to kiss me . . .

A loud shriek makes us both turn our heads. My eyes scan the lake's edge, until I spot the source: it's just a child being chased around by his mum. The little boy is wearing a bright paper crown marked with a big '6' and following a few steps behind are ten or eleven more children and one or two mums and dads.

'Oh, it must be a birthday party!'

'Great. A bunch of noisy kids to ruin the mood,' Callum mumbles.

I don't think I agree with him, although I suppose it does interrupt the romantic atmosphere somewhat. Then a drop of water lands on my head. (Where on earth have those clouds come from? They seem to have materialized out of nowhere.) 'Somehow,' I say, 'I don't think the *party's* going to ruin it.'

At which point, as if my words are a prophecy, the heavens open, and our beautiful picnic is drenched by the rain.

★ ★ Chapter Eighteen ★

All Callum's careful arranging goes out of the window as we hurriedly toss everything back into the hamper. The birthday group are now *really* screeching and running for shelter.

When everything is put away, Callum grabs my hand. 'This way!' he says.

I still have a paper plate in my hand, which I hold over my head as a very poor substitute for an umbrella. We run towards the park gates and into the welcoming dry of a coffee shop near the station.

Even from that short downpour, my hair is soaked. My make-up, so carefully applied earlier, is also letting me down big time. I look up at Callum, who hardly seems wet at all. His short hair is as perfect as ever. How *do* boys do that?

He wipes a drop of rain from the tip of my nose. To my surprise, his shoulders slump down. 'Sorry about this. The weather forecast this morning didn't say anything about rain.'

'That's OK. You can't always rely on what those guys say anyway, right?' I grin.

'Clearly not.' His eyes glower.

'Hey, don't worry about it – really.' I put my hand on his arm.

He shakes me off. 'Meh. Would you mind ordering me a latte? I'm going to the loo to get dry.' He hands me a fiver and storms off.

I'm left staring at his back, the five-pound note limp in my hand. Then I shake out of it: the rain's ruined his plans for the day and he's mad. That's OK. I get in the (now) long line for coffee.

'Oof, what a nightmare!' cries the woman behind me. I turn round and recognize her as one of the women from the birthday party. 'That wasn't forecast, was it?'

'Apparently not!' I say.

'What *am* I going to do with a dozen screaming kids expecting an outdoors party? Any ideas?'

I shrug, but the woman keeps on talking. 'All I have is a nearly sodden birthday cake. I guess I'll just have to serve it here. Great! Add sugar high to my growing list of problems . . .'

I look over her shoulder at the swarm of bored children and I feel her disappointment. 'Can I do anything? Can I get your drink so you can start cutting the cake?'

'Oh, that would be wonderful! Thank you.' She hands me a couple of pounds. 'Just a tea for me. Lord, do I need it!' She rushes back to the kids, one of whom – the six-year-old birthday boy – is climbing up on to a table. 'Get down, Lucas!' she shouts irritably.

I laugh. Finally, when it's my turn at the counter, I order a latte and two cups of tea with milk.

'Who's the third drink for?' Callum pops up behind my shoulder and I jump. He looks relaxed again, I'm pleased to see.

'Oh, the poor mum looking after that gaggle of kids.'

'That's nice of you.' Callum takes the latte from out of my hand and walks to the furthest seat away from the birthday party.

'Do you mind if I pop to the loo first?' I ask. Callum waves his hand dismissively, so I take that as a yes.

Under the harsh lights of the cloakroom, I lean against the sink and stare at my reflection in the mirror. I brush away some of the mascara that has drifted off my lashes, and try to fluff some sort of life back into my damp hair. But it's the look in my eyes that's shaking me. I just don't look at all . . . happy.

I can't quite put my finger on what's wrong. Callum has been a perfect gentleman – with a couple of little blips about the alcohol and then the rain. But there's a weird swirling feeling in my gut that has nothing to do with being hungry. There's just none of the . . . the excitement, the spark, that I was expecting to feel. In fact, it almost feels as if the tiled walls are closing remorselessly in on me and all I really want to do is come up with a reason to leave without seeming rude. I'm enjoying hiding away in here far too much.

I half think about texting Elliot for advice, but I know he'll scold me for being on my phone during a date, so I decide to pull myself together. *You're just not being fair, Penny,* I tell myself. *Give him a chance at least.*

Mood bolstered, I put on a big smile again and head out into the coffee shop.

'Thought you'd got lost in there,' says Callum.

'Nope, all good.'

'Well, you look beautiful. Even drenched by the rain.' He touches my hand as I sit down and I blush furiously. Although I'm unsure where my feelings are at right now, he looks absolutely, meltingly gorgeous and any uneasy feelings I've been having seem to vanish. Am I really that fickle?

'Thanks,' I say.

'Sorry to interrupt, sorry to interrupt!' The woman from earlier comes hurrying over, and I can't help noticing the flicker of frustration that distorts Callum's perfect features. Luckily, the woman doesn't seem to notice, and I give her a warm smile. 'Thank you so much for my tea. In return, here's a couple of slices of birthday cake.'

She plops two smooshed-up pieces of chocolate cake wrapped in a brown napkin on the table and dashes back.

I pick up one of the slices and take a bite. It's delicious. 'Wow, free cake!' I say. 'And it's really, really good!'

Callum shrugs. 'I'm not really a big cake fan.'

'Hey, this is so weird, we've just been given free cake!' I feel excitement bubble up through my veins. It's the perfect opportunity to see what Callum is really like.

Callum stares at me like I've gone off the deep end. 'Uh, yeah, and . . .?'

'And . . . OK, hear me out. In my family, we have this tradition called Magical Mystery Day. We haven't done it for a little while, but it always used to start with cake – and then we'd have to go from place to place, having cake with every meal.'

'Sounds a little dumb . . .' There's a forced smile creasing his face, which is followed by an awkward chuckle.

'Yeah, I guess it is . . .' My face falls.

Callum notices and backtracks. 'Not dumb, but . . . childish. You know, fun when you're a kid, but . . . Your parents sound like they were great fun. Now, though, when you get given free cake in London you have to be careful it's not spiked with anything.'

'That's kind of a cynical way to look at life.'

'Hey, you can't be too careful. And we can do better than cake. Since it's raining, why don't we catch a movie?'

I look down at my watch. It's still over an hour before I have to catch the train, but I don't have time for a film. His reaction to Magical Mystery Day has taken whatever wind was left in my sails clean away. When I mentioned it to Noah, he immediately joined in the fun. Can I really be with someone who can't enjoy the awesome cake-moments in life? I'm just not sure this is going to work. I shake my head. 'I have to catch the train home – but maybe another time?' The words slip out of my mouth before I can stop them.

There's disappointment in Callum's eyes, but then they light up again. 'Maybe I'll see you in Scotland next week then?' he says.

'Yeah, that would be nice,' I say. I immediately wish I hadn't told him. But then again, I'm going to be so busy helping Mum, I'm not really going to have time to see Callum. I'll have to let him down gently another time or skilfully avoid him like a Charlie's Angel.

'Come on, let me walk you to the station.'

'Oh . . . you don't have to do that, really . . .'

'Yeah, I do. This date has already gone wrong enough. Serves me right for trying to impress, I guess.' He gestures to the hamper.

He looks so sad that my heart goes out to him. Instinctively, I grab his hand. 'No, it's been great. You can't help the weather. Let's try again – maybe on your home turf it will be better.'

He smiles, and my heart jumps. He *is* incredibly cute. WHY AM I SO *FICKLE*?

He puts an arm round my shoulders and walks me out of the coffee shop and back towards the Tube station. The rain is still coming down hard, so we half jog towards the entrance.

'It's really good to get to know you better, Penny,' he says, stopping outside the barriers. 'For instance, now I know the way to your heart maybe is through chocolate cake.' He winks.

'Yeah,' I say, the word coming out as more of a sigh. His hand traces down the length of my arm, from my shoulder to my palm.

My heart beats wildly inside my chest, and I feel like I've run a mile – even though we're standing still. I tilt my chin up and catch his eyes, and my breath catches in my throat.

'Until Scotland, then.'

'Until then.'

His hand grips mine, pulling me closer. His other hand drifts to my chin and gently, ever so gently, his lips touch mine.

4 October

First-Date Jitters

Even writing the title for this post will be enough to shock you into clicking on it. Yes, that's right . . . I have been on a date. With a boy. Who is not from Brooklyn. I'll give you guys a moment . . .

. . .

. . .

Having only ever been on a handful of first dates before, I don't have an encyclopedia of positive experiences to draw from. In fact, most have been downright disastrous. If I'm honest, after *everything* that's happened in the past year, it felt quite strange agreeing to meet with someone, but I figured I had nothing to lose. Whether we never spoke again, parted on friendly terms, or completely hit it off, how would I ever know unless I at least tried?

For a while I was in denial that it was even a date at all, but after numerous friends drilled it into me, I decided I'd better come to terms with the fact that it actually COULD be a date, and that it was OK. I think once you label something with the word 'date', everything becomes a lot more terrifying.

— *What if* it's *awkward*?

— *What if* we run out of things to talk about?

— *What if* he eats with his mouth open?

— *What if* I fall over and flash my *pants*?

The possibilities are *ENDLESS*.

Before my date, I managed eventually to run out of '*what if*'s. I'd exhausted all possible horrors, gone through all possible scenarios.

Anyway, who knows if this will amount to anything, but I found it was *nice* to spend some time with new company – and we were given *free cake* so, all in all, not bad for an afternoon! I'm also pleased I was able to step out of my comfort zone and leave any niggling thoughts at home.

Do you get nervous before a first date? Do you have any awful date experiences to share? Spill the beans to make me feel better.

Girl Online, going offline xxx

Chapter Nineteen

'So, how was *the* kiss?' Elliot asks, lying on his front in my bed, his legs kicked up behind him. I've just finished telling him all about our semi-disastrous date – from the picnic to the rain to the Magical Mystery Day comments.

'It was really nice,' I say, leaning back against the headboard.

'"*Nice*". Ugh, that's like the kiss of death!' Elliot's nose wrinkles as he talks. 'Really? *Nice* is all you've got? Nice is like . . . the Middlesbrough of all compliments.'

'Have you even been to Middlesbrough?'

'No, but I don't have to. It just *sounds* like it fits.'

'And anyway,' I say, 'I said "really nice".'

Elliot throws his hands up in the air. 'Oh wow, big whoop. So honestly, it was only nice?'

I shrug. 'Yeah. I mean, on the surface he's like my perfect guy, but there just isn't that spark.'

'These things can take time, I suppose.' Elliot still sounds doubtful. 'So are you going to see him again?'

'I kinda don't have a choice. It turns out he's been invited to the wedding that Mum and Sadie Lee are organizing, so I would have seen him there anyway . . . After that, though, I don't know. We'll have to see how it goes.'

'What is it with you and guys at weddings? Still nothing from Noah?'

I shake my head. Having Sadie Lee and Bella around has only intensified my desire to hear from him, to contact him, to let him know people are thinking about him. But every time my finger hovers over his number, I force myself to put the phone away. I've tried to reach him in the past; now I'm going to follow Sadie Lee's lead and wait until he's ready. He wants to lock himself away; that's his decision. Even if it does seem like a pretty selfish one to me. And the longer he cuts himself off, the angrier I'm becoming about it.

'Well, in the meantime, *I've* been reading up on Castle Lochland and it looks amazing. Do you think it's too much for me and Alex to wear matching kilts already? Also, I hope it doesn't rain *all* the time.'

'Matching kilts? Please, no! And as for the rain, I think you're not going to get much of a choice with that one.'

'And you're going to have to introduce me to this Callum guy, anyway. Then I can decide for myself whether it matters that your first kiss was more *blah* than *wow*.'

'It wasn't blah,' I say, feeling defensive. And it wasn't. It was exactly what I said . . . nice. It just didn't blow me away. But wasn't I expecting too much? Everything else about him screams that I should give him another shot. Maybe in his home environment he'll be more relaxed. And, even though

Sadie Lee and Bella will be there, I'll be so far away from all the other reminders of Noah that maybe *I* can relax too.

Elliot spins over on to his back. 'I can't believe Megan got kicked out of Leah's studio session. Have you spoken to her since?'

I shake my head. 'No. I debated sending her a message but I think she's the one who needs to come to me this time.'

'Yeah, too right. You're always way too nice to that girl. She's trouble on two legs. I still haven't forgiven her for that *Celeb Watch* stunt and I can't believe you have. Are you forgetting Milkshakegate? The only time I've ever genuinely found Megan funny was when she was dripping with the milkshakes we dumped over her . . .' A smile spreads across my face, but I instantly feel a tiny pang of guilt and I regain my serious composure.

'I know. But I'm sure she won't do anything like that again – she's learnt her lesson.'

Elliot snorts.

'Something else interesting happened yesterday,' I say. 'I took this photograph and sent it to Melissa . . .' I clamp my mouth shut. Suddenly I feel shy about it. Elliot knows I've been searching for something 'uniquely Penny' that would be worthy of the opportunity François-Pierre Nouveau offered me, but he doesn't know I've been sending photos to his office manager. I have a feeling this photo might be the start of something, but I don't want to jinx anything by sharing the news with Elliot.

Like the fact that Melissa's response to my latest photograph was her most enthusiastic yet.

'*Annnnd . . .?*' Elliot prompts.

A big thump on the other side of my bedroom wall jolts us both upright. 'Wait – did that come from your room?' I ask him.

His eyes are wide with alarm. 'Uh, I think so.'

There's another crash, so violent it shakes the pictures on my wall and one of my posters, giving up the ghost, comes fluttering down.

'What on earth's going on?' I ask.

Then we hear a voice. A woman's voice. Elliot's mum. And she sounds mad.

Elliot leaps to his feet and rushes out of my room. I follow him down the stairs as quickly as I can, swinging round the banisters to keep up with him. In a flash, we're on the ground floor of my house, out of my front door and round the steps to Elliot's. Elliot fumbles with the key, allowing me to catch up. I want to tell him to slow down, not to rush into what might be going on, but he's a man of single-minded focus.

By the time we reach his attic room at the top of his house I'm totally out of breath. And if I wasn't winded already, what I see now would take my breath away from me anyway.

Mrs Wentworth, Elliot's mum, is in his room, tearing it inside out and upside down. His clothes are strewn everywhere, his normally uber-neat, colour-coordinated wardrobe a big mess on the floor. She looks like a mad woman, a glint in her eye. She's normally so put together (that's where Elliot gets his neat streak from) but today her hair is tumbling out of its ponytail and the buttons on her shirt aren't even done up straight.

Elliot lets out a sound that is barely human: half groan, half scream. '*MUM!* What . . . the . . .'

'I know you're helping him hide things from me! Where is it?'

'Where's WHAT?'

'Evidence! Trust me, I've searched every inch of this house except your room and I haven't found anything, so I know it must be in here somewhere.'

'Mum, I'm not helping Dad hide anything! I barely even talk to the guy! He hates me and "my kind", remember? All those hours of therapy were for nothing.'

'That would be just the sort of manipulation your father would love.' Abandoning the wardrobe as a lost cause, she's now turning her wild eyes on Elliot's desk instead. Elliot leaps in front of it, holding his arms wide.

'Penny! Get in front of my wardrobe,' he says, drawing his mum's attention to me.

'This is a *family* matter, Penny. Go home,' she commands icily. Elliot's parents are normally perfectly nice to me, but then again, in all the years we've lived next door, I've never seen his mum like this.

'Penny *is* my family now,' says Elliot. 'She's certainly a lot closer to me than either of you!'

Now I cringe for real, wishing I could disappear through the floor.

Thankfully, his mum's eyes slide away from me. 'While you're living under this roof, I still have the right to look through your things,' she says. Instantly, I know it's the wrong thing for her to have said.

'THEN I WON'T LIVE UNDER YOUR ROOF ANY MORE. Come on, Penny.' Elliot storms over to me and grabs my hand.

As we leave his bedroom, he spins round. 'Search under every floorboard, Mum. There's nothing there. What you're looking for can't be found in your son's bedroom. Just remember that.'

When we get outside, we don't go back to my house – despite the drizzle that's just started. We walk down the hill, towards the park. When we're far enough away for Elliot's mum to not see which way we've gone, Elliot breaks down into heaving sobs. I drag him inside a bus shelter, wrap my arms round him and pull him tightly to my chest. 'It's OK, Elliot. It is.'

'It *isn't*,' he says after a snotty sniffle. I give him my tissue.

'Did you really mean what you said?' I ask. 'About not going back home?'

'Yes. If . . . if it's OK with your parents, I mean.'

For a moment, I'm taken by surprise. 'Wait – you want to live with us? What about Alex?'

'Don't get me wrong, I *love* Alex, and I do want to live with him. Just not yet. When I move in with him, I want it to be for all the right reasons – not just because I'm living in the fifth level of hell from Dante's *Inferno* right now.'

'Dante's what?'

'Honestly, Penny, don't you read? Even Dan Brown? The fifth level of hell is dedicated to anger. Our house is drowning in anger right now.'

I gently squeeze his hand. 'See, even when you're an emotional, snotty mess you're still the geekiest person I know.'

He sniffles. 'Thanks, Pennylicious. Sorry you had to see that.'

I shrug. 'Don't mention it. You *are* my family, you know that. You know everything about me too.'

He sighs and leans his head on my shoulder. 'Did they have to do this to me in my last year at school? Couldn't they have waited until I'd gone off to uni or something? The worst thing is, I think Mum is probably right. Dad has been acting totally weird lately, making more of an effort with his appearance – I swear I actually caught him *working out* the other day – coming home even later than normal, signing up for more and more business trips. At first, I thought he wanted out of the house to get away from *me*, but now I think it's something else. That, or Mum's paranoia is contagious.'

'I think sometimes paranoia *is* contagious. But also your instincts are normally pretty good.'

'In this case, they're pretty bad.'

'They're both grown-ups. They have to figure this out for themselves.'

Elliot dabs his eyes with my tissue. 'I know that. I just wish they'd sort it out without dragging me through it too.'

'It's not fair at all.'

'It's not fair, but it's reality. God, never did I think I'd be so desperate to go to Scotland! Couldn't your mum have arranged a wedding in Ibiza, or somewhere *hot* at least?'

I nudge his shoulder. 'Hey, you love Scotland.'

'I know. The Highlands were one of the few places my

parents took me to as a kid. They'd pretend to be all out-doorsy and buy all new camping gear: tents, mattresses, sleeping bags, the lot. Then halfway on the drive up, some-where near Watford Gap services, they'd have an argument about how much dehydrated food they should have bought, then they'd pack it in and Mum would book a last-minute hotel in Edinburgh at some outrageous price. Sounds dumb, but it was actually enjoyable. It's not like we're great at family activities in the Wentworth household.'

Elliot leans his head against the glass panel of the bus shelter, where the streaks of rain trickle down on the outside like the tears staining his cheeks.

'At least Alex will be with me this time. Then we can make new memories in Scotland. I have a feeling I'm going to need them.'

Chapter Twenty

'Can we stop? Can we stop?' I tap Dad on the shoulder as we drive out on the road from Inverness. I'd survived the plane journey – just – with the help of Mum's huge woolly cardigan, which I've stretched out so much now it looks like a lumpy blanket with arms. Just when I think I've turned my back on my anxiety, a plane journey will come along to remind me I still have a *lot* of work to do before I'm truly fine. Maybe I'll never be one hundred per cent how I want to be, but as long as it doesn't stop me from doing the things I love, I'll be OK.

Now that we've landed and we're here, though, my anxiety has been banished to the back of my mind. Out of the window, a glittering loch stretches as far as the eye can see, surrounded by golden fields of long grass. We've barely been in the car for half an hour, and already I'm totally smitten with the Scottish countryside going past my window.

'Penny, if we stop every five minutes, we're *never* going to get to Castle Lochland.'

'Just this once more, please?'

'OK, darling daughter of mine.' He pulls over on to the rocky verge, and I leap out of the car. I've never done much in terms of landscape photography, but round every corner is a view that's even more inspiring than the last. I look down at the screen to preview the photo I've just taken. I grin. This landscape doesn't need any kind of filter or editing to look fantastic. It just is.

I take a deep breath and clean, fresh air fills my lungs. It's different to Brighton, where the air is always tinged with salt from the sea. This feels pure and restorative.

An impatient toot of the horn from Dad brings me back to reality, and I slide back into the car. 'Sorry, Dad. It's just too beautiful!'

'You'll have to go on some Highland walks when you're settled at the castle,' says Mum from the passenger seat. 'You'll love it. Just make sure to take a guide with you – you don't want to get lost out here.'

'Maybe I do,' I say wistfully.

The castle really is up in the middle of nowhere, and as we get further away from the city, the countryside gets even more wild and craggy. Dad only lets me stop one more time for photos, and that's when we pass a circle of standing stones perched high on a moor – just as atmospheric and mystical as Stonehenge. Maybe even more so, because there aren't scores of tourists milling around everywhere.

'Careful,' Mum says. 'They say there's magic in stone circles like these.'

'Wow, I could totally believe that,' I say. 'Magic . . . or

maybe they were just built by giants.' Who else could have carried up such huge stones to such a precarious location?

'Just *wait* until you see the castle, Penny. It might be a struggle to get you home.'

'You keep saying that, but how long until we get there?'

Dad consults his map. For some reason the satnav doesn't like it up here, so far away from everything. 'Not far,' he says. 'Probably half an hour or so.'

'Eek, I can't wait,' I say.

'Now,' says Mum, 'where did I put my notes?' She pats her sides, looking around the footwell of the car.

Now that we're on Scottish soil, I can sense the tension building in the air, radiating from Mum. She always gets like this before a big wedding. And with this one having such a big budget, there are even more to-do lists – and only three short days to complete it all in. No matter how big or how small the wedding is, she always tries her best to make sure it runs perfectly. But with something this size, the logistics are almost overwhelming.

'Ah!' she says, finding her notes, and she starts flicking through the pages. I can hear her muttering out loud, checking off the items on her lists.

'Is there anything I can do to help when we get there?' I ask.

'Oh, I'm *sure* there is, honey! One of the things you can do for a little while is man the phones. We won't have any phone signal up there so everything is going to have to be done via landline.'

'Wow, that's so old-school!'

'Trust me, a *lot* of this wedding is going to be old-school. Also, if you could keep Bella out of Sadie Lee's hair during the wedding preparations, that would be *so* helpful.'

'Of course!'

'Brilliant. The rest of this stuff will be down to me . . .'

I reach over the headrest and stroke my mum's hair. 'Don't worry, it's going to be great.'

'Speaking of great – keep your eyes peeled, Penny.'

I turn back to the window. The road, barely wide enough for our car now, is surrounded by tall trees, blocking the light and casting spooky shadows. It twists and turns sharply, up and down, and we pass over an old stone bridge that looks as if it was constructed hundreds of years ago. It probably was.

Then, like a curtain parting to reveal the set of a play, the trees stop and in the clearing I get my first view of Castle Lochland.

'Oh. My. God.' They are the only words I can say, and I plaster my face to the window.

The castle sits at the top of a high, rocky island in the middle of a vast lake, connected to the mainland by a single, long bridge. The water is covered by a thick layer of mist, making the castle look like it's floating on clouds. All round the lake is the extension of the thick forest we've been driving through, bright bursts of orange and red streaking across the autumn foliage as the leaves turn.

It's perfect and magical and everything that I imagined it would be.

We drive down towards the castle, but at the last minute Dad takes a turn that leads *away* from it. 'Aren't we going to the castle now?' I ask, unable to hide the disappointment in my voice.

'We can't drive across the bridge,' says Dad.

'Argh, yet *another* logistical nightmare I'm going to have to deal with!' says Mum.

'So we're going to go to our home for the week first,' continues Dad, 'to drop off our things.'

'I suppose that makes sense,' I say with a sigh.

When we pull up in front of a little stone cottage with a thatched roof, however, I immediately forget all my disappointment at the delay in seeing the castle. The cottage is absolutely adorable, and I can't wait to get inside and see my room.

There's already another car in the yard, which means Elliot and Alex must already be there. They'd come up a day early because Alex had wanted to do a tour of Loch Ness – he has a thing about mythological creatures.

They've obviously heard our car arriving, because soon the door opens and 'Greetings, lads and lassies!' says Elliot – already wearing a tartan beret. He looks mildly ridiculous. I think you have to actually be Scottish to pull that look off. 'We've got some bannocks warming on the Aga and a cuppa waiting for you inside.'

'Oh, Elliot, you are a *star*,' says Mum.

'What's a bannock?' I ask.

'A kind of flatbread . . . a bit like a scone, but Scottish,' says Elliot with a wink.

'Ooh, I love scones,' and I give him a big hug. 'But since when did you know how to use an Aga?'

He winks again. 'That's not me – that's all Alex. Turns out his family used to have one when he was growing up. A person of many talents, my boyfriend . . .'

'Well, I can't wait to try these bannocks!'

'Come on, I'll show you to your room.'

Inside, Elliot has to keep ducking his head to avoid bumping it on the low wooden beams criss-crossing the ceiling. It's exactly as humble and romantic as I imagined: there's a fire burning in the living room, which, along with the Aga, keeps the place toasty warm, and there's a deep window seat in the stone wall below the window, covered in embroidered cushions that I can imagine curling up among with a good book.

'This used to be the gamekeeper's cottage,' Elliot says, as he climbs up the stairs. 'Built in the early 1500s!'

'Wow, that's awesome! But not for tall – or even medium-sized – people,' I say, as I nearly crack my head on a beam jutting from the roof.

'I don't think it originally had an upstairs. Your parents' bedroom is downstairs and is much roomier. C'mon, this way.'

My room is in the loft, and the ceiling is so low it doesn't even have a proper bed, more like a mattress nearly on the floor that I'll have to crawl on to. But I don't mind and squeal with delight when I see it. The room's been decorated in such a sweet way, with a white sheet canopy hung from the ceiling so that it drapes down round the bed as if it belongs to a princess. Pale triangles of pink and green bunting trim the edge of the sheet. And the best part? When I lie down on the bed, I have a perfect view through the dormer window of the castle on the lake.

'Happy?' Elliot asks with a grin.

I smile back. 'I couldn't have imagined anything more lovely, even if I tried.'

Chapter Twenty-One

The smell of freshly baked bread makes my mouth water. It drifts up through the rooms of the castle and crosses even the thickest stone walls to reach us in one of the higher towers, where Bella and I are playing with an old set of marbles. Sadie Lee and Bella are staying in two rooms in an extension adjoining our cottage, but we've all come down to the castle itself to get on with the wedding preparations.

I'm taking my responsibility of keeping Bella out of Sadie Lee's hair very seriously, and together we've explored much of the castle, but I have to keep Bella's hand in mine just in case we come across any spooky suits of armour. The first one she saw almost made her jump out of her skin – probably because he was wielding a huge axe bigger than my head.

For me, it wasn't the suits of armour that were creepy, but all the animal heads on the wall, relics of the castle's hunting past. But everything else is just so cool, I quickly get over my fear. Enormous portraits hang on the walls, but they're not like the 'boring' ones I've seen in some other castles nearer home. These are of muscular men in brightly coloured tartan and big feather caps, surrounded by the animals of the Highlands – great stags and eagles. There's even plenty of bare leg on show, thanks to their kilts! I almost expect them to come to life. Being inside this castle makes me feel like I've received my invitation to Hogwarts and at any moment I'll run into Harry, Ron or Hermione.

'Shall we go see what your grandma is cooking up?' I ask Bella.

'OK!' she says. She scoops up the marbles, which have rolled all over the stone floor and under the carpet. I put them back into their little bag and place it on top of the armoire we found them in.

As we walk downstairs towards the kitchen, we pass an army of Mum's helpers busy dressing every inch of the castle. Mum calls this a 'wedding of two halves' – the bride has requested that the first part of the day be white and bright and fresh everywhere, with bundles of white roses that have to be shipped in at eye-watering expense because they're out of season. Then, once the sun sets, she wants a gothic, 'Halloween – but classy' vibe for the masquerade. It's going to be a challenge to pull it off in time, but there's nothing Mum loves more than a challenge.

Meanwhile, Sadie Lee is hard at work on the cake of a lifetime. It's also a cake of two halves – one side complementing the white theme (dozens of white sugar flowers cascading down five huge tiers), the other side iced in black (with red roses dripping blood). If you look at it straight on, you can only see one side or the other, so they'll rotate it throughout the night. If you look where the sides join, the white side seems to peel away to reveal the dark. When it's finished it will be absolutely stunning.

'How are my girls?' Sadie Lee asks as we walk in.

'All good! Although I think Bella is exhausted,' I reply. Almost on cue, Bella releases a big yawn.

'I think you're right, little lady.'

'I'll take her back, Mrs Flynn,' says one of Sadie Lee's assistants. Bella has managed to enchant everyone she meets, and they all vie for her attention.

'That's lovely, thank you, Gemma. Now, Penny, can you pass me that piping bag?'

I look down at the array of piping instruments on the stainless-steel table in front of me. Sometimes, when Sadie Lee's working, she resembles a surgeon more than a baker. 'Uh . . . which one?' I say.

'The one with the star-shaped nozzle on the end.'

I spot it and pass it over.

'Great,' she says. 'Now why don't you pick one up and you can make some decorations for me too?'

'Really?' I ask. 'What if I mess up?'

'Practice makes perfect! And, OK, we're making some little cupcakes for the young ones too . . .'

'Oh good, that's less pressure than doing decorations for the *actual* cake!' I say with a laugh.

My mum's voice echoes around the draughty room, louder than normal.

'Everyone look sharp,' says Sadie Lee. 'The bride's coming.' She lowers her voice and winks at me. 'Your mum and I have a system – if the bride's on her way, we try to speak louder than normal to give the other some warning! No one wants to have an angry bride sprung on them.'

Sure enough, a few moments later, Mum appears in the kitchen followed by the bride, Jane.

'Something smells good in here!' Jane says. I'm surprised – even though she's Callum's cousin, she doesn't have his accent. She has the same tall, willowy figure, though – and the hint of a thorn tattoo peeking out by her collarbone. Now the reason why it's a 'wedding of two halves' starts to become clearer.

Sadie Lee kisses Jane on both cheeks, avoiding touching her with her sugary hands.

'Jane,' says Mum, 'this is my daughter, Penny. She's going to be helping me out tomorrow.'

'Oh, so *this* is the famous Penny!'

Mum and Sadie Lee both look at me questioningly.

'Do you know Penny from her blog?' Mum asks.

Jane frowns. 'What's that? No, I've heard about her from my cousin, Callum,' she says with a wink.

I cringe. I haven't exactly told Mum yet about my date with Callum – it just seemed too premature. In hindsight, I probably should have mentioned it. Oops. 'I met Callum at Megan's school. He's also at Madame Laplage.'

'Oh!' Mum's arched eyebrow raises even higher. I know she knows there's more to the story.

'It's such a wonderful coincidence!' says Jane. 'He's going

to get here later on this afternoon. He thought maybe you'd like to go for a walk and see where he grew up? I can drop you off there on my way back.'

'Oh, uh . . .' I look to Mum and Sadie Lee, who are now staring at me expectantly. It feels rude to refuse a suggestion from the bride. 'Sure, that would be great,' I answer.

'Sorted then. Be at the front gates in an hour and I'll drive you down. Sadie Lee, tell me, how are the canapés coming on? I really want the smoked salmon to be incredibly fresh . . .'

Sadie Lee whisks Jane off to the other side of the kitchen, leaving Mum still staring at me. 'So . . . who is this Callum?'

'He's just this guy I met . . . We went on one date and he wants to see me again.'

'Oooh, check you out. What about Noah?'

I cringe. Ah, Mum. Always straight to the point. 'I haven't heard from him in so long, and besides we're supposed to be just friends now . . .'

She puts her hand on my shoulder. 'I understand. It's good that you're meeting new people. I know you'll follow your heart.'

'Do you think Sadie Lee will mind?' I ask. I can't help feeling like I'm betraying their whole family.

Mum shakes her head. 'Don't you worry about that. Noah is his own person, and what he's doing isn't fair to you – or to them. Frankly, I hope he snaps out of it soon. A creative break. Really . . . If only all we creatives were so lucky as to get a break.'

'Thanks, Mum,' I say.

'Now, if you have an hour, here's a list of all the things you can do in the meantime . . .'

I look down at the list and inwardly groan. It's packed with errands that will mean running all over the castle. But the last thing Mum needs from me is any more stress.

Instead, I plaster a smile on my face and say, 'You got it!'

Chapter Twenty-Two

With all the errands I have to do for Mum, the hour flies by, and it's not long before I'm sitting in the car with Jane – who might just give Kira a run for her money as the chattiest person on earth. I could put it down to pre-wedding jitters, but something tells me she's always like this. I'm still not quite sure how planning to avoid Callum wherever I could while I was here has turned into being driven to his family home by his cousin.

My stomach swirls with guilt at leaving Mum a man down (or, rather, *a girl down*) at the castle, but I hope I can make up for it later. It is strange how circumstances keep throwing Callum and me together. Maybe I should listen to them?

'Did you grow up in Scotland too?' I ask Jane.

'Do I sound like I did?' she says with a laugh. 'No, it's just Callum's family who live up here now – but I used to come up here every summer to play in the Highlands and around the castle. I always knew that when I got married it would be here. It's practically a McCrae family tradition! Perhaps one day it will be your turn,' she winks.

I swallow hard. What on earth has Callum said about me? I try to laugh it off, but it comes out as more of a croak.

'So do you visit the castle a lot then?' I continue.

A strange look passes over Jane's face. 'Visit? All the time! It's the ancient family seat of the McCraes, after all. It's only recently that it's been converted into a tourist attraction and the family moved into a more modern country house a few miles away. Callum's parents are still very involved in the restoration work, of course, and you can often find his mum doing the tours.'

My eyes open wide. *Callum's family* own *Castle Lochland?* 'Oh, I didn't know that.'

'Ah, well I guess you two are still getting to know each other. Don't let it change your view! Callum is still one of the most down-to-earth guys you'll ever meet.'

'Yeah, he seems that way.'

'Ah, here we are.' We pull in to the driveway of the country house and I almost groan out loud. It's *huge*. There are four gigantic windows on either side of the front door, which is double the size of ours, and it's three storeys high, the stonework covered in ivy. It almost looks like a castle in its own right. Why don't I ever attract an average Joe, living in a three-bed family terrace who works in Starbucks on the weekend?

'This place is beautiful,' I manage to choke out.

'*And* it's got all mod cons. There's even an indoor/outdoor swimming pool in the grounds at the back. You can tell why the McCraes wanted to move here – much easier to take care of than a draughty old castle.' She pulls up in front of the house and toots the horn twice.

Callum steps out of the front door, in full Scottish countryside gear: a flat cap, olive jacket over tan shirt, and khaki trousers tucked into dark green wellingtons. He looks like he's walked straight out of a Barbour catalogue. He couldn't fit in more if he tried. In his hands are another pair of wellies, this time in pink. A real gentleman, he even opens the door for me to get out.

'Hi, cousin!' he says over my head.

'Lovely to see you, Callum. Well, you two lovebirds, I have a mani-pedi appointment to be getting to! But I'm sure I'll be seeing a lot more of you soon, Penny.' Jane waves at me and drives off the moment I shut the door. I smile awkwardly up at Callum. I guess I'm stuck here now.

He holds out the wellies to me. 'Ready for a walk?'

'I guess so!' I say with a laugh. Balancing on his shoulder, I remove my Converse and replace them with the wellies. They require a bit of manoeuvring to get on, but once my feet are inside I'm surprised how comfortable they are.

'They suit you! Come on, this way.' He starts walking away from the house, but before we can go very far, we're interrupted by a loud 'Oi!'

I spin round and have to duck as a rugby ball is thrown over my head. Standing in the doorway is an even bigger version of Callum, in a polo shirt and chinos.

Callum catches the ball, then effortlessly tosses it back to his almost-twin in the doorway. 'All right, Mal?' There's a hint of hesitation in his voice.

The guy grunts and steps out, followed by another, this one also tall and blond. *How many of them are there?* But I can't think for too long: I jump out of the way as the two guys tackle Callum, roughing up his hair. I can't help but laugh.

'I'm glad someone's finding it funny,' says Callum, caught underneath Mal's arm in a headlock. He grimaces. 'Penny, these nutters are my older brothers, Malcolm and Henry.'

'Hi, Penny,' they say, almost in unison. Mal releases Callum, and I finally get a proper look at them both and realize they're not as alike as I first thought. Malcolm is taller and broader, with a nose that looks like it's been broken, and Henry's hair is cropped short and he's much more muscly than Callum. But from a distance you'd be forgiven for thinking they were triplets.

Rowdy, sporty triplets, I think, as I watch them wrestling the ball from one another. I grin as Callum's cheeks flush with colour and snap a photo of them all on my phone.

Seeing Callum loosen up with his brothers makes me look at him in a new light. Either he notices my scrutiny or they all finally run out of energy, because a breathless Callum jogs over to me, his brothers smiling and chuckling. 'See you later, you two!' shouts Malcolm in a sing-song voice.

'Come on, let's go before they drag us into a game of rugby!' says Callum.

'Yeah, let's – I'm rubbish at sports!'

We clamber over a fence and walk through the short yellow grass of a fallow field. Out in the open, the breeze cools my skin, sending a delicious shiver down my spine.

'You're so lucky to have grown up here,' I tell Callum. 'It's absolutely beautiful.'

He grins. 'So, Jane spilled the beans, did she? I hope you don't think any differently of me.'

'Of course not!' I say.

'No, I suppose you wouldn't. You did date a sell-out pop star after all, so you're probably used to it.'

My jaw drops open. 'Well, I hope *you* can get used to dating a normal person,' I shoot back.

He stops and takes my hand. 'Sorry, I didn't mean to touch a nerve. Come on, let me show you something. Do you like ruins?'

I search his face, but it doesn't give away any hint of malice. Maybe he's just the kind who makes bad jokes, like calling Noah a 'sell-out pop star'. So I give him a small, tentative smile. 'Sure.'

'Then I have just the thing,' he says. We start walking again, and I have to pick my feet up to avoid squelching in the mud. 'There are these old ruins of a castle, about a mile away along the coast. Well, I say "castle", but it's actually a single tower with a few turrets on top. The man who owned it was a pirate and a rogue.'

'Ooh, sounds scandalous!'

'He was. As a third son, he never expected to make anything of himself by legitimate means, so he became a pirate. But then he inherited the lairdship and suddenly he was a pirate *and* the rightful landowner of an estate. It didn't change him much. He still led raids on his neighbours and scandalized the local village. His castle was ruined when he was finally defeated by a rival clan and that put an end to his pillaging ways.'

My eyes open wide. 'Wow! There's so much history here. You talk about it like it happened yesterday.'

'The past is all around us. In Scotland, you don't have to scratch too deep before you find a tale or two that will chill your blood or shake your bones, or both. It's why I love it here so much. It feels one step away from being wild again. Not like in London, where the history is either buried or it becomes assimilated, so you're just not aware of it.'

As if eager to provide a suitable atmosphere for his words, the wind picks up as we near the cliff edge and sends my hair flying round my face. Callum reaches out and grabs one of my hands to steady me and I pull my jacket closer round me with the other, but I don't hate the wind. It feels bracing and, Callum's right, it feels *wild*. I lean into his grip, burrowing against his muscular chest. This is not so bad.

As we walk along, the waves crash against the foot of the cliffs, sea spray leaps hundreds of feet into the air. A few gulls squawk overhead, but apart from that it's as if we're the only creatures for miles.

'There, can you see it?' Callum points to where the cliff juts further out into the sea.

I squint in the direction he's pointing. 'Is it . . . is it that lump of rock?' I ask.

He laughs. 'That about sums it up! When you get closer, you'll be able to see it clearer. And, if it's not too overgrown, we might even be able to clamber inside.'

'Oh, cool!' I say. 'It's a pretty desolate place to put a castle, though.'

'Welcome to Scotland,' Callum says with a wink. 'And, like I said, the man was a pirate, so he wanted to have a good lookout over the sea.' He breathes in deeply and looks out over the ocean too. He seems much more at home here than he did in sedate St James's Park.

'How did you end up in London?' I ask.

Callum shrugs. 'I won an Arts Scotland photo competition, and I've always loved taking pictures. I never thought I was good enough to make a career out of it, but when I was offered the place at Madame Laplage, it seemed like too good an opportunity to miss. A place where my hobby was suddenly something worthwhile. If it doesn't lead anywhere and it turns out I have to go to law school or be an accountant or something, at least I got to do it for a little while.'

I nod. 'I know how you feel. It's a privilege to be able to do what I love and hope to make money from it. I've been so lucky so far, but I can't help thinking the rug is going to get pulled out from under me at any moment.'

'I think that's called being a creative,' he says.

'I guess so.'

He squeezes my shoulder, bringing me tighter towards him. 'You shouldn't worry about that, anyway. Yes, you've had some luck, but you've also worked hard to put yourself in a position where you can be lucky. Not everyone does that. Plus, you're *really* good. Don't underestimate that either. FPN doesn't do charity cases.'

I smile up at him gratefully.

'When was the first time you knew you *had* to be a photographer?' he asks.

I pause. 'I've never really thought about it. I think it was when my friend Megan got a Polaroid camera for her birthday and asked me to take photos at her party. I loved the anticipation of seeing the picture develop right in front of my eyes. It felt like . . . a dream coming to life.' I blush as I think how cheesy I sound, but Callum nods thoughtfully.

'For me, it was getting my first roll of film developed. Taking a little black bottle to the shop and an hour later receiving an envelope full of memories. It felt like magic. What was your first camera?'

I scrunch my nose up trying to remember. 'It was a Canon Sure Shot, I think.'

'Me too!' he says with a laugh. 'I used to spend all my pocket money on getting the films developed in Boots. Most would come out blurry or the composition would be pants, but it was fun. There were certainly a few gems in there.'

I grin, nodding at his words, amazed at how much we have in common – at least, when it comes to photography.

We walk the rest of the way to the ruins wrapped in our own thoughts, and I'm grateful for the comfortable silence. The harsh wind whips away our words anyway, and the salty sea air stings my nostrils.

When we reach the castle, I run forward, excited at the prospect of getting up close to the ruins. The big, dark stones are fluffy with moss and I can see now that the tower must have been much taller in its heyday.

'Over here,' Callum says, walking round the other side. I follow him over to a window – or rather, just a hole in the stone – and he hoists himself up to climb through. 'Come on, I'll help you,' he says.

'OK,' I say, and swallow hard. I tuck my camera bag behind my back, tugging the strap tight round my body. Then I take Callum's outstretched hand and let him help me through the window.

Inside the castle is so much quieter than outside, the wind buffeting the stone but unable to break through. The Scottish wildlife has completely taken over inside, though: rough brambles with juicy blackberries punch up through the soil and thistles huddle low to the ground.

'Wow, this place is amazing,' I say.

'I know,' he says with a grin.

Callum has his phone out and is searching for something online. It looks such a funny juxtaposition – this modern Scottish boy in an ancient castle on his brand-new phone – that I whip my camera out and snap a picture.

'Ah, a couple of months in London and I forget how bad the signal is out here,' he says, with a shrug of apology at having his phone out. He plucks a couple of berries from the bush and hands them to me. 'Try one? They'll be really sweet at this time of year.'

I take a couple from his palm, the purple juice already staining my fingers. I pop them in my mouth and he's right – they're deliciously sweet, with only a hint of tang. I savour the taste on my tongue, closing my eyes.

'You know, if you want, you could come to the wedding

with me. As my guest. Jane doesn't mind a bit – I've already asked her.'

I open my eyes wide with alarm, and swallow down the rest of the berry as fast as I can. 'Oh no, I couldn't – I . . . I need to help Mum anyway. That's the whole reason I'm here.'

'Well, you have to at least come to the masquerade. There won't be anything left for you to do in the evening. I insist.'

I wrinkle my nose. 'There's *always* things to do on a wedding day but . . . I'll see if I can spare an hour.'

'Good,' he says, stepping close to me. 'It would kill me to know that you were so near but I wasn't seeing you.' He lifts his finger to my chin. 'You have some blackberry juice here,' he says, gently wiping at the corner of my lip.

Then he leans down and kisses me again.

And I curse my stupid mind and heart for not feeling a thing.

Chapter Twenty-Three

My alarm goes off at six in the morning and I wake up, bleary-eyed.

'Come along, sunshine!' Elliot peeks his head round my door, *way* too perky for this early in the morning. But he's been like a different person all week. Sunnier. Happier. More like the old Elliot. Plus, he's brought me a cup of tea, so I can't be mad at him for long.

'You're so excited, anyone would think it was *your* wedding day!' I say with a laugh.

'*Dahling*, if this was my wedding day, I'd be bouncing off the walls! Plus, there's no way I'd be able to afford something *this* extravagant, but my goodness me, I'll enjoy helping your mum put it all together. She's a genius!'

'I know,' I say with a grin. 'But do we really have to wear these costumes?' In the corner of my room, laid over an armchair, is the purple crushed-velvet monstrosity that I have to wear for the majority of the day. When Mum showed it to me last night, I almost called Callum right then and there to take him up on his invitation, just so that I could wear *normal* clothes. But I also knew I couldn't let Mum down, even if she was making me wear 'historically accurate' dress for the wedding.

I shouldn't have been surprised. I'd been dressed as a maid in New York. But at least those outfits were black and designed to not draw attention. *This* is going to cause a stir. Elliot and Alex's costumes have a similar historical theme, but they'll look downright cool in their kilts, naturally. I can already imagine the guests pointing and whispering, wanting to take selfies with us.

And I'm not allowed to bring my camera. Jane has hired a world-famous wedding photographer (and videographer) for her big day, and he's coming with two assistants, so I'm not needed. Plus, my Canon won't exactly look authentic with my costume.

It's for Mum, for Mum, for Mum, I keep thinking, over and over.

'You'll look adorable,' says Elliot, following my gaze and my grimace. 'But your mum said you might need some help with the corset, so that's why I'm here!'

'Ugh!' I say, groaning at the thought of wearing a corset all day.

'Now, now. I do have something *else* to cheer you up.' He brings out an exquisite gold filigree mask with two red velvet ribbons, one on each side, for ties. I'm stunned and I actually gasp at how beautiful it is. 'Since you told me last night you'd be going to the masquerade, I thought you'd better have a proper mask to wear.'

I take it out of his hands, holding it delicately as if it may disintegrate in my fingers at any moment. 'It's gorgeous . . . Where did you get it?'

'Oh, you know me. I always keep something up my sleeve.'

I throw my arms round him. 'Thank you!'

'No problem. Now, let's get this dress on!'

It takes us a good half-hour to put my dress on and tie every lace, ribbon and bow. By the time we've finished, I look like a genuine seventeenth-century Scottish lass.

Elliot hurries away as he and Alex have to get ready too and suddenly Mum's calling up the stairs. 'Penny? Are you ready to go to the castle?' I can tell she's keyed up as her voice sounds edgy and brisk.

'Coming!' I shout, and I run down the stairs as fast as my cloth slippers allow.

'Oh, Penny, you look amazing!' Mum says. She isn't in costume. It's a stunning dove-grey suit for Mum, her wedding-planner finest – suitable for a wedding guest but also comfortable enough for running around solving problems all day.

Andrea, Mum's assistant, is dressed in character like me. We're going to be mingling with the guests, adding to the set-ting as we role-play our historical counterparts, but also solving any problems that come to light – in short, being Mum's eyes and ears on the floor.

When we get to the chapel, Andrea's and my first task is to go round lighting every single candle – and trying not to set fire to our purple velvet skirts in the process. Then it's not long before the guests start arriving, but we're too busy help-ing Mum with last-minute checks to spend long watching them and, as always, the day starts to disappear fast.

As soon as the bride arrives at the door, it's non-stop for all of us and, before I know it, she's walking down the aisle, they're making their vows, the minister is declaring them husband and wife, and they're walking back outside for the photographs . . .

Somehow, I manage fairly successfully to stay out of Cal-lum's sight, though he does find me once – and I swear I spot him covering his mouth to suppress a giggle. I consider stick-ing my tongue out at him, but that wouldn't be very lady-like.

It's only after everyone has sat down for the wedding breakfast that Mum and her team of helpers are allowed our first few moments of rest.

Mum's looking more relaxed now, pleased that the day seems to be going so well. 'Go on, Penny,' she says, 'you can go off to get changed,' and she scoffs down one of Sadie Lee's leftover canapés.

'Really?' I ask. 'You don't need any help with the changeover?'

'I think I've got it covered. Thank you for all your help today,' and she gives me two big kisses on the cheek. 'Now go and have fun. I don't need you to think about anything else for me, OK?'

I nod, and give her a tight squeeze-hug back. 'Thank you, Mum.'

As I slip out of the castle there's a definite chill in the air. I make my way across the bridge and back to the little cottage and for the first time all day feel thankful for the layers of petticoats under my dress. I pull my tartan shawl closer round my shoulders for warmth.

Back in the cottage, I suddenly realize I don't know what I'm going to wear to the masquerade ball. I survey my options: I haven't really brought anything suitable for a ball and only have a simple black dress with me. It's pretty, with little lacy sleeves in the pattern of roses, but it isn't grand. Still, it's the only thing I have.

Then I remember the mask Elliot gave me this morning. I take it out of its tissue-paper wrapping and put it on. It's a surprise how light it is on my face; the velvet ribbons are soft against my skin and I love the way the gold of the mask off-sets the auburn in my hair. I look in the mirror and admire how the mask elevates my dress into a gown worthy of a ball.

You are Autumn Girl, I think. I shake the thought from my head. I don't want to be Autumn Girl. I don't want to be just a lyric in a song. I want to be loved for who I am, in a relationship that's equal.

Maybe Callum will be that person. Maybe not. But does it really matter? I want to be able to make mistakes. I want to throw myself in at the deep end, without worrying about the consequences. I want to make a fool of myself and not be self-conscious.

I smooth down the front of my dress.

'You look so pretty,' says a small voice by the door.

I smile at Bella. 'I thought you were supposed to be in bed, little lady,' I say. She's in her nightie and her feet are bare. Then I sweep her up into my arms.

'I don't like my room; it's scary,' she mumbles.

'Well, don't worry – I'll be back to protect you before you know it.'

'OK,' she says, leaning her head against my shoulder. 'I miss No-no.'

I give a start and my chest tightens, as if a hand is suddenly gripping my heart. *Noah*. I stroke her hair with my free hand. 'I know, Bells. Me too.'

Chapter Twenty-Four

Before very long, Bella is snoring gently on my shoulder and her breathing evens out. I carry her back to her room, lay her gently down on her bed and kiss her forehead. As I tiptoe through the living room, I wave at Gemma, Bella's babysitter for the evening, and put my finger to my lips to signal that she's asleep. Gemma gives me a thumbs up, and then a double thumbs up for my dress.

I grin back, smoothing the front of the pretty lace.

There's no more time to lose. I wrap myself up in my coat and scarf, then slip back across the bridge.

Now that night has fallen, the atmosphere of the castle is completely different. Mum has replaced the white candles with the black ones, and red fabric drapes the walls where there had been white before. Jane's gothic-themed evening is coming to life. I half expect to see a ghost or two drifting through the halls or the suits of armour stretching their metal-clad limbs. I'm glad that Bella, who wouldn't like this at all, is safely asleep in bed.

I can hear the string quartet playing somewhere and head towards the music. Later, there will be a disco but for now the ambiance is more refined. The laughter of the guests mixes with the haunting music, and I'm glad everyone is having a good time. Mum will be so pleased and relieved.

I step into the dining hall and gasp. It's been absolutely transformed for the evening. Thousands of candles are set at different heights round the walls and project flickering shadows towards the ceiling. Many of the guests are dancing, waltzing round the dance floor, and those who aren't are helping themselves to the wonderful buffet laid out by Sadie Lee, admiring the gorgeous half-white, half-black wedding cake. The bride and groom will cut the cake together later in the evening.

'Penny,' a voice says, 'there you are.' And Callum steps out from the shadows, his face hidden behind an emerald-green mask. The combination of the mask and his tuxedo makes him so dashing tonight.

'Hi, Callum,' I say with a genuine smile.

'Your mum has really done an amazing job. I don't think I've ever seen Jane so happy.'

'Oh, I'm really glad. I'll tell her.' It's obvious Callum wants to dance – he's already swaying slightly to the music – but it's too slow. I don't want to dance to something so . . . romantic. I scan the room until I spot Elliot and Alex in a corner. 'Hey, do you want to meet my friends?' I ask.

He hesitates, but then shrugs his shoulders. 'Sure thing.'

'Great,' I say, taking his hand and leading him over to Alexiot. They're deep in conversation, lost to the crowd around them, until I manage to catch Alex's eye. The surprise on his face makes Elliot spin round.

'Penny!' Elliot has a huge grin on his face. 'Love the dress.' He gives me two kisses on the cheek and squeezes my arm. 'And who's this?'

Callum stretches out his hand before I can answer. 'Callum McCrae.'

'Wonderful to meet you.' Elliot blatantly looks Callum up and down. When Callum turns to shake Alex's hand Elliot gives me a thumbs up of approval behind his back.

Unfortunately, however, my diversion technique doesn't last very long, because Callum's ears suddenly perk up on hearing a change of song. Still a slow one. I suppress my sigh.

'Ready for a dance?' he asks.

'OK,' I say.

'Good, because I've been waiting for this all night.'

He kisses my hand and guides me into the middle of the dance floor.

The music is quite slow and, because I don't know how to waltz and feel awkward, we end up doing an odd sort of shuffle.

'I really enjoyed our walk yesterday,' he's saying close to my ear.

'Me too.'

'I hope you don't mind me telling you, Penny, but I really like you,' he continues, and he laces his fingers through mine. 'I . . . I was wondering if you felt the same way.'

I can feel myself blushing beneath my mask and I'm lost

for words. His eyes are searching mine, hoping to find his own feelings reflected back . . . but the truth is, I just don't feel the same way.

'Callum, I . . . I –'

But before I can say another word a hand taps him on the shoulder. He tenses with annoyance and stops dancing, but his hand stays firmly attached to mine.

'Mind if I cut in?' says the voice. An American voice.

My heart flutters then starts beating wildly. It isn't . . . It can't be . . .

But it is.

It's Noah Flynn.

Chapter Twenty-Five

'Mind if I cut in?'

Noah's words ring in my ears.

'Uh, OK,' says Callum. He's too polite to refuse. His eyebrows join together in a frown beneath his mask. *The mask!* I whip my head round to look at Noah. He's wearing a mask too, a black one that covers the top half of his face. Callum doesn't recognize him. At least, I don't think he does.

Before I can regain the ability to speak again, Callum has stepped back and Noah's hand is in mine and his other hand is round my waist. He pulls me away into a spin, but with every turn I can see realization dawning on Callum's face . . .

'Hi, Pen,' Noah says in almost a whisper, his soft American accent lingering on my ear.

I put my cheek on his shoulder, leaning into his warm embrace and closing my eyes. I feel a wave of goosebumps prickling my skin from top to bottom like an electric current and the crowds of people dancing round us are blurry and out of focus. I'm struck by an eerie sense of calm, of immense relief: he's OK, nothing bad has happened to him.

'I've missed you,' he continues.

I'd forgotten how much I've missed him.

Not just as a boyfriend; as my friend too, having him around, the smell of his hair, the touch of his skin . . . OK, so maybe *mostly* as a boyfriend. I forgot how neatly my head tucks into the crook of his neck, and how comforting his hand is round mine; his fingers, with their tiny calluses from playing guitar, rubbing against mine. The way his smile, with those gorgeous dimples, show off his perfectly straight teeth. And how his big brown eyes crease slightly when his face lights up. I forgot how he smells like rain and leather and a hint of musk.

'I'm back now,' he says.

Then it all comes crashing down on me, like a bucket of ice water tipped over my head. Noah *left*, with just a single, short note, ignoring all my other messages and texts. He selfishly left me to stew while he swanned off for a break, with no thought for his family or for me . . .

And he shows up now? Just when I was thinking about moving on?

He squeezes my fingers. 'Are you going to say something?' he asks.

That's what breaks me. I stop dancing and step back out of his embrace. I frown, looking up into his warm eyes, but I have to look away again or else I risk losing all my nerve.

'What are you doing here?' I demand.

His hands are outstretched towards me, like he wants to bring me back into his embrace, but I don't step towards him. I fold my arms over my chest. 'I wanted to see you,' he says.

It sounds pretty feeble to me. Somewhere behind Noah I sense Callum staring, and the room isn't a blur any more. Everything has been pulled back into focus and the music is loud.

'After all this time? You just show up out of the blue and expect everything to be how it was?'

His lips part, but no words come out. I don't care. I can feel white-hot rage racing through my veins, making my cheeks tingle. How *dare* he? I can tell Noah's never seen me like this. He looks . . . stricken.

A comforting hand grips my shoulder. Elliot. 'Are you OK, Penny?'

I just shake my head. He turns to look at Noah. 'You shouldn't be here,' Elliot says, much more gently than I would have been able to manage.

'I'm sorry, Penny. I didn't mean to hurt you . . .' Noah mumbles. I realize I've never seen him this way: so apologetic, so afraid of how I'm going to react . . .

I want to tell him to just go away. That I'll deal with it when we get back home, not in the middle of someone's *wedding*. That's when I look up to see Jane over by her wedding cake, pointing at us, her face crinkled in anger. Callum is next to her. My face drains of colour. 'We're causing a scene,' I say to Noah through gritted teeth.

'Is there somewhere we can go talk?' he asks.

Reluctantly, I nod.

'Are you sure, Penny?' Elliot asks.

'I'm OK, honestly,' I tell him, and force a small smile across my lips.

'Well, if you need anything, message me. I'll be right there.'

'Thanks,' I say.

But we've taken too long already. One of the wedding's security team comes striding over, Callum only a couple of steps behind. The security officer taps Noah on the shoulder. 'Excuse me, sir, but do you have an invitation?'

Noah turns with a start, then straightens his back. 'My grandmother is doing the catering.'

'Are you on the official staff list then?'

Noah shuffles his feet. 'No . . .'

'Then I'm going to have to ask you to leave. Now.'

'We were just going,' I say. I lift my eyes to Noah's briefly. 'Come on.'

'*You* don't have to go, Penny,' blurts out Callum. 'It's only the gatecrasher who has to leave.'

'I know. But it's fine. Actually, I'm not feeling that well anyway. I'll see you tomorrow?' I say. Before he can say anything else to try to change my mind, I storm off towards the wide double doors that will lead back out to the entrance of the castle. I don't even look to see if Noah is following, but I can hear his footsteps echoing along the flagstones behind me as I get further away from the ballroom.

I push through the heavy wooden doors of the main entrance and stride out on to the bridge that leads across to the mainland. It's raining – *typical* – and windy, but there wasn't a chance to grab my jacket before I left the party. I wrap my arms round my body, aware suddenly of the cold.

The rain slicks my hair to my cheeks and the wind covers the sound of Noah's steps behind me.

I jump with a start as he wraps something warm round me. 'Here, take my jacket,' he says.

But I shrug it off. 'No!' I half shout into the wind. I spin round and stare at him, looking into his eyes as boldly as I can. 'You don't just get to come back here and pretend like everything is OK! You left – and only one stupid note.'

'I know . . .'

'You ignored my messages.'

'I know . . .'

'You even told your *grandmother* not to contact you. I mean, I know I'm not your girlfriend any more, but you could've at least made sure the people who love you knew you were safe.'

'Penny . . .'

'Why are you even here?' I ask again. I start to shiver, slowly at first, but the water is gathering in the soles of my shoes and even Noah's jacket wouldn't have kept out the bitter coastal wind.

'Give me a chance to explain,' Noah says, 'and I'll tell you everything.'

We stare at each other, and the moment stretches until it seems like it could last a lifetime.

I break eye contact first. 'Fine,' I say. 'Let's go inside.'

Chapter Twenty-Six

I let us into the house, ushering him towards the living room. 'It's all right, Gemma,' I say, as she looks up from her paperback. 'We can look after Bella now. You can take off early if you want.'

'Sure thing.' She looks curiously at Noah, but doesn't say anything. I know she's heard a lot about Sadie Lee's infamous grandson, but she's too good an assistant to mention anything. 'See you tomorrow,' she says, throwing on her coat and heading out into the rain.

There's a low fire in the hearth, and Noah kneels down in front of it, adding more logs and coaxing it back to life. I sit on the sofa, shivering uncontrollably. I pull the faux-fur throw draped over the back of the sofa round me, sighing as I loosen up into its warmth.

'Do you want something?' Noah asks, once the fire is roaring again. 'What is it you Brits normally have in this kind of situation . . . a cup of tea?'

I shake my head. 'I don't want tea.' I kick off my heels, letting my stockinged toes sink into the deep pile of the carpet. The sofa dips next to me as Noah sits down, but I don't look at him, and I'm still gazing at my feet when Noah starts to speak.

'Penny, I want to explain everything. So . . . I'm going to start from the beginning. After leaving you in Brighton, the tour just wasn't the same. I felt like I was going through the motions – like I was having this incredible opportunity and seeing all these amazing things, but all I wanted to do was be back in the UK with you. But I knew that wasn't fair. We'd agreed to be friends, and I had to give you that space. I owed that to you, even if I couldn't stop thinking about you – even for a moment.

'My new management are great, by the way. I owe you for that. You'll have to meet Fenella one day, my new manager. You'd love her. She noticed I was feeling down and suggested I write some music on the road. New material. But I couldn't. It was . . . scary. No – more than that: it was terrifying. I could barely play a note; my mind was blank; I had all these feelings but no lyrics were coming. When Fenella realized that wasn't working, she'd send me demos from other artists, to see if I could find my next single. But I didn't want to listen to anything. Even my performances went downhill. Then it got really bad. One night, before a show, I started drinking. I ended up so wasted I couldn't go on. They had to invent an excuse for me. That's when I knew it had to stop, so I told Fenella I needed a break.'

I look up at Noah, searching his warm brown eyes. 'I

didn't know it had got that bad. You could have told me. Even though we're . . . we're not . . .' I barely know how to describe what we are. I give up trying. 'You could have called and I would've been there for you.'

He smiles. 'I know that. Of course I know that – but it wasn't right either. We took this time because we needed to figure out who we are without each other.'

I think back over my internship with François-Pierre Nouveau, travelling to London without anxiety. I think about my new friendship with Posey. I think about the photos I've taken, trying to find my style. I *have* grown a lot in the few months I've been apart from him. But that's also because of the confidence he's given me. I know I wouldn't have been able to do it without him. It doesn't feel like the right time to tell him that, though. Instead, I let him continue.

'So I quit the tour. I needed to go somewhere where I could find inspiration – and I didn't want anyone to know where that was. Not even Sadie Lee. Not even you. Only Fenella knew, but she also had *very* strict instructions not to disturb me unless it was urgent.'

'Did it work?' I ask.

'It did. Not at first – I was in a really bad way. I just lazed around on the couch and binge-watched Netflix, worrying about how dropping out of the tour would affect me and whether I would ever be invited to join a band again. Then something clicked. Maybe I ate one too many grilled cheese sandwiches or watched just one too many episodes of *Breaking Bad* in a row, but I got fed up with myself. I told myself that I wasn't allowed back in the real world without at least five songs that I loved. So I wrote and wrote and wrote. It was like a fever dream. I couldn't stop. I remembered what it was like to be creative again, to focus again.

'A few days ago, I was done and I felt ready. I had about twenty songs I hated, ten I liked, and five I *loved*. I was ready to rejoin the world again. I got in touch with G-ma first. That's when I found out she was in Brighton with Bells. She told me about Scotland. I thought I would surprise you here.'

'So this had *nothing* to do with Callum?'

'Callum? Who's Callum? The guy you were dancing with?'

Despite the fact that I have nothing to be ashamed of, I feel my face burn. 'It doesn't matter,' I mutter.

'Penny, it's OK. I get it. I kind of assumed you'd find someone else. I can't expect you to wait for me – that wouldn't be fair. He's a lucky guy . . .'

'No, it's not like that . . .' I think about how to explain it, but it's too complicated. I shake my head. 'So, what are we? What do you want us to be?'

He reaches over and puts his hand on mine. 'I want whatever you want. I just want to be part of your life again. And for you to be part of mine. If it's as your boyfriend – great! If it's just as your friend – I can live with that too. In fact, I've pretty much proven to myself that I can't live *without* that.'

They're the words I've wanted to hear for so long. But I know we can't rush into a relationship again. All the same issues that drove us apart in the first place – our careers, his fame and, most of all, the distance – are the same as they were. Nothing has changed on that front. But his friend? That I *can* do.

Now that we're here, away from the wedding and the drama and all the other people, I relax and my anger dissipates. What do I know of the pressure Noah's under? I'm just glad he's here now. He's safe. He's happy. And we're OK.

'Of course I want to be your friend,' I say. 'I couldn't live without that either.'

'Perfect.' He smiles, and it seems genuine – even if there's a shadow of disappointment in his eyes. 'And if you ever want anything more . . .'

'I'll let you know.'

I can't hold it in any longer. I lean forward and wrap him in a huge hug. He squeezes me back, and for an instant everything feels normal and right with the world again.

'You're still my everything, Penny,' Noah whispers into my hair. 'My forever girl.'

Chapter Twenty-Seven

Waking up under the canopy the morning after the wedding, I feel like I'm swimming in soft, golden light. The sky outside is tinted rose-grey, and dust motes shimmer in the thin beams of sunlight that filter through. The cottage is quiet; like it's taken a deep breath after the madness of the previous night. It's colder too. I pull the blankets up to my chin, working myself further down into the warmth. I don't want to get up just yet.

I roll over and my eyes fall on my golden mask from yesterday, discarded at the side of the bed.

Yesterday.

A day that passed in an instant yet seemed to last a lifetime.

I can't believe I'm sleeping under the same roof as Noah again. He ended up crashing in the room with Bella. He's back. I almost have to pinch myself, to make sure it's not a dream.

I replay our conversation from last night in my head, and a warm glow spreads from my toes to my head. It's *good* to have him back. But still something about what he said doesn't add up. Did he really just happen to appear the moment I was dancing with another guy? He wouldn't have known that there was no spark for me, that I would have ended things before they'd even had a chance to begin. He didn't know that Callum wasn't right for me. He said he didn't mind – that he even *expected* it – but how can that be right?

How could he think I'd be ready . . .?

And if I *did* feel like that, why did he think he could show up and ruin it?

I realize I'm not as over his 'missing period' as I thought I was. Yes, I'm glad he's back. But I'm definitely not ready to rush into anything other than a rekindled friendship.

Plus, I can't shake off the niggling feeling that there's something he hasn't told me. Something important. A missing piece that would make the whole matter of his absence hang together a bit better.

My phone buzzes and reluctantly I stretch an arm out from beneath the warmth of my duvet to nab it from the bedside table. I have quite a few texts to read – from Megan, from Callum, from Mum. But the most recent is from Elliot. That's the one I open first.

Are you awake, my wee Scottish gal?

I sit up in bed just as there's a soft knock on the door. 'Come in!' I call.

Elliot's head pokes round the door, then he slips inside, quiet as a mouse. He puts two cups of tea down on the bedside table and gets in under the duvet next to me. 'So . . . what happened? Tell me! Is Pennoah a thing once more?'

I toss my pillow at him, but he ducks the blow, grinning triumphantly.

'Pennoah is *not* a thing. Neither the name NOR the relationship.'

Elliot's smile immediately changes to a frown. 'Are you OK?'

I nod. 'Yeah, I'm fine. It was me who made the decision.'

'You did? What did he say about the creative break?'

'Actually, it sounds like it had got really bad for him and he really needed the time off.'

Elliot grimaces. 'Well, if it helped him, maybe it was worth some of the trouble,' he says.

'He said it was just coincidence that he was ready to talk again last night.'

'Oh, sure,' says Elliot sulkily. 'He just happened to come in as you were dancing with Callum, having just introduced him to *moi*. Coincidence? I don't think so.'

I shrug. 'That's what he says.'

'Hmm. Is it because of Callum that you don't want to get back with him?'

I shake my head. 'No. To be honest, I don't think Callum is right for me – and I knew that well before Noah showed up. I'll have to find some way to let him down gently.'

'So, no Callum, and no Noah?'

'Yeah, that's about right. It's going to be *just Penny* for the moment.'

'Well, *just Penny* is just great. Alexiot supports her all the way. Maybe you can be PenPo . . .'

'I do *not* need a nickname for a relationship with myself!'

'Why not? You could start a new trend for "single and loving it"! Just imagine all the celebrities doing it . . . *LeaBro, TaySwi, HarSty . . .*'

I hit him with the pillow again and again, as he continues to shout out celebrity names, until we're both rolling around in a fit of giggles.

I grab his hand. 'So, Scotland's been good for you?'

He squeezes my hand back. 'Yes. Alex and I have had so much fun – and there's still more to see. I'm really looking forward to carrying on to the Isle of Skye and seeing what else Scotland has to offer. And I spoke with your mum. She's OK with me staying with you guys until things settle down at home. I texted my mum and told her the plan. She's not happy, but she's not stopping me or demanding I come back home. She's come to her senses more or less.'

'That's good,' I say.

'I just need some space to breathe. It's stifling in that house. Anyway, though: how are you going to tell Callum?'

I cringe. 'I have no idea.'

'I get the feeling from the brief millisecond I've seen

him that he's not going to be the type who's used to being rejected.'

'I know what you mean,' I say. 'Oh well.'

Quite suddenly, Elliot sits up in bed, his nose sniffing the air like a bloodhound. 'Is that bacon I smell? Come on, let's go grab some breakfast.'

There's lively chatter in the kitchen as we head downstairs, but it all stops the moment I walk in. Mum, Dad, Sadie Lee and Alex all turn to look at me. The only people who aren't there are Noah and Bella.

'Morning,' I say, as brightly as I can.

'Everything OK, honey?' Mum says.

'Absolutely fine. Never better. Ooh, Dad – is that eggs?'

Thankfully, everyone starts talking again now that they've seen I'm normal and not some emotional wreck. Inside, it's a slightly different story. My ears are primed for every sound of a Noah-like footstep on the stairs, my eyes peeled for messy brown hair coming round the corner. But it's actually my nose that gets the first clue. Noah's signature cologne drifts into the kitchen (even overpowering the bacon) and my heartbeat speeds up to a million miles a minute.

'Morning, everyone,' says Noah, as casual as ever.

'Noah!' Mum stands up from the table and gives him two flamboyant kisses on the cheek – she must have come in so late last night she hasn't had a chance to say hello yet. 'Lovely to see you again. I hope you're feeling . . . refreshed?'

'Yes, thanks so much, Dahlia. And now I'm feeling pretty darn hungry too. What you got cooking for us there, Rob?'

Mum laughs. 'Sit yourself down, Noah. Breakfast is almost

ready. I'm afraid I won't be joining you, though – I have to go and put the castle back into some sort of order and make sure nothing disastrous happened in the night!'

'Do you really have to rush off, Mum?' I ask.

She sighs dramatically. 'Afraid so. But I'll see you before you head off with Elliot and Alex.'

'Great!'

Noah turns to me. 'Are you going somewhere?'

'Alexiot have planned a little Scottish road trip for their last day here, and they've asked me to go too instead of heading back today with Mum and Dad.'

'Oh, sounds cool,' Noah says.

Oh god, do I invite him? I suddenly think with a pang of alarm.

But it's Dad who speaks next. 'What are your plans, Noah?' he asks.

'I'm not sure. I have a few things to talk about with G-ma, so I'll be here for a bit, then I'll probably go back to get some studio time booked and work on some of my new songs. I was hoping to have some time to talk to Penny, but if she's not going to be around . . .'

Noah's going back to New York already? My heart sinks, even though I can't figure out if I'm sad or a bit relieved. I don't know what to say in reply, but then there's a loud buzzing noise – saved by my phone. Again. I'm aware of Noah staring at me as I glance at it to read the message.

'Oh wow!' I say.

'What is it?' asks Elliot.

'It's from Posey! I think . . . I think seeing Leah might have helped her!'

I turn the message round so that Elliot can see.

Penny!! Guess what? We had our first dress rehearsal
yesterday and a bunch of the older students were invited
so we had a proper audience. And . . . I DID IT!
WITHOUT STAGE FRIGHT!!

'Nice work!' says Elliot.
I can't keep the grin off my face. I text back.

That's amazing! How did you do it?

It was strange . . . I used that technique Leah described to
me – about the tree? It really worked. Before I went on, I
pictured the tree inside me, anchoring me to the stage. Then
when it was time for me to go on, I stopped being scared.
Instead of worrying that I'd disappoint everyone, I knew I
wasn't alone up there: I was part of a company, so I was
joining the others when I walked on. I think that's part of
what's held me back – thinking the focus was all on me. But
a show is about everyone. Listening to Leah made me realize
that as a soloist she faces more pressure than me so has had
to be much braver

Glad you've found a way to perform. But don't think you aren't as brave as Leah. She's one in a million and so are you! Does this mean you're going to keep the part?

Maybe!

Well, 'maybe' is definitely better than what you've said before ☺☺☺

'I wish I could see her and give her a huge hug,' I say.

'Who's Posey?' asks Noah.

'She's . . .' But how do I even begin to explain to him everything that's gone on over the past month? I realize that in the time Noah's been gone, a lot has changed. I'm finding it too hard to speak to him . . . even to look at him. Suddenly the emotions everyone thought would afflict me before, the emotions I'd kept down inside me for so long, rise up to the surface –

'I . . . I just . . .'

But I can't stay in the same room as him any longer. Pushing back my chair, I grab my coat blindly and run from the kitchen. I run outside, and keep running till I reach the edge of the lake, where I collapse down on to the stone wall of the bridge.

As tears sting my eyes, I tell myself sternly not to be so silly: they're only from the harsh wind blowing across the water. *You've had months to get over this, Penny Porter.*

He wants you back, another voice in my head replies, however – this one not as sensible as the first. *You should be with him. You're meant to be.*

But he left, says the first voice firmly, *and you're OK on your own. You're PenPo, remember?*

I stare down at my reflection. My auburn hair blazes as it's caught in the morning sun and blown by the lively wind. All round me, the trees in the forest make a frame of burnt oranges, bronzes and reds.

It's autumn and I'm his Autumn Girl ... but whether that's for 'forever', I'm still going to have to wait to see.

Chapter Twenty-Eight

When I return to the cottage, I avoid the kitchen and head straight upstairs in order to hide in my room. But before long Elliot sticks his head round the door and says, 'Noah's gone out with Sadie Lee and Bella, if you want to come downstairs.'

'Thanks, Wiki,' I say. I pick at a loose thread on the duvet, my head hanging low. I feel the mattress shift underneath me as Elliot sits down beside me.

'Listen – Alex and I won't mind if you want to go back with your mum and dad, like you originally planned. I know it's been a tough couple of days for you. You can, you know, handle *The Return of the Flynn*.'

'Really?' I say, looking up.

'Yeah, of course,' he replies gently.

It's as if Elliot has read my mind. I just don't want to be here right now. I don't even want to be in Brighton.

I smile, but then it changes into a grimace. 'I'm so embarrassed about Callum too,' I admit.

'Has he been in touch?'

'Yeah. He texted to see if I was OK. I guess I owe him an apology.'

'You don't owe him anything. But it might make you feel better.'

'I think you're right. I'll see if I can get Dad to drive me over to his house before we go to the airport.'

Elliot leans forward and gives me a huge hug. I squeeze him back tightly. He slides off the bed and leaves me to gather up the last of my things into my suitcase. The only thing I can't fit in (it's only a small weekend case) is what I wore on the night of the wedding, so I pack that into a plastic garment bag and bring it down over my arm.

'Are you coming with us then, Penny?' Mum asks as I stand in the doorway of the kitchen.

'If that's OK?'

'Of course!' She kisses me on my forehead. Dad takes my suitcase to load it into the car.

'Do you mind if we stop by Callum's parents' house on the way? I need to have a chat with him.'

'No problem at all. Are you all packed up? We want to get on the road soon.'

'All done!' I confirm.

I help Mum and Dad load up the rest of the car and say goodbye to Alex and Elliot. I feel bad for not saying goodbye to Sadie Lee and Bella, but I know there'll be another opportunity to see them before they go back to New York.

On the short drive to Callum's I bite my nails down to the

quick, trying to decide what I'm going to say. I know I need to apologize for running off, but do I have to apologize for not feeling the same way as him?

We're there before I know it, pulling off into the big drive-way and parking our tiny rental car between the flashy Range Rovers. Mum and Dad say they'll wait in the car, and I'm glad to have the excuse of our imminent flight not to have to stay too long.

My steps crunch on the driveway as I walk up to the front door. I ring the bell and rock back on my heels, jamming my hands into the front pockets of my jeans.

It's Callum who answers, and I let out a nervous breath. 'Hi,' I say quickly.

'Oh, hi,' replies Callum, leaning up against the side of the door. I notice he doesn't invite me in, but I'm OK with that.

'So, I just wanted to apologize for last night. That was really . . . rubbish of me,' I blurt out.

Callum softens then, his arms uncrossing. 'Come round the back – if we go inside we'll just get bothered by my brothers.' He steps out and leads me round to the back of the house where, beyond the garden, there's a view over fields sloping down to the coastline we walked along before. I join him as he leans over an aging wooden gate, watching the sheep nibble the grass.

'So . . . are you OK?' he asks.

'Yeah, I'm fine. I was taken by surprise and I didn't react well in the moment.'

'Well, that's understandable. That guy did just show up out

of nowhere.' Callum's fingers curl into fists, but he relaxes them just as quickly. 'So, are you and him a thing now?'

'No, not exactly . . . I don't know.'

He turns round so that he's leaning with his back against the gate.

'Does that mean I can still take you on another date?' He looks at me, his eyes sparkling.

This is the moment I've been dreading, but I know it will be better to get it over with quickly, just like it's best to rip off a plaster. 'I need some time to get my head straight. Can we just be friends?'

Callum looks away, then down to the ground. 'I guess I'll settle for what I can get,' he says. 'But you'll still give me your tips on portrait photography, right?' He catches my eye again, smiling.

'Any time.' I smile back. The sense of relief is overwhelming, and I'm grateful to him for making this so easy.

'Do you want to go for another walk? I can show you this cool little waterfall nearby . . .'

'Oh – I can't. I'd better get back to the car as we have a plane to catch.'

His face falls, and by the way he shoves off abruptly from the gate I can tell he's annoyed again. But, I tell myself, I suppose I would be too. Even though I'm trying not to give him any hope, I feel like I'm still leading him on.

'No problem,' he says, and we head back towards the car.

He waves as we drive away, then Mum turns round in her seat. 'Did everything go OK?'

'Yeah, fine,' I say, leaning my head against the window.

With Callum, there was no big scene, no games – he just wanted to see me again. And with Noah . . .? *Oh!* I just don't know how to feel.

My mind is a tangle I can't even begin to unpick.

I need to get away from it all. To focus on what makes *me* happy, not on the boy-drama in my life.

But I have an idea. And I'm going to need Posey's help to pull it off.

Chapter Twenty-Nine

From: Melissa.Iwobi@NouveauStudios.com
To: Penny Porter

Penny, these are just G.R.E.A.T. I think you really have an
opportunity to grow this idea. Keep working on it! I know you'll
get there.

Mel xx

PS I showed FPN a couple of these and he nodded, which you
KNOW means he thinks you're on the right track!

I close the email, feeling a grin spread over my face. Melissa's
message has given me a boost of confidence that I've
sorely needed – and just the motivation to put my plan into
action.

I filled my parents in on the plan during the flight back, and
my mind was so distracted by how I was going to pull it off

that I barely gave my anxiety a look-in. Posey – fresh from her *second* wobble-free rehearsal – was all set to meet me that very afternoon. I've asked her to come with me to the National Gallery, where I have an idea for my photography series that I want to try out.

'Can you tell me *anything* about your project?' Posey asks.

'It's all a bit top secret for now,' I say. 'But I'll tell you in time. Just be on the lookout for any kids on their phones.'

'OK, will do.'

We cross Trafalgar Square, which is packed to capacity with tourists lounging on the steps or on the plinths of the huge lion statues at the four corners. You can tell the tourists by the obscenely large cameras they have round their necks, and I wonder how many of them know how to use their impressive (and expensive) bits of kit. Maybe if my dreams of being a professional photographer don't work out I could run courses – or teach. Then I think of all the times I've been out with my big camera. Maybe people mistake me for a tourist too.

As we walk up the steps to the National Gallery, Posey says, 'I still can't believe you've come all the way down here. Aren't you supposed to be in Scotland somewhere?'

'Near Inverness. But don't worry – the wedding is over and I was supposed to be coming back anyway. Plus, I just had to get away from there.' I bite my lip. 'Noah came back.'

'He did?'

'Yeah, but I couldn't face him, not properly.'

'Oh.' She sees how red in the face I go, and doesn't push me. 'How about over there?' she says, as we walk into the first gallery. She's pointing towards a group of teenagers who look as if they're on a school trip from somewhere. As we approach, I can hear some of them speaking French. They're all on their phones, sitting in front of a gigantic sixteenth-century painting of a battle.

'That's perfect,' I say.

Next to me, an older lady glares at the students and tuts to her friend. I swear I hear her mutter something about 'that generation' before she wanders off into the next room.

She means our generation, the generation who are always on their phones.

Except, as Posey and I walk round to the other side of the group, I glance down at some of the students' screens and realize they're using an app for the National Gallery. They're all completely absorbed in reading about the painting they're sitting in front of.

Hmm, yes, 'that generation'. The generation who are always on their phones . . . using them to communicate, to game, to connect, and yes, to learn too.

One of the students catches my eye and I smile back. I normally hate talking to strangers, but I know if I want to be a great photographer I'm going to have to conquer my nerves. 'Hey, do you speak English?' I ask.

'Yes, I do,' the girl says in absolutely perfect English.

'Um, do you mind if I take a photo of your group? I'm doing a school project and it would be amazing if you could be involved.'

Unexpectedly, the girl lights up. 'Oh, sure! *Écoutez donc, les mecs!*' she calls, turning to her friends. '*Elle veut prendre un photo de nous . . .*'

They all start to arrange themselves into various formal poses and I have to laugh. 'No, uh, just as you were, if that's OK?'

They shrug, then resume reading up about the painting, quickly losing interest in the weird girl with the camera. I snap a few photos of them then say '*Merci*' to the girl, and Posey and I move on.

'Did you get what you need?' Posey asks.

I nod. 'I think so.'

'Still not going to tell me what you're up to?' she asks with a sly smile.

I wink and put my finger to my lips. 'I promise you'll be one of the first to know.'

She laughs. 'I'd better be! Actually,' she continues, 'I'm really thirsty. Fancy a drink or something?'

'Sure! But we should go somewhere to celebrate how well you're doing with the rehearsals now. Where do you fancy?'

Posey grins. 'I know this sounds really silly, but . . . how about McDonald's?'

I can't help laughing.

So, in what may be Guinness-World-Record-breaking speed, we dash back across Trafalgar Square and up the Strand to the nearest bustling restaurant. We both order milkshakes and we sit on the red plastic stools kicking out our legs like we're ten years old again.

'Have you told Leah about your successful rehearsals?' I ask. 'She'd love to know.'

Posey shakes her head. 'Not yet. I kind of don't want to jinx it.'

I tilt my head. 'OK. Well, once you've had your successful *opening-night* performance, you can tell her yourself!'

My phone rings and when I see who's calling I almost cry out in delighted surprise.

'What is it?' Posey asks.

'Just, speak of the devil . . .' I turn the screen round and let Posey read for herself: the caller ID shows 'Leah Brown'.

'Wow, weird!' says Posey.

'Don't worry, I won't say anything right now,' I say and slide the bar on my phone to answer the call. 'Leah?'

'Hey, P.' Her voice sounds tired and dejected.

'Is everything all right?' I ask. 'Are you OK?' But I already know something is really wrong.

'My label is going nuts. I have to call anyone who's been in my studio recently.'

'Why? Oh my god, what's happened?'

There's a long pause on the other end of the line. 'It's my album. My first single's been leaked and it's all over the Internet.'

★ ★ Chapter Thirty ★

Posey's face is drained of colour, our shakes abandoned, a pool of vanilla-flavoured goo in the bottom of each cup. Straight after getting off the phone with Leah, I call Megan and ask her to come and meet us here.

'I just can't believe it,' Posey repeats for the hundredth time. 'Who would do that?'

I shake my head. 'I have no idea.' As we wait for Megan, I search on my phone for 'Leah Brown leaked song'. The search loads with hundreds of results from different gossip websites. It seems that the leak didn't happen via download sites; it's rather that someone has emailed a low-quality copy of an audio track to a journalist. I expect if it was any other artist, the poor quality of the recording would put people off. But the leaked song is something so different for Leah, so new and raw, and she is such a huge star, that the Internet has gone crazy. I scroll down post after post linking to the pirate copy. It's already got out of hand – there's no way Leah's team could put the lid back on the leak now, however much money or influence they brought to the problem.

The only good thing is that all the comments about the track are positive. People are loving it – and they want the full version. I listen to a snippet of it, but don't recognize it as one of the ones she played for us, and I feel the tightness that's been building in my chest suddenly release. It can't have been one of us.

'I hope she doesn't think I would do anything like that,' says Posey.

I grab her hand. 'Of course not. None of us would.'

'Hey, guys!'

I look up to see Megan waving as she comes towards us, glowing as a result of her brisk walk. Thankfully she seems to have reactivated her 'niceness' gene since the other day because she gives both Posey and me a big hug.

'What's up?' she asks. 'What's so urgent that I had to rush over here?'

'I had a call from Leah Brown,' I begin. Then I take a deep breath, my eyes searching Megan's face. 'Someone's leaked a song from her unreleased album and it's all over the Internet.'

Megan hops on to a stool, her hand over her mouth. 'No way? Is it bad?'

'Well, it's *everywhere*. She needed to contact us all to make sure we're not involved.'

'Of course not! She said we couldn't record.'

'I know. It's just a precaution that the studio had to take, getting in touch with anyone who's been in there over the past week or so.'

Megan relaxes, her shoulders dropping, but Posey's eyes well up with tears. 'Hey, don't cry,' Megan says softly.

'I hate that Leah thinks we might have done this. She probably already has so much to deal with and she was so nice to us,' says Posey.

'But sometimes leaks can be a good thing, right? No publicity is bad publicity and all that . . .' replies Megan.

I frown. 'I can safely say that's *not* true.'

'OK, but, hey . . . she wouldn't be the first singer to have had leaks!'

'But how does that make this leak any less serious?'

'I'm not saying it's not serious. I'm just saying she'll be OK.'

Posey and I share a look, then I nod. Megan's right. One leaked song isn't going to ruin Leah's career. But I've seen first-hand the effort that she puts into all her songs, and I know that this is the first time she's written anything so personal. Plus, like Noah, she's a perfectionist – she wouldn't want anything to go public until she was ready.

My phone rings and we all look to the screen. It's Leah again. I swipe immediately, then gesture to the girls to keep quiet, so I can hear her better. 'Hello?'

'Hi, Penny. More news – not good, I'm afraid.'

'What is it?' My heart leaps into my throat.

'They isolated the track so that it's really clear and I remember exactly when I was singing it. It was during *our* session in London. It can't have been any other time.'

'But . . . how is that possible? I've never heard the song before, I promise you. It's not one of the ones you sang for us.'

Posey's face goes white, and Megan swallows hard.

As for me, my pulse is racing.

'I did sing it that day – maybe it was when you were upstairs setting up for the photoshoot? Anyway, point is, it has to have been one of your friends.'

'Seriously?' My voice is shaking as I talk to her. 'Oh, Leah, I am so, *so* sorry.'

'Look, I have to go. I have to . . . figure out what my next steps are. I'll talk to you later.'

'OK,' I say, but she's already hung up. I stare with disbelief at the phone in my hand. I look up at Posey and at Megan. They both look guilty. They both look innocent. 'I . . . she . . .' I can't even find the words.

'What is it, Penny?' Megan prompts.

'Leah recognizes when she sang that version of the song. It was during her session with us.'

'But I haven't even heard it before!' says Megan. I remember now. She'd come upstairs and gone to the bathroom when I was setting up for the photographs. That leaves only one person it could have been.

But it can't be.

We both turn to Posey.

'I . . . I didn't do anything,' she says, her voice coming out in a stutter.

'But you were the only one there,' says Megan. 'It has to have been you. How could Penny or I record it if we weren't even in the room?' Her voice is hard, and I can see tears spring up in Posey's eyes.

But I can't feel any sympathy for her. All I feel is . . . empty. And then I feel something else too. I feel betrayed.

'Penny, you have to know that I would never . . .'

'No wonder you didn't want to tell Leah how you've been getting on,' I snap, almost shaking with anger. 'What did you think you could gain by selling her song to some website?'

Posey's face goes from white as a sheet to red as a beetroot, and tears stream down her cheeks. 'I . . .' But she never finishes the sentence. Instead, she snatches her bag from under the table, jumps off her stool and runs out of the restaurant.

I just shake my head in disbelief.

'Wow,' says Megan, breaking the silence.

'I can't believe Posey would do something like that!'

'I know. It's hard to believe,' says Megan, 'but then – I guess we barely know her. You only met her a few weeks ago –'

'That's true, I suppose.'

'And she's always been really quiet at school, despite getting the lead.' She shrugs. 'Madame Laplage is a great school, but it's really cut-throat, and, at the end of the day, she wants to be a star some day. Getting ahead of the competition, a foot in the door – it's worth a lot to a Madame Laplage student.'

I shake my head. 'She'd have way more to gain by being Leah's friend than by betraying her trust. I can't believe someone can be that stupid!' I say, exasperated. Even so, the doubts lurking in the bottom of my stomach grow. Megan's hit on an uncomfortable truth: even though I *thought* I had the kind of connection with Posey that makes us true friends, I really don't know much about her at all.

I text Leah:

> Turns out it was Posey. She was the only one in the room while you were singing

Leah texts back:

> Wow! She seemed so nice. I'm sorting out with my lawyers what we're going to do. I'll keep you posted

> Sorry again

Megan puts her hand on mine, breaking me out of my thoughts. 'You're doing the right thing, Pen. There are always people who want to bring down big pop stars like Leah.'

I force a smile. 'You're right.'

'Want to get out of here and do some shopping in Covent Garden?'

'OK,' I say.

'Awesome. I'll show you this make-up that I *really* want.'

Shopping feels like the last thing I want to do, but I still have a few hours before my train. Maybe it will cheer me up. Megan grabs my hand and pulls me through the doors, out on to the bustling streets off the Strand. We wind our way up to the huge Covent Garden piazza, one of my favourite places in London. The weather, for once, is bright and clear – a beautiful autumn day that reminds me, again, just why this is my favourite season.

There's a juggler performing to a large crowd, his microphone-enhanced voice bouncing back off the stone buildings that surround the square. Megan and I stop for a moment to watch him, and I stand on my tiptoes to peer over the sea of heads. The juggler tosses a flaming baton high in the air, catching it at the very last second, and Megan and I gasp along with the rest of his audience.

She tugs at my arm. 'Come on, let me show you before this crowd breaks up.'

She takes me to towards a beautiful high-end make-up store decorated with large mirrors that remind me of some of the ones I've seen inside dressing rooms I've been in with Noah. The make-up is all way out of my budget, but Megan and I have fun trying on the different lipsticks and highlighters.

'Check out this colour. It would look *so* nice on you,' she says, unrolling a lipstick and running it over the back of my hand. It is a really lovely pink, but the price tag makes my eyes water.

'I think I'll skip it for now,' I say.

'OK, suit yourself. I'm just going to get this stuff and then we can go.'

Megan takes four or five different items to the counter and pays. Then she links her arm through mine and leads me out of the store.

'So, what happened with you and Callum? You were going to meet up with him in Scotland, weren't you?'

'Oh . . .' I can't help the flush that rises to my face. Even though I spoke to him briefly before leaving Scotland, I still feel bad for the way I left it. I shove the niggling feeling of guilt to the back of my mind. 'Well, the biggest news is that Noah is back.'

'WHAT? HOLD UP.' We come to a standstill in the middle of the street. 'Noah's back? And you saw him? What did he say? What did you say? Are you getting back together?'

I laugh. 'Whoa with the questions! We're *not* back together.'

'Aw.' Megan pouts.

'We didn't really get to talk properly, because I came back down here.'

'You ran away.'

'No! I wanted to surprise my . . .' I would say 'friend', but I don't know any more. 'I wanted to surprise Posey.'

'*Annnnd* you needed to run away.'

'OK, I needed to run away a little bit,' I concede. 'I just didn't know what to do with him, and with Callum and everything . . . It was too complicated.'

'Well, that's OK. I'm glad you told me. I'm sure you'll clear things up with Callum. He'll understand about Noah. True love always has to come first.'

I grimace. 'I'm not sure a guy who abandons you for a month with no word or anything can really count as a true love.'

'You and Noah are meant to be. I know it.'

I smile weakly. 'Can you keep quiet about his return for a little bit? I don't know how public he wants it to be.'

Megan runs her finger across her lips. 'Don't worry, your secret is safe with me.'

'Thanks,' I say with a smile.

'Awesome. And if you ever need any advice on the Noah thing, you know who you can come to.'

Chapter Thirty-One

Elliot's jaw almost drops into his bowl of cornflakes. 'But she seemed so sweet!'

'I know.'

I've just filled him in on the drama with Leah and her leaked song, which he's listened to about a hundred times. 'At least the song is amazing. I love it! I bet everyone at school is going to be talking about it.'

'Same.'

'Are you ready? I'm going to be late. I have this huge history paper due and I can't miss the start of the lesson.'

'Yeah, I'm ready.'

We continue our routine of walking as far as the corner together, where we break off to go to different schools. Except now, of course, it's different because the routine starts as soon as we wake up. Elliot's moved in to Tom's room temporarily. It's still strange to have him in the same house, rather than next door. While I love having my BFF living under the same roof as me, I wish it was under better circumstances. Still, I know my family will do anything and everything they can to make him feel safe and loved. He needs that more than anything during this turbulent time.

As I reach the bottom of the steps to my school, I get a long WhatsApp message from Posey.

Dear Penny, I'm sure I'm the last person you want to hear from, and I know you must hate me, just like Megan does. But I wanted you to know I'd never do what you and Megan accused me of. You have to believe me. I don't know who leaked the song, but it wasn't me. Hope you write back. Posey x

My stomach churns as I read it. I want to believe her, but the proof is too glaring. I know it wasn't me, and Megan's alibi is sound. So I shut my phone without replying.

The day disappears in a blur as I try to put the whole situation between Posey and Leah to the back of my mind. It's hard, because Elliot is totally right. Everyone at school *is* talking about it, even though they don't know I had anything to do with it.

Even at lunch, when I walk into the canteen, Kira and Amara are talking about it. 'I wish there was a version I could listen to on Spotify,' Kira is saying. 'It would go straight to the top of my playlist!'

The sisters both look up at me as I put down my tray. 'Hey, Penny! Have you heard Megan's news?'

'Megan's?' I raise an eyebrow.

'Yeah! She's having a party. I bet you have one of these invites in your locker.' Kira pulls out a black envelope that

shimmers under the bright fluorescent lights. It has a seal –
now broken – made with blood-red wax.

'Oh wow!' I say as I pull out the stiff piece of card that's
inside. It's an invitation to a Halloween party at a farm outside London.

'Yeah, she's invited basically everyone in the sixth form
and apparently a bunch of people from her new school too.
Are you going to come? I bet your new guy is going to be
there.'

I swallow, disguising my blush by staring down at the invitation. I haven't had time to fill anyone in on the new Callum
situation.

'Hmm, I guess,' I say. 'Is it fancy dress?'

'Uh, how could it be a Halloween party without costumes?'
says Amara. 'We should think of something *great* and then all
go together.'

'I don't know . . . big parties aren't really my thing. And I
should probably check that I'm actually invited first.'

I finish my lunch and head straight to my locker. Sure
enough, as soon as I open it, a black envelope tumbles to the
floor.

I snap a picture of it on my phone and send it to Megan.
Within a millisecond, she's ringing me.

'Please say you'll come!' she jumps in, without even saying
hi. 'I'll make sure you have a good time . . . and I'll make sure
you have a safe place to retreat to. It would mean a lot to me.
This is my chance to really make my mark on the school,
and . . .' She finally takes a breath. 'It's the day before my big
stage debut.'

I blink with surprise. 'What do you mean?'

Megan's voice lowers, like she's surrounded by loads of people and she doesn't want them to hear. 'Posey dropped out of the show today. She claimed it was because of her stage fright, but I think it was guilt.'

'Wow,' is the only thing I manage to say.

'So, you're going to come? Pretty please?' Megan's voice brightens again.

'All right, I'll see what I can do.'

'Yay!' Megan says with a loud squeal. 'I promise you, this is going to be the best party *ever*.'

Chapter Thirty-Two

'What do you think, Elliot?'

Elliot leans back in his chair and strokes his chin as if it's covered by a thick beard. 'I think you three look like the spookiest witches I've ever seen . . . but that's probably not the kind of costume Megan had in mind.'

He's probably right. Kira and Amara have come over so we can get ready for the party together, and we've raided Mum's collection of costumes for the most elaborate witchy outfits we could find. We've decided to go as the three witches from *Hocus Pocus,* my favourite Halloween-themed film since I can remember. I've bagged Sarah Jessica Parker's role as Sarah Sanderson, while Kira is Winifred and Amira is Mary. Alex has been on hand to provide some equally outlandish make-up – long fake fingernails and crazy back-combed up-dos. Looking in the mirror now, I wonder if we may have overdone it a tad – but there's no going back now.

Kira giggles. 'I feel like a true Sanderson sister.'

'Hang on, your wig is wonky,' says Alex to me, as he adjusts my long, newly blonde and very knotty locks.

'What happens if you bump into Callum?' Alex asks.

Callum sent me a text asking if I was going to the party and whether we could talk again. 'I'll have to talk to him,' I say, 'just to be honest once and for all. At least he won't be able to see how embarrassed I am under all this make-up and fake hair.'

Amara points her broomstick at me. 'We're going to have a good time. *You're* going to have a good time. We're not going to make this all about Callum.'

'So, where is this party again?' Elliot asks, examining the invitation.

'It's at a farm in Surrey, about thirty minutes' drive away. Kira's got their mum's car, so she's going to drive us.'

'How the heck is Megan affording all this? Since when did she have the megabucks to throw around for a big party?'

It's a question that's been niggling at me too. 'I'm not sure,' I reply. 'But her parents have money . . . Maybe it's to celebrate her getting the lead role in their school show. It's a pretty big deal.'

There's a pause, silence hanging in the air, which is suddenly broken by Elliot having a fit of giggles. 'I'm sorry,' he says between laughs. 'I just can't take you seriously with you looking like that!'

I look at Kira and Amara, and they look at me. Then, on cue, we pretend to beat Alexiot with the ends of our broomsticks.

'OK, we better get going, before we ruin our glorious make-up!' And I hop off the bed.

'Have fun, you crazy witches. You know I'm going to want all the details,' calls Elliot.

'Of course!'

We hurry downstairs, and Dad lets out a genuine yelp when he sees us. 'Girls! You scared me!'

'That's the idea, Dad!' I say back, then add my best witch's cackle for good measure.

'I'd tell you to be safe, but I think it's everyone else who's going to have to look out for you three.'

'Ha ha, very funny,' I respond, and I raise a sarcastic eyebrow, but then I catch a glimpse of us in the hall mirror and almost jump myself. I've always been a fan of 'go big or go home', and I think, between us, we've definitely gone *beyond* big.

Kira and Amara's mum's car is parked outside our front door. 'Can you imagine if we get stopped looking like this?' says Amara.

'I hope we don't have to stop for petrol!' I say.

'Don't worry,' Kira replies. 'I filled up on the way here.'

We leave the Brighton traffic behind, pulling on to the motorway that will take us north through the Sussex countryside towards London. I check my phone but then put it back just as quickly: I have several missed calls from Noah and I know I've been avoiding the situation. It's true – we do need to talk again, but I just can't face it.

When we come off the motorway and get stuck at some traffic lights, we end up terrifying a little boy in the car next to us. We collapse into giggles and only just recover by the time it goes green.

The satnav takes us down a winding country road, so narrow that the wing mirrors almost brush the hedges on either side. I'm thankful it's not me driving – this would definitely make me nervous.

Eventually we get stuck behind a bus full of people in fancy dress who must also be on their way to the farm. That must be the party bus that Megan talked about, the one for people who didn't have access to a car. I'm glad I'm not on that – just the thought of it makes me start to sweat.

'Glad I'm not on the bus with all those people,' Kira says, echoing my thoughts.

'Oh god, me too! I can't imagine anything worse,' I say.

Amara smiles at me. 'Are you going to be OK, Penny? Do you want to have some kind of signal or code word or something? For when one of us is ready to go back?'

I think about the film *Hocus Pocus* and how when the sisters want to regroup or club together, Winifred shouts 'SISTERS!' With that, they all gather together in a giggly mess, so I suggest, 'If one of us wants to go, we could cry "SISTERS!" just like in the film.'

'Love it! It's a deal,' the others say enthusiastically, and I smile back gratefully. I really appreciate my friends; they understand my anxiety and are trying to make me not feel so alone. We all know full well that it's not going to be either of the twins who blows the whistle on time at the party.

The bus ahead of us turns into a large farm gate, and we follow suit.

Our jaws drop in awe. The place is Halloween on steroids: hundreds of carved pumpkins line the track, creating an eerie kind of red carpet. Ghostly spiders' webs hang from the leafless trees and, to complete the scene, hay bales are stacked up all around.

The wind blows, sending the candles flickering, and there's a chill in the air. I'm glad I decided to wear tights underneath my dress and corset.

We walk up the avenue of pumpkins, clutching our invitations tightly. A burly security guard (with a pang, I instantly think of Larry, Noah's bodyguard) checks our invitations and waves us through. I'm amazed by how many people there are here, but then I realize that it's not just Megan's party at the farm tonight – there are other events on here too. The guard shines his flashlight along the ground for us, in the direction of a huge barn. That must be where Megan's party is being held.

'This is crazy,' Kira says. 'Is it OK if I'm a bit scared?'

'Are you kidding? I'm terrified!' I reply.

There's a queue of people waiting to get into the barn, and we huddle together at the end of it. A creepy man in a Joker costume is at the front, opening and closing the door and ushering people in, and as we get closer I realize it's Luke, Megan's date. She must really have him eating out of her hand to get him to do door duty.

'Welcome to the House of Horrors . . . if you *dare*,' he says, his painted mouth twisted into a leer.

'Uh . . . thanks?' I say tentatively. It's so obvious that Luke is a drama student.

'I suggest you hold hands as you start walking through . . . And remember, *don't stop until the very end . . . Mwahahaha!*' He opens the door, and then Kira, Amara and I all scream as we are pushed inside. The door slams shut behind us. We're plunged into pitch-black darkness.

I'm sandwiched between the twins and their fingers squeeze mine tightly as we take tentative steps forward. 'Oh my god, Penny, I swear something is touching me. I don't like this,' says Kira.

I don't like it either, but I grit my teeth. 'Come on, this is supposed to be fun. I'm sure it's not – *AHH!*'

I scream at the top of my lungs as a man in a hockey mask lunges out of the darkness towards me, wielding a knife. Amara screams a second after me as a girl – her face covered in weeping sores – jumps on to the bars of a cage barely a foot away from her face. On cue, we begin to run through the dark maze, adrenaline coursing through our bodies. Even though I'm screaming, it's weird because I actually think I'm enjoying myself. Something about being scared witless when you're (almost) sure you're not going to come to any real harm *is* pretty fun.

We come across two doors, one labelled DANGER! DO NOT ENTER!! and the other THIS WAY. Before anyone can stop me, I push through the door marked DANGER!

It must be the right one. As soon as my eyes adjust to the light, we're inside the huge barn and there's music and a packed dance floor, coloured lights swirling overhead to the beat of a bouncing DJ in the corner.

But that's not who I see first.

The very first person I see is . . . Noah.

Chapter Thirty-Three

He's dressed as a ghost, which is appropriate considering how much he's been haunting every moment of my life. He's all in white – even his face and hair are covered in white powder. I blink, wondering if maybe he's a *real* ghost and I'm imagining things.

He's busy scanning the rest of the crowd so isn't looking in my direction, which is lucky – because I'm not ready to face him yet. I grab Kira's hand and pull her away from the door and into a shadowy corner. Amara looks round, wide-eyed, wondering what spooked me. I'm glad we're wearing such full-on costumes and I've come as a peroxide blonde this evening, because it means that Noah will take more time to find me.

'What is it?' Kira asks.

'I've just seen a ghost,' I reply.

Kira peers round the crowd. 'I think you'll have to be a bit more specific . . . There are quite a few ghosts in here!'

'I mean . . . Noah.'

'Oh, *seriously*?' Then her eyes open wide. 'I get it now. Just look for the gaggle of girls, right?'

'What do you mean?' I say, following the direction of her eyes, and my shoulders slump. I hadn't even noticed before; I was so focused on him. But all round Noah there's a circle of girls, all standing *just* far enough away so as not to appear too creepy-keen, but also *just* close enough that they can easily catch his eye if he should look at one of them. But suddenly Noah turns away and heads outside.

I let out a big sigh of relief.

Amara raises an eyebrow at me. 'You don't want to talk to him?'

'No . . . yes, I do . . . just not right now, though,' I say. 'But what's he even *doing* here?'

If he's here then Megan must have invited him. After her *promise* that she would keep quiet about it, she decided to just go ahead and invite him to a party where hundreds of people would see him and start talking about him again. Sure enough, just as I expected, all the girls who were surrounding him are now on their phones. They exchange a flurry of whispers – *This is going straight on my Snapchat! Was that* really *Noah Flynn?* – which echo off the walls of the barn.

Kira nudges me in the ribs. Before I can ask what the matter is, I see Megan sauntering towards us, looking gorgeous in a tight-fitting, iridescent cat costume. She even manages to make whiskers look good: a snub of black paint on her nose complements her chestnut hair, which is falling in large, bouncy curls over her shoulders.

'You look great, Megan,' we chorus.

'You guys look positively wicked!' Megan says. She leans forward and gives us air kisses – 'I don't want to get lipstick all over me!' she squeals.

I can't bring myself to return the kisses. 'Megan, what is Noah doing here?' I say.

Megan pouts. 'Oh, you've seen him already? I wanted it to be a surprise. I kind of want to be there when you guys make up.'

'When we make up? What do you think this is, some kind of intervention party?'

Megan finally catches my tone and she frowns. 'Why are you mad? I thought you'd be happy.'

'I remember asking you specifically to keep quiet about him being back!'

Megan rolls her eyes. 'Whatever, Penny. This is *my* party and I can invite whoever I want. Noah didn't have to come if he didn't want to, then no one would know he was back in the world of the living, if that's how he preferred it. Don't blame me. Just use this as an opportunity. Anyway, *I'm* going to enjoy my party. You do what you want.'

She flounces off, as seriously as anyone can while wearing a cat tail. I sigh and turn to Kira. 'She's kind of right, isn't she? I mean, if Noah wanted to keep hidden away, he wouldn't have come to some cheesy party.'

'Yeah, but Megan could have given you a heads-up.'

I smile weakly. 'Look, you don't have to hang round with me. I have some people to talk to and it's . . . well, it's not going to be fun.' *Callum, then Noah, then an apology to*

225

Megan . . . No, I'm not really looking forward to having *any* of those conversations.

'Are you sure?' Amara asks.

'Yeah, go ahead. I'll find you guys again later.'

'Remember,' Kira adds, '*SISTERRSSSS!*'

'I got it!' And I watch them as they walk away, then wrap my arms across my tummy, remembering just how much I hate parties like this.

Despite the chill in the air outside, inside it feels too warm – the mass of bodies moving and writhing under the heavy spotlights, the fog machines, the air thick with spray cologne, cheap perfume and sweat. I hope it doesn't take too long to find Callum.

I take a deep breath, then I begin to do a circuit of the room. Knowing that I have an escape route makes it feel easier, and the task at hand takes the focus away from my anxiety. *I can do this.*

I hurry round the perimeter of the throng, but there's no sign of Callum. I spot Megan's cat tail weaving through the crowd, and I catch sight of Kira and Amara a couple of times, but thankfully I don't see Noah. I wonder what kind of costume Callum has chosen.

There's a staircase leading up from the edge of the room to a mezzanine level, where the bar is set up. I climb the stairs, hoping I'll have a better view from higher up, but as soon as I come to the top I don't need to look any longer. There's Callum, standing round the punch bowl with a few of his mates, pouring gold-coloured spirits out of a couple of flasks and into the punch. They're all dressed as vampires, which seems kind of appropriate. A drop of blood oozes from the corner of Callum's mouth as he laughs.

His eyes start to widen in surprise as he takes me in – although at first it's obvious he's not completely sure it's me. 'Penny?' he asks, after gawping at me for a couple of seconds.

'Hey, Callum,' I say.

'You look . . .' I can see he's struggling to think of something complimentary to say, but the words never come. I knew that my choice of costume, not going along with the 'cute-kitty-in-a-tight-catsuit' thing, would put me in the minority, but I didn't think Callum would be fazed.

'Did you want to talk?' I ask.

'*Oh-oooh*,' his friends chant at once, wiggling their fingers in our direction.

I scowl at them, but Callum just laughs again. 'Yeah. Do you want some punch first?'

I shake my head, so he shrugs and follows me to the railing overlooking the floor below. A string of little light-up orange pumpkins is wrapped round the rail – not quite the fairy lights I love, but atmospheric all the same. I know that by staring at them I'm just distracting myself from the conversation I need to have. I look up into Callum's eyes, and it's him who takes a deep breath first.

'Penny, when I found out you were coming to the party, I knew I had to speak to you one more time.' He reaches out and takes my hand, long pointed nails and all. 'Look, so Jane's wedding didn't quite turn out like I planned but I meant it when I said I enjoyed spending time with you, and that I'd like to do more of it. Plus, I think you're an insanely talented photographer and I bet I can learn a lot from you. That and you're incredibly beautiful –' he looks at my smeary black eye make-up and back-combed blonde wig – 'most of the time.'

Despite myself, and my resolutions, I feel my cheeks go pink. Even Noah wasn't this complimentary about me.

'So I know I'll only kick myself if I don't try one more time. Do you think we can hang out again?' he asks.

'Callum ... I think I just want to be on my own for a while.' I'm not sure if he hears me, because he's focused on something over my shoulder.

'Oh no, not this again,' he mutters, and he snaps his hand out of mine, his eyes narrowing.

'What?' I spin round. There, at the top of the stairs, is ghost-Noah. How is it possible for someone in a ghost costume to look so jaw-droppingly hot and effortless? How does he make being a ghost so smoulderingly beautiful?

'Noah, please,' I say, 'I just want to have a conversation with Callum.' But it's like I'm not even there. Noah has his eyes fixed on Callum, and they're squaring up to each other.

I hate it.

Callum, feeling more confident now as his friends move in for support, draws up to his full height – a few inches taller than Noah. 'Look, *dude*, why don't you leave Penny alone for a while rather than stalking her like some creepy ex?'

'"Stalking her"?' Noah snaps back, almost laughing.

I look frantically between them, my head switching back and forth like I'm watching a match at Wimbledon. And I'm not the only one. All around, phones are pointed at us, recording every moment. The last thing Noah – or I – need is for this to go online and be the next viral hit. I come to my senses.

'Both of you, stop it!' I shout, but suddenly the floor starts to sway, and I feel a wave of heat wash up through my body. My palms are slick with sweat, and I know this isn't an attack I'll be able to dismiss with a few deep breaths.

'Penny –' Noah recognizes the signs, and he takes a big step towards me. Callum doesn't know me as well, but he grips my arm and tries to put himself between me and Noah.

'Leave me alone,' I manage to choke out, as I push past both of them and lurch towards the stairs. The crowd parts to let me through, phones still tilted in my direction.

Thankfully, at the top of the stairs, I see Kira's familiar face. Even under her fake nose, I can tell she looks pale with worry. 'I heard the names "Noah" and "Callum" and came rushing up . . .'

'Sisters . . . *sisters* . . . *SISTERS*!' I repeat, between breaths.

Kira's lips set themselves into a thin line and she grabs my hand. 'Let's go.'

I'm so thankful to her; she takes charge immediately and whisks me down the stairs and out of the barn. I go with her, breathlessly, blindly, stumbling along. She talks constantly, and her stream of chatter is soothing.

'I made sure I found out all the routes to the exits as we were walking in. I know that sounds lame, but I really care about you, Penny, and I like to think of these things in case you need me. I always know the fastest way to leave.'

I don't reply, but I squeeze her hand and my heart goes all warm and fuzzy. I don't think I could talk even if I wanted to. My head is whirring with questions. *Why was Noah there? What did he want? Why did Megan invite him?* And most of all: *Why do boys think they can fight over someone like she's some kind of trophy?* He didn't seem like the Noah I knew at all.

When we get to the car, I climb into the passenger seat while Kira turns the cold air on high. She strokes my hair as I try to get my breathing under control. 'You're safe, you're OK, nothing's going to happen to you,' she whispers.

I wish I could believe her.

It feels like we sit that way for ages, but in reality it's only a few minutes. When I feel my heartbeat is back down to normal and my breathing less shallow, I lift my head. 'Thanks, Kira,' I say. 'When did you learn how to do that?'

She shrugs. 'We may have googled *help someone having a panic attack* a few times. We wanted to know what to do if you were ever in that situation again.'

My eyes go wide. I can't believe how lucky I am to have such amazing friends. 'Thank you,' I say, and it hardly seems enough.

Amara jogs up to the car and climbs in. 'Shall we go home? This party's kind of lame anyway.'

I've never been so happy to have such solid, caring friends. As we drive away I try not to think about what just happened and put all my efforts into concentrating on my recovery.

One thing at a time, Penny, I tell myself. *One thing at a time.*

Chapter Thirty-Four

In the light of day, with the last of the make-up rubbed (and scrubbed, and buffed, then scrubbed some more) off my face, I know I need to confront the situation. Before I can change my mind, I open my phone and press Noah's number.

He picks up within a few rings. 'Penny?'

'Noah. I'm sorry I ran off last night.'

'No, I'm sorry – I didn't realize you were in the middle of another conversation or I would have never interrupted you. Turns out my timing is terrible.'

'You could say that,' I say with a small laugh.

'Listen, do you have any time today so we can talk in person?' he says.

'Um . . . sure. Are you staying at the Grand with Sadie Lee and Bella?' The Grand Hotel is right on the seafront in Brighton, and has become their home from home.

'No,' he replies, 'but I'll text you the address. Are you sure?'

'Yeah.'

'Cool. I'll see you soon,' and he rings off.

I walk back into the kitchen, where Mum is busy washing dishes. 'Is everything OK, darling?' she asks.

'Noah wants to meet up. I think I'm going to go out for a bit – unless you need me for anything?' I bite my lip.

She walks round the worktop to give me a big hug. 'You'll be fine. Be strong, my brave, my precious Penelope.'

'Thanks, Mum.' She hasn't called me that since I was a little girl, and it makes me smile.

I double-check the address that Noah's sent me. Like the hotel, I know it's on the seafront, but I don't recognize it – maybe there's a new cafe there that he wants to meet in. I frown. I kind of want to be somewhere much more private, especially after last night. Just as I expected it would, the Internet lit up with footage of Noah and Callum arguing over me. NOAH FLYNN: BACK AND UNLUCKY IN LOVE read the headlines.

I start walking down the hill towards the sea, pulling my jacket collar up tightly round my neck against the cold wind biting at my skin. Last night, the calendar flipped from October to November, and instantly the weather has changed too. I think back to the summer, and how I wished it would last forever.

But nothing lasts forever.

Not even someone's forever girl.

When I reach the seafront, I stop and stare at the roiling sea. It looks so different now than it did back then: under the sunless sky and huge clouds the sea is grey and cold. The

once colourful beach huts look muted, like there's a sepia filter across my eyes. I'm used to Brighton being bright and
sunny – but even this wintry version has its own kind of
beauty. Something more solemn.

According to my phone, I've reached the address that
Noah gave me. But there's no cafe here – there's not even a
little shop. We're far down the coast from the Pier and the
bandstand, and there's nothing but rows of Victorian houses,
most of them now converted into flats.

I'm about to text Noah when he messages me:

Buzz flat 5

I look up, arching my neck to see if I can see him at one of
the windows, but there's no sign of him. I shrug and stare at
the line of buzzers. Next to number 5 there's a neat card that
says *F. JONES*. I press the button anyway, and a few seconds
later the door clicks open. The lobby is beautiful, with a big
wrought-iron chandelier hanging in the centre, and my footsteps echo on the marble floor. There's a board with notices
and flyers pinned all over it, and little bunches of mail tucked
into cubbyholes like birds in a dovecote.

I get another message:

Take the elevator up to floor 3

I frown. The lift? That's when I see it, and gulp. It's one of those old-fashioned lifts, with a gate that you have to slide open and closed. It's small, only big enough for one or two people – cosy, some would say. It looks *much* older than me – probably older than Mum and Dad – and the thought of going in doesn't thrill me. Still, my curiosity is piqued. I step into the lift, press the button for the third floor, close my eyes and hope for the best.

The lift rattles ominously, but the ride up is mercifully short. I still rip open the gate when it stops, almost tearing a fingernail in the process. But the sight I'm greeted with is enough to make me gasp in a different way. The lift opens directly into an apartment – no front door or anything to push through. But before I can take a proper look around, my nostrils flare. There's a distinct smell of burning in the flat.

'Sorry!' Noah's head peeks round the corner. His hands are wrapped in floral oven gloves and they're holding a cake tin with a scorched sponge inside. 'I attempted to make a cake, but . . . I don't think I inherited any of G-ma's baking skills. Go chill on the couch while I . . . toss this.'

Chill? My feet feel rooted to the floor in front of the lift. Every surface of the hall is covered in Noah's things. He must have opened a window to get rid of the burning smell, because a breeze picks up in the apartment and the scent of the sea snaps me out of my paralysis. It also swirls a sheet of paper towards my feet. I bend down to pick it up: it's a piece of sheet music, with Noah's characteristic scrawl all over the page. Snippets of lyrics, some crossed out and rewritten, lie underneath the dancing notes of a melody. I place it safely back on the little entrance table it fell from, weighing it down with a set of keys.

I take my first steps into the flat properly and round a corner and my jaw drops at how spacious it is. The kitchen (where Noah is unceremoniously dumping the burnt cake into the rubbish bin) is open plan into the living and dining area, and two giant bay windows – with cute window seats that just beg to be curled up in with a good book – offer what seems like an infinite view over the sea.

Apart from the view, everything is distinctly . . . Noah. It's a Noah Flynn haven. I count at least four different musical instruments as I look around. Where a dining table *should* be, there's a piano, and several guitars are propped up against the back of the L-shaped sofa. Even the sofa is distinctly Noah, with its beaten-up chocolate brown leather, a dark grey throw with bright yellow accents carelessly tossed over one of the cushions. Huge pieces of art hang all over the walls – some photos of iconic rock musicians like Robert Plant and Jimmy Page from Led Zeppelin, others just huge canvases of riotous colour. Noah's slim MacBook, covered in band stickers, sits on the low table and there are mountains of empty paper coffee cups on almost every flat surface.

This place looks lived in, even though Noah's only been here a few days. I wonder who the place really belongs to, and whether they know that Noah has completely taken over and made the space his own. The more I look, the more I can only see Noah. Over the fireplace (which doesn't look as if it is ever used) there are even propped-up photos of Sadie Lee and Bella.

My heart twinges as I spot a Polaroid of us. My arms are wrapped round him on Brighton beach, our grins wide as we goof around for the camera. His fingers are on top of mine, holding me close. The good times.

'OK, so I suck at baking, but I can at least pour a drink. Want something?' he asks.

My throat is parched and I need *something* to do with my hands, so I nod. 'Water's good, please.'

'One water, coming up.'

I take the glass from his hand and gulp down half of it at once. When I can finally speak again, I look up into Noah's gorgeous dark eyes. 'Noah, this place is amazing. Who owns it?'

Noah smiles. 'I do.'

Chapter Thirty-Five

'You're kidding me!'

'Nope. This is mine.'

My mind races. 'But . . . what . . . how can that be? Who's "F. Jones" then?'

'Oh, that.' Noah frowns. 'I haven't gotten around to changing the door sign yet and, besides, it's good for privacy. But F. Jones is Fenella Jones, my new manager in the UK. When I dropped out of the tour, we had a long chat about what I really wanted. She said she had a bolthole down in Brighton that she wanted to sell and it seemed like the right thing for me to do. Plus the view is . . . pretty cool.'

I follow his gaze out of the window, and I have to agree with him. If you look at it from the right angle, it looks like the sea comes right up to the edge of his living room. But then I shake sense back into my brain. 'But that means . . . how long have you been living here?'

'Since I left the tour,' he says sheepishly.

'Huh?' I blink several times, unsure of how to process this new information. 'You've been living in Brighton this whole time?'

'Yeah.' He gestures for me to sit down, and I'm glad because I'm not sure my legs will hold me up much longer.

'But . . . why? I thought you loved New York? If you were going to buy a place anywhere, I figured it would be there.'

'Have you *seen* the price of NYC real estate? Heck, it puts even London to shame!' At my confused expression, he softens. 'OK, so it wasn't about real estate prices at all. I wanted to see if I could do this. If I could really live here.'

'And if you couldn't? Buying a flat is a pretty big deal.'

'I had some money from the tour and if I didn't like it then it's still a good investment. Trust me, this new management company is much more on me to be wise about my financial decisions.'

'Oh, that makes sense, I guess.' I pick at a loose thread on my jacket. I haven't even felt comfortable enough to take it off yet.

Noah shifts closer towards me, so that our knees are almost touching. 'Penny, I want to be with you more than anything. But I also know that I can't expect you to just drop your life – your dreams – to come on tour with me all the time. And then, what – I'm in New York in the off-times and we do long distance? Nah, you still have two years of studying left. It's too hard. We figured that out pretty quickly before.'

I nod, miserable to be reminded of all the ways 'Noah and me' didn't work.

'So I wanted to see if I could be here in Brighton, but without the pressure of you thinking I'd moved here just for you. And, Penny, I *love* it here. Fenella introduced me to some awesome musicians who live down here and we've been jamming all the time. I've written more new music staring out at that sea than I ever did in Brooklyn. The streets just feel alive with creativity. It feels . . . it feels weirdly like home.'

'Really?'

'Yeah, really. Since Mom and Dad . . .' He releases a long, sharp breath that reminds me just how hard it is for him to mention them. 'Since they died, I haven't felt like there's a place that's mine. Sadie Lee has been amazing, but her house isn't where I belong, not any more. I used music to escape. When I first met you I was running away from all my problems, but you're the one who grounded me. I wondered if the effect would extend to this cool little British seaside town. And it has. For now, this is where I want to be.' He reaches out and grips my hand. 'That is, if you don't mind. Because if this is going to be an issue I can move or I can . . .'

I lean back in the sofa, letting my body sink into the leather. 'Noah . . .'

'I know, it's a lot. You don't have to say anything just yet. I wanted to tell you all this in Scotland, but I thought it would make more sense if I could just show you.'

He's right. Now that I'm here and can see how . . . how at home he is, it does feel real. I don't think I could have imagined it if he hadn't shown me.

I lift my eyes. 'And the party?'

Noah laughs softly. 'I thought you knew I was going to be there. That's what Megan told me. So when I saw you with that guy again . . . I just saw red. It's not an excuse. I'm trying to explain.'

'You surprised me by being there.' Before he can speak again, I think back on all those times I *thought* I saw Noah. Maybe it really had been him. 'Have you seen me since you were in Brighton?'

'It was hard not to! This town is a lot smaller than I thought. I tried to stay out of your way, though. Like I said, I wanted us to figure this out independently.' He bites his lip. 'Did I do the right thing?'

I think about how much his absence and his silence hurt. I think how I tried to move on, but something was holding me back. I think about the ghost-Noahs that have been haunting my every step. And I think about how far I've come – with my panic attacks, with my new friends, with my photography. All I want to do is share that with the person I love most in the whole world. With the person who makes me better. If that means letting go of the hurt – I can do that.

I can do that with my whole heart.

There's just one more thing, though. 'What about Sadie Lee and Bella?' I say.

'Well . . . that's the main thing I had to talk to Sadie Lee about up in Scotland. But she surprised me too. So you know how the partnership with your mum works so well?'

'Yeah . . .'

'They've been talking for quite a while about properly

going into business together. That way they can keep doing these big, high-profile events.'

'Seriously?' My stomach flutters with excitement: this could be the perfect thing for Mum too. Mum and Dad have always worried about how to make sure they can keep the business going, but with Sadie Lee as a partner . . . they would be unstoppable.

Noah nods. 'They want to at least try it out. And since Bella loves it here . . . they're going to stay for a while.'

I can't help myself. I launch off my corner of the sofa and land in his arms. 'Is this really happening? You're really serious about this?'

'Deadly.'

For a moment, words totally escape me. Noah pulls me tight into his chest, and I let myself relax in a way I haven't in months. Then I lift my chin, studying his dark brown eyes, remembering every fleck of gold in his irises, the way his eyelashes curve softly, pointing up to his thick brows. My gaze drifts lower, over his strong nose, the day-old stubble on his chin, and finally to his wonderfully full lips.

He leans forward, his hands caressing my back, preventing me from falling. Then his lips brush against mine, softly at first, then with greater urgency.

Suddenly the fireworks I've been missing are all lit up at once inside my mind, bursts of silver and gold sparks in front of my eyes. He pulls away slightly but I bury my hands in his unruly hair and bring him back again. He tastes like caramel and sea salt, and his familiar musky scent fills every intake of breath. I want to kiss like this forever.

A kiss that feels so right I expect angels to start singing and trumpets to sound at any moment.

When he pulls away again, our faces remain so close we might as well be kissing. He strokes my cheek and whispers to me softly:

'This is you and me, Penny. I meant it when I said "forever".'

1 November

Brooklyn Boy Is Back

Good evening, my lovely readers!

I promised you that this new iteration of *Girl Online* was going to be more honest and upfront, so I have to share the news with you guys . . . Brooklyn Boy is back, but he's no longer Brooklyn Boy . . . now he's Brighton Boy!

Sometimes the ghosts of our past come back to haunt us and it's just whether they're friendly ghosts or not that takes a bit of time trying to work out. So, that's right: BB is back in my life. He's back in all our lives.

It's strange – I really thought that if I put my mind to it, I could bury all these feelings I have towards him. Turns out, however, even a charming Scottish guy couldn't erase them. That's when I *knew* they were so deep and real I couldn't NOT act upon them!

I've worked out that when it comes to both your heart and your head, heart wins every time. No matter how loud your head is screaming, your heart is always louder and stronger. I'm not sure how this will go, and I'm a little nervous if I'm completely honest with you, but I've put my worries to one side for now and I'm just taking each day as it comes.

I'm so happy I'm almost brimming every waking moment of every day, and I'm making the *absolute most* of it. It feels so normal – but so new and exciting all over again.

Got to dash. I can't *think* above the racket of my completely, ridiculously, utterly beautiful, talented boyfriend playing his guitar. (Feels *so* weird to say that ☺☺☺)

Girl Online, going offline xxx

PS Would you like some fries with all that cheese? ;) x

★ ·Chapter Thirty-Six· ★

'Cheers, to the *second* best couple in the world getting back together,' says Elliot, raising a glass to us. I'd invited Elliot and Alex over to Noah's apartment for a bit of a celebration – we'd ordered in Pizzaface pizza, which we ate on the floor (since Noah had no dining table), off mismatched plates that we found buried in Noah's cupboard. He wasn't kidding when he said he didn't cook much. Most of the kitchen stuff looks like it's never been touched.

I snuggle into Noah's shoulder and 'Cheers' back with my fizzy water.

'I must say, it's awesome that you're sticking around, Noah,' Elliot continues with a grin. 'Now maybe we can get normal, happy Penny back – rather than the grump who's been hanging round these parts lately.'

'Hey!' I say. I chuck a piece of garlic bread at his head, but it lands directly in his glass with a loud plop.

'My vintage!' he squeals.

'Good shot!' says Alex, laughing.

This is how it should be. The four of us, hanging out and not having a care in the world.

'So, tell me, what else have you guys been up to while I've been away?' says Noah, turning to Alex first.

'Same old, same old for me,' says Alex. 'I've moved jobs, and I'm making more money as a waiter than I did at that vintage shop. I think they want me to train as a manager, which would be great. Other than that, I've just been hanging out with this nutter.' He nudges Elliot in the ribcage, causing him to almost spill his wine again.

Noah turns next to Elliot, who sighs dramatically. 'Well, you know that I'm living with Penny at the moment?'

Noah's brow furrows in concern. 'I gathered, but I don't know all the details.'

Alex gently strokes Elliot's hand as Elliot shrugs. 'Not really any details I'd want to divulge. My parents are psychopaths, so I had to move out.' He laughs, but it doesn't quite ring true. When we don't respond the way he expects, Elliot continues, his finger running round the top edge of his glass. 'They're just fighting a lot. I think they'll probably end up getting divorced, but I can't be in the house while they're figuring it out. It's not long until it's not my problem anyway. I have bigger things to worry about, like getting into uni and making sure Alex here comes with me.'

'I'll come with you and you know it. Let's be honest, what choice do I have?' Alex says with a laugh, lifting Elliot's hand to his mouth and kissing it.

'I'm sorry, man. That's hard about your mom and dad,'

says Noah. 'Have you decided which uni yet? Last time I heard, you had a school in London in mind?'

'Yeah, University College London, if I can.'

'If anyone can do it, you can,' Noah says. 'You're, like, the smartest kid I've ever met . . . besides myself, obviously . . .'

Elliot waves his hand in front of him extravagantly and takes a bow. 'Why, thank you, kind sir. I *was* going to be worried about Penny missing me, but that probably won't be a problem now that you're not hiding away like Miss Havisham any more,' he says with a wink.

'Hey, I'll still miss you!' I protest. 'But in case you hadn't noticed, since going to visit Megan, I'm a pro at whizzing up to London now.'

'Speaking of the she-devil, has she been in touch since the party?'

I shake my head. 'No. It is Megan after all . . . plus she's probably busy with rehearsals for the show. Opening night is tomorrow.'

'Well, tell her I hope she breaks a leg. Literally.'

'Elliot!'

'What? Inviting Noah to the party just so she can become queen bee of her stupid school, not caring about your feelings or what sort of drama it might bring up – that does *not* make me like her any more than I already disliked her before. I had maybe shifted from Hatred Level Elevated down to Guarded, but now it's ratcheted right back up to Severe again.'

'What are you talking about, Wiki?'

'I use the US Homeland Security threat levels scale – and Severe is the highest.'

I frown. 'She's not *that* bad. She had a really hard time at the school in the beginning. And you know Megan – she always goes over the top when it comes to these things.'

'You don't have to keep defending her, Penny,' says Elliot. 'It's exhausting just listening to you doing it all the time. Sometimes I wish you'd just open your eyes. That woman is evil incarnate.'

Noah's arms stiffen round my shoulders, but I don't need him to fight my battles for me. 'I'm Megan's oldest friend,' I say levelly, 'so I have to believe the best in her.'

'I wish you wouldn't; you're being wasted on her,' my BFF grumbles. Then he waggles his eyebrows at me. 'Noah, you should ask Penny what *she's* been up to while you've been away – with her photography, I mean.'

'Oh?' Noah leans back so that he can look into my face more easily. My cheeks are rapidly turning a horribly bright shade of red.

'I don't want to talk about it yet . . .' I mumble.

'That's right, it's a *secret* project,' Elliot persists.

'Does it have to do with your A-level stuff?' Noah asks, the words sounding funny in his mouth. Coming from the United States, where they have a different system – SATs and Advanced AP classes and other weird stuff like that – he hasn't quite got to grips with the difference between my GCSE exams I took last year and the A levels I'll be taking next year. (I've already had to explain the intricacies of sixth form to Noah. Him: 'So it's called "college", but it's not college like I know it?' Me: 'No, it's not "college" as in "university". It's what you take in order to get into university.')

I shake my head, but keep my lips tightly zipped.

'OK, does it have anything to do with that internship you did over the summer with that fancy photographer?'

'*Mayyybe*,' I say, regretting even giving away that much. 'I promise to tell you all when it's ready. It's just an idea at the moment and I feel like if I talk about it or even think too much about it then it might fly away.'

'I feel that way about songs sometimes,' says Noah. 'I'm glad you're still concentrating so hard on your photography. I didn't realize how much I missed that side of you until I tried to take my own pictures of the sea and they just came out crap. I honestly think Bella could have done a better job.' He kisses my shoulder, and I beam.

'You two are so sweet it makes me sick,' says Elliot.

'No, I think that's just too much pizza!' I shoot back.

Elliot grips his stomach as it lets out a growl. 'Oh my god, I think you might be right,' and he stands up.

'Bathroom's down the hallway and to the right, dude,' calls Noah after him.

Just then, my phone rings, and when the caller's face pops up on the screen and I see it's Leah, I say, 'I better get this,' to Noah.

He nods, raising his eyebrows in concern, but I whisper, 'I'll explain later,' before stepping out into the hall.

'Hey, Leah,' I say when I answer. 'How are you?'

'Oh, you know, getting there. I saw that Noah's back – his Twitter is active again. Does that mean he's been in touch?'

Even though she can't see it, I smile. 'Yeah,' I say, feeling sheepish even though I know I have no reason to. 'And some. To cut a long story short, we've decided to give it another go.'

There's a squeal on the other end of the line. 'Yay! I'm so happy for you guys,' she says. 'I want to hear all about it, but I'm calling this time to give you an update on the whole song-leak thing. Do you have your laptop around?'

'No, I don't . . .' I say, 'but I can see if I can borrow Noah's.' I walk back into the living room and gesture to the MacBook on the table. 'Do you mind?' I ask Noah.

'Go ahead,' he says. He lifts it up and gives it to me. I walk over to the kitchen, put the laptop down on the worktop and boot it up.

'Is anything going to happen to Posey?' I ask. Even though she did an awful thing, I hope nothing more is going to happen to her. Losing her part in the show is bad enough.

'Listen, I've had my lawyers and tech guys going over things for days,' Leah explains.

I let go of a long breath. This is a huge deal for Leah. 'I'm really sorry this happened to you. Do you have a plan?'

'We're not going to press charges for now. And my label has decided to use the noise to help drive pre-order sales. I'm going to be working my butt off for the next few days, but we're going to get the single ready for release ASAP.'

'Well, that's good at least. What a nightmare.' I breathe a sigh of relief that Leah can be so nice about it. She could have pressed charges, but I get the feeling Posey has had enough punishment already.

'Anyway,' she continues, 'yesterday they came up with something *very* interesting. I've sent you an email with a link in it. Once you watch it, I'll leave it to you to decide what to do. Now, I better run. I am so happy for you and Noah. When I'm next in town, we'll all have to meet up.'

'It's a date,' I say.

Leah hangs up before I can question her any more about the link she's sent me, so I immediately log in to my emails, my fingers flying across the keyboard. Leah's email is sitting at the top. STRICTLY PRIVATE AND CONFIDENTIAL is the title, and it makes me gulp.

I open it and click the link, which leads to a video on a private channel. I watch the video once, then I instantly rewind and watch it again.

And again.

'What's up, Penny? You've gone as white as a sheet.' It's Elliot standing in the doorway, staring at me staring at the computer. Noah and Alex swing round to look at me too.

I swallow hard. 'Looks like you were right after all, Wiks. Megan can't be trusted one little bit.'

Chapter Thirty-Seven

The video footage that Leah has sent me is from the CCTV cameras inside the recording studio at Octave. Megan's on there, doing something with her phone, and then you see her leaving it on the mixing table, right on top of the button that brings in the sound from the live room. Then she gets up and leaves. That would be when she came upstairs and asked me where the bathroom was, I think. So, even though she's not there in the studio herself at that point, she's still recording the song.

I can hardly believe my eyes. Why would Megan do something like this again? And why would she be so stupid as to think she wouldn't get caught?

I show Elliot, Noah and Alex the video, and Elliot's face screams *I told you so*.

Noah puts his arms round my waist. 'What are you going to do, hon?'

I snap his laptop shut, then spin round so I can bury my

face against his shoulder. 'I don't know,' I mumble, and I pull away, shaking my head.

'Milkshake, milkshake,' Elliot starts chanting, harking back to the time we threw our milkshakes over Megan when she needed standing up to.

I laugh bitterly. 'Elliot . . . this is serious! Somehow, if Milkshakegate didn't get through the first time, I don't think it's going to work now.' I let out a strangled groan. 'Leah's not pressing charges, and she's leaving it up to me to do what I think best.' Then my hand flies instantly to my mouth and I let out a cry: 'Posey! I was so mean to her! I didn't believe her when she was telling the truth this *whole* time!'

'You can make it up with her,' Elliot says gently. 'But, if I were you, I wouldn't tell Megan that Leah's not pressing charges. Some guy went to jail for a couple of years for leaking Madonna songs.'

'Seriously?'

'Yeah, copyright breaches are serious business in the music industry. Especially if someone's done it for profit, which is what it looks like in this case.'

I think of all the money that Megan's been throwing around lately: the expensive make-up in Covent Garden, the lavish Halloween party. The thought makes me shiver. She messed with me before, and I managed to forgive her for that. But now she's messed with not one but two of my friends: Leah in a big way, and Posey too. Megan convinced me that *Posey* was the one who'd leaked the song, when she knew all along that *she'd* done it. She destroyed my new friendship, got herself the big role in the show and catapulted her status at Madame Laplage from nobody to Miss Popular.

You have to hand it to the girl. She knows how to play to win.

It makes me seethe with rage, and I know I will never be able to trust her again.

Elliot comes up and whispers in my ear: 'Revenge!'

Luckily, all it does is break me out of my fury. I laugh. 'Elliot, I wish she was worth it. But this time I don't think she is. All I want is to never speak to her again. I think I just want her out of my life.'

'Aw, there must be *something* you can do. She can't get away scot-free.'

I drum my finger on my bottom lip. 'You know what, Wiks? You're right. I think there *is* something she can do to make up for it.' I allow myself a small smile. I won't take no for an answer and I'm not going to let her wriggle out of it.

'Do tell,' says Elliot, his foot tapping impatiently.

I shake my head. 'No . . . but you guys are free tomorrow night, right? Do you want to come to London to see a show?'

Once Elliot and Alex have gone and it's just Noah and me, I can't help the tears that well up in my eyes. Megan might have been a terrible friend to me on too many occasions now to count, but she was also a good friend, once upon a time. Even recently, she's seemed to really open up to me. And she was so great about my anxiety. But I guess you never really know some people. Sometimes they can be wonderful;

sometimes they can be the absolute worst. You just have to decide how much of either you can accept.

But I've had enough of accepting Megan.

'Penny, it's OK. You couldn't have known.'

'Couldn't I? Elliot's right: the signs were there. She's basically made a fool out of me.'

'And like a good friend, a good *person*, who gives other people the benefit of the doubt, you chose to believe she could be better. That she couldn't be isn't your fault at all.'

'The things I said to Posey . . .'

'Posey will forgive you. You didn't know.'

'Oh, I hope you're right. This is something I need to apologize for in person – some things can't be said by text.'

'So, can you give me any hints as to this secret project of yours?'

'Nice change of subject,' I say with a small smile. 'But just because I'm upset doesn't mean I'm going to give away all my secrets.'

Noah puts his hand on his chest in mock outrage. '*Moi?* Try to get your secrets out of you?'

'I promise you, you'll know when it's ready.'

'OK, I can live with that.'

I sigh, and we curl up on the sofa. There's a DVD on low volume in the background, an old BBC nature documentary that Elliot had put on. We lose ourselves watching it, my head on his chest, and I marvel at how well we fit together.

'What about you?' I ask, my eyes drifting over the array of musical instruments in the room.

'Hmm? What do you mean?'

'When am I going to get to hear what *you*'ve been working on?'

'Ah, you're not the only one who can make someone wait.'

'Aw, really?'

'Nah, you think I can resist that face? I have something super special I'm working on that you *will* have to wait for, but for now let me play you something a bit different.'

He moves over to the piano – which takes me by surprise, because I've never heard him play it before. He settles down at the keys, his fingers flexing. Then he starts playing a beautiful melody, his hands flying up and down the length of the keys with practised speed.

Then he sings the first few lines, and at first it's just so amazing to hear him sing live again (I've been listening to his album while he's been away of course) that I forget to listen to the lyrics. When I do focus on them, I realize the song is about someone who feels he's drowning, overwhelmed by a dark sea. The song is sad and slow, but so moving, and as it nears the end it builds up with an epic crescendo.

And when the last note hangs in the air between us I burst into applause.

'You like it?' Noah looks nervous but pleased.

'It's incredible!' I enthuse.

'I wrote it during the darkest time, when I first got to Brighton after quitting the tour. Like I said, the words and the music just kind of . . . flowed straight out of me. But this had to be a piano piece, not guitar. It needed that more solemn, grounded sound. I haven't sent it to Fenella yet.'

'She's going to think it's as great as I do, I promise.'

'Why, thank you kindly,' he says, imitating Sadie Lee's southern drawl.

'You know, I still can't believe you're going to be living here.'

'Yeah, it's crazy, right? I want you to take me to do all the British things. Maybe I'll start talking in a British accent.'

'*Noooo!* I love that you talk like a *New Yorker*.' I attempt an American drawl for that, but it comes out a terrible mix, somewhere between Irish, Indian and French.

'OK, OK, no accents!' he cries. 'But I do want to do the whole British thing. Maybe we can go visit the queen at Buckingham Palace?'

'And go for afternoon tea!'

'Watch the footy!'

At that, I grimace. 'Oh no, don't become a football nut either.'

'Ha, no worries about that!' Noah laughs. 'If I wasn't a sports fan in the USA, I don't think a move across the pond is going to change things.'

'And we can do other things too. Like visit the Roman baths or go to a festival or learn how to talk about the weather non-stop.'

'As long as you're with me, I'll be up for anything.'

'This is going to be so much fun,' I say. I can't remember the last time I felt this happy, this content. I snuggle closer against Noah's chest, our feet entwined on one side of his L-shaped sofa. The moon outside casts its beam through one of the big bay windows, landing directly on our toes. I wish I could bottle the moonlight and take it home with me.

The thought triggers an unwelcome reminder.

'I better be getting home,' I say, looking at the time.

'I'm so glad we're doing this.'

'Me too.'

'Are you sure you don't want me to come with you and Alexiot tomorrow?'

'No, this is something I have to sort out on my own.'

'Well, don't worry. You got this. I believe in you.'

It's just the boost I need to settle my stomach. Tomorrow's going to be one of the hardest days I've ever had to face.

Chapter Thirty-Eight

School the next day is pure torture. Everyone is talking about Megan's party – how cool it was and how they hope she holds another one next year. Her popularity plan is going off without a hitch. Well, except for *my* planned hitch.

I can barely concentrate the whole day, so much so that Miss Mills has to call my name three times before I finally look up.

'Penny?' She sounds exasperated.

'Sorry, miss, my mind's elsewhere.'

'You're telling me! Can I see you for a minute after class?'

'Uh . . .' I look down at my phone. I was hoping to leave straight after my photography lesson. My free period means I can get up to London in plenty of time to intercept Megan and put my plan in motion.

'Penny . . .?'

'Yes, sure, of course,' I say. I can spare a few minutes, and I feel guilty enough for ignoring my favourite teacher.

So, when the bell rings, I walk over to her desk, where she's laying out papers.

'I haven't seen you much lately,' she says without looking up.

'I've been working. I'm just . . . not ready to show my project quite yet.'

Now she looks up at me, her eyes scanning my face. I try to put on my best innocent look. It's not like me to hide work from her – even unfinished stuff – but this is something different. Only one person has seen it so far, and they had encouraged me to keep going. The idea still feels too much like a shimmering bubble in a bath of bubbles. It's too fragile and I'm afraid that if too many people look at it before it's ready it might burst.

'OK. Well, as long as you're not too distracted. This is an important time for you.' She gives me a small smile. 'I read your blog. I'm glad you're happy. Just make sure it doesn't mean you waste all the progress you've made so far. You're pretty brilliant on your own, Penny.'

'I won't, I promise.'

'See you tomorrow then.'

'See you, miss.'

As soon as I step outside Miss Mills's door, I'm accosted by Kira. I bite my lip. If I don't get away soon, I won't have enough time . . .

'Are you going to London later? Us too. Can we come with? You've been to the school before, so you know where it is and we won't get lost.'

She speaks so fast I almost don't have time to register what she's saying. 'Wait, what? You're going to the show later this evening?'

'Uh, where have you been, Pen? Megan wants us *all* to come to her show.'

'Megan invited all of you?'

'Yeah, she said she had a load of extra tickets and, you know how it is. She wants us all to see her big debut.'

I swallow. This is going to make my plan even more difficult.

'So, are you going up?' asks Kira again.

'Yeah, I am, but I have a free period now, so I was going to leave straight away and catch Megan before the show.'

'Oh, boo. OK, well, we'll see you there then.'

'Sure. See you.'

I just about have enough time to make it to the train. I need to get this earlier one if I've any hope of putting my plan into action. I bite my bottom lip at the thought.

My phone buzzes suddenly with a text.

> Hi Penny. Look, I'm sorry but I don't have time to meet up with you before the show. It's a bit crazy. Sure you understand

There's no kisses at the end, no emojis . . . Megan's definitely still holding a grudge after the party. And now that she has everyone at school – her old school *and* Madame Laplage – eating out of her hands again, she has no need for her old friend.

She was never your friend, I remind myself.

She only used you.

Tears well up in my eyes. I thought, through everything, I knew Megan and she knew me. But then her words come back to me, what she said about students at Madame Laplage.

Everyone wants to be a star.

No one wants it more than Megan.

She's prepared to do whatever it takes . . . no matter what the cost.

And the only person who can stop her is me.

Chapter Thirty-Nine

The theatre is quiet in the last few hours before the show. Everything's ready and the place feels empty – like the calm before the storm. The stage set is designed to transport us all to New York City, and I'm reminded of when we did our school production of *Romeo and Juliet*. Our drama teacher had set that production in Brooklyn. Maybe he'd been a fan of *West Side Story* too. I can see, however, that this is a much better quality set than we had for our school show, and if I close my eyes I can almost picture myself on a Manhattan street. I'm grateful that Megan gave me such a thorough tour the last time as I don't have any difficulty finding my way.

I reach the main dressing-room door, which has a piece of paper pinned on the outside with the name MARIA scrawled across it. I take a deep breath, then give a knock.

'Come in!' says Megan's melodic voice.

She has a huge smile on her face that falls to the floor when she sees that it's me who comes in. I don't know who she was expecting, but it clearly wasn't me.

'Oh. Hi,' she says irritably. 'Didn't you get my message?' She turns back to the mirror, where she's busy applying the first layer of her make-up. Her chestnut hair has been brushed to a mirror shine and I have to admit she does look like she's made to be a show diva. It's just a shame she chose to go about it in such a deceitful way.

'Yeah, I did,' I reply. 'But this is important.'

'So important it couldn't wait until after?'

I decide to just say it, before I lose my nerve.

'I know it was you who leaked Leah's song.'

Megan pauses for a moment, then puts her brushes down. She turns to look at me.

'How dare you! I told you it wasn't me. I wasn't even there. It could only have been Posey . . .'

I roll my eyes, folding my arms across my chest. 'Just stop this, Megan. Leah has the CCTV footage.'

'OK,' Megan says unsteadily. At least now she has the decency to look less sure of herself.

'You know she can press charges,' I go on.

Megan's face blanches. 'Is she going to?'

'No,' I tell her. 'You're *not worth it.*'

'Well then, I guess we've got nothing more to say to each other. If this means I don't have to be your friend any more, I guess it's win-win.'

My jaw drops. 'What have I done to you?' I gasp.

'What have you done? This role was as good as mine; that

264

girl was going to drop out. And then you had to give her this *big* confidence boost – and you had the nerve to bring me along with you? I thought you were supposed to be *my* friend! You meet some random girl and after a couple of weeks you take her side? What kind of "friend" does that, Penny?'

I frown. 'What? I am your friend. Or at least . . . I was your friend. But you've gone too far this time, Megan.'

'What exactly do you want, Penny? If you don't mind, I need to get ready for the show.'

'Give Posey back her role.'

Megan laughs, but stops again quickly. 'Are you *kidding*? No, Penny. I've worked too hard for this and you're not going to take it away from me now.'

'I've got the CCTV footage of you recording the track. I could tell everyone you did it.'

Megan stands up now, shaking her hair out behind her. 'Honestly, Penny? Who cares? It's a song leak. I got a bit of money. Leah got some great exposure . . . It's all good. I think you should go now. And, besides, I know you don't have it in you to release any video. That would make you as bad as me. And you're too much of a goody-two-shoes to *actually* do anything.'

I realize my plan is beginning to crack and crumble. Megan's right – I couldn't release the video to hurt her. But I have to try again to make her back down – for Posey's sake.

'You know,' I say, 'I'm not sure where this all went so terribly wrong for you, Megan. I've given you the benefit of the doubt before, but you've changed. For the worse. You aren't who I thought you were. The Megan I once knew was kind and considerate. She actually liked making people happy. She wasn't this hard, self-centred person who steamrollers over other people to get what she wants. I think the least you can do is to give Posey back her role.'

'No,' she snaps.

'Are you sure about that?' A soft voice comes from over my shoulder, and Megan's face has drained of colour.

I spin round.

'Madame Laplage?' Megan exclaims in surprise.

Behind me is a tall, stern-looking woman carrying a large bouquet of yellow and white flowers, which she drops unceremoniously down on to a table just inside the dressing room. This must be the renowned principal of the school herself. She folds her arms across her chest.

'Would you please explain what's going on here?' she says to me.

'She doesn't even go here!' Megan jumps in. 'She's trespassing.'

I see then for myself the formidable Madame Laplage I've heard so much about, because she's able to silence Megan with a look. Then she turns back to me. Fortunately, her eyes now are softer again. More encouraging.

My mouth opens, but no words come out. I don't know if I can tell on Megan – not to someone as important as Madame Laplage anyway. Then I realize I have to tell her, if only for Posey's sake. It's Posey who should be in this dressing room.

'Megan took money for leaking one of Leah Brown's songs,' I say in a rush, 'and she blamed Posey Chang, who dropped out of the production because of it.'

Madame Laplage shakes her head slowly. 'Is this true, Megan?'

Megan stares at her shoes, not responding.

'We don't like thieves here at my school.'

'Thieves?' Megan squeaks.

'I'm afraid so. We are a prestigious school for the arts. We take copyright theft extremely seriously. And the fact that you falsely accused another student and took advantage of her lack of confidence to take her role – well, I've known understudies who've schemed to get the main role before, but this is the worst example of such dreadful behaviour *by far*!'

She draws herself up to her full height, and both Megan and I shrink back. 'You have forfeited your right to a place at my school. Your place is temporarily withdrawn.'

'No . . . please!' Megan is trembling now. 'I promise I've learnt my lesson! Madame Laplage, I didn't mean it . . . Penny's right, that's not who I am . . . not deep down . . . I just wanted this so much. I didn't think about anybody else . . .'

But Madame Laplage's mouth is a hard line. 'If you want a second chance, it will have to wait until *after* the production, when we can review this properly. For now, you aren't welcome here and I need you to leave this dressing room.'

Megan barges past me, shooting me the dirtiest glare she can muster as she goes. I'm stunned. But Megan made it clear she wasn't even going to apologize for what she did. She wasn't going to even try to make amends by giving Posey back her role. She deserves to be kicked out.

Madame Laplage turns her steely gaze on me as if really seeing me for the first time. 'Tell me, are you a student here?'

I shake my head. Suddenly I feel extremely out of place in the backstage of the theatre.

'But you know Posey Chang?'

I nod.

'Then I suggest you go and find her quickly, and let her know she has to get ready for the performance tonight. We're all looking forward to it.'

I nod once more then dart out of the door, remembering just in time to say, 'Thank you, Madame,' as I go past.

She is *SOOO* terrifying! I really wouldn't want to be in Megan's shoes right now.

This time when I knock on a door, I'm in a very different mood. There's a huge grin on my face and I can barely keep my toes from dancing with excitement.

'Hello?' says Posey as she opens the door.

'Hey, it's me,' I say.

I'm half expecting Posey to close the door in my face, but instead she smiles when she sees me. Then she remembers what's happened and the smile drops. Suddenly she looks afraid.

My stomach churns with guilt. I can't believe what I've done to this girl, this person I was supposed to be friends with. I put my hand on her door. 'Posey,' I blurt out, 'I wanted to say that I am so, *so* sorry I didn't listen to you.'

'Oh?' She opens the door a tiny bit wider.

'I know now that it wasn't you. And I should never have believed it in the first place. I may not have known you for long, but I already know you better than that.'

Posey's eyes shine with tears. 'Thanks, Penny. You don't know how much that means to me. I've been so sad at the prospect that our new friendship might have been ruined by something that wasn't true.'

I take a deep breath. 'And I also have some news. Megan's not going to be able to play Maria tonight.'

Posey's eyes open wide. 'What? Why not?'

'She's been kicked out for breaking the rules.'

'No way! That can't be right.'

'She falsely accused you of stealing Leah's song and forced you to leave your role – Madame Laplage is furious. And it was *her* all along.'

'You mean . . . Megan was the one who leaked Leah's song?'

'That's right! I should never have trusted her. I should have seen the signs long ago. I was an idiot.'

'Oh my god!' Posey backs into her room and falls on to her bed, as if her legs won't support her any longer. I'm feeling wobbly too, so I go inside and sit down next to her. 'But there are so many people coming to see her,' Posey says. 'And it's been all over her blog and Twitter and Facebook . . . What's she going to tell people now?'

I shrug. 'That's her problem. She probably should have thought of that *before* she went and stole the song.'

'Wow! I can't believe it was her. But, gosh, how do you feel about it, Penny? Are you OK?' Her eyes shine with concern.

'I'm fine. A bit rattled, but . . . I'm glad it's all working out. Anyway – the *really* big news is that when Madame Laplage heard how she got the role of Maria, how she lied about it being you who'd done the recording and everything, she said you must play Maria tonight. She sent me here specially to find you and tell you to go and get ready.'

Posey's eyes turn towards the ground. 'But, Penny, I still don't think I can do this. I've got used to the idea of just having a small role in the show . . .' Her hands begin to shake. 'See? I can't even think about it without my stage fright coming back. Surely one of the other cast members can do it. I don't even know if I remember all the lines . . . and the cues . . . I've been busy learning all the chorus stuff. What happens if I mess it up? I'll get a terrible mark and get kicked out myself.' Her words begin to run together until they're a babble.

'Posey,' I say, gripping her shoulders. 'Close your eyes. Breathe.'

She closes her eyes and it takes a few slow intakes of breath, but gradually she begins to breathe normally again.

'You can do this,' I continue. 'You were born to do this. You know this role inside out. Just acknowledge the nerves. Acknowledge the fear. Picture it . . .' I think back to Leah's tree metaphor. 'Think of it like a shower of rain. Most people want sunshine all the time, but you know there has to be rain. The tree needs it to survive. You can use the fear to drive you so that you give the performance of your life. Don't try to pretend the fear isn't there. Remember that nothing truly bad will happen to you – you'll survive, your friends and family will still love you. Give your fear the respect it deserves and move on. There may be nights when it gets too much. But tonight won't be one of them. You *can* do this, you *WANT* to do this. I believe in you, Posey.' I reach down into my bag and pull out a brown paper bag and hold it out to her. 'Here,' I say, 'I've brought you something.'

She takes it and looks inside. 'Oh!' she exclaims, then she reaches in to pull out a tiny bonsai tree. Relative to its tiny size, the bonsai tree has a thick trunk, with a cap of bright green leaves, each the size of my little fingernail.

'I thought you needed a little reminder of what's inside you – that tree of confidence that gives you the courage to go on. It's not too difficult to look after either!'

'Penny, I love it!' She places the tree down on her desk and gazes at it for a few moments.

When she looks back up at me, there's something different in her eyes. A determination I haven't seen before. Then she looks down at her watch and shrieks in alarm.

'Right, I've got thirty minutes . . . I'd better be quick!'

'Yes!' I cry out, wanting to jump and scream all at the same time. She's going to do it. She really is!

Posey leaps into a hug and we jump around in delight. Then she dashes everywhere, throwing clothes and make-up into a bag.

As we leave her room, she stops me just inside the doorway. My immediate thought is that she's changed her mind. But instead she smiles at me. 'You know, Penny, you're really good at this.'

'At what?'

'At helping people.'

I blush furiously at her words. 'What do you mean?'

'I mean that no one has ever really listened to me before about my stage fright. They thought it was a phase I would grow out of.'

'But the thing is, I knew a bit about what you must have felt, because of my own anxiety. And I know it can be triggered by things that aren't your fault.' I think of the near-miss car accident that triggered my own panic attacks. 'We mustn't let the bad experiences ruin our life. And for you that means making sure they don't stand in the way of your dreams. Right, I must go. I'll see you after?'

She grabs my hand. 'Come backstage with me. I might have another blip. But if you're there . . . I *know* I'll be able to do it.'

I grin. 'With pleasure!'

Chapter Forty

The backstage area couldn't be more different from how it was only a couple of hours ago. It's mayhem. There are people running around everywhere, flinging costumes over their heads, and the stage lights keep flickering on and off as the technicians practise the different sets. I skip out of the way to dodge a trolley full of big flouncy underskirts.

'Oh good, you found our star!' comes Madame Laplage's distinctive voice as we hurry to Posey's dressing room.

'Madame Laplage! It's so nice of you.' Posey almost curtseys like she's meeting royalty, but she stops herself at the last moment.

'No, my dear, not at all. I've had reports from several of your teachers about the wonderful audition you gave, and you've had some good rehearsals too. But don't worry, everyone has at least one dress rehearsal that goes badly,' she says with a wink. 'It practically guarantees a good opening performance. Now, go and get ready.' Posey hurries on to her dressing room and I'm left alone with the formidable Madame Laplage.

'Please, Madame, is it all right if I stay backstage? Posey thinks it will help her.'

She looks down her severe, straight nose at me and purses her lips. 'Well, I hate having idle hands backstage. Is there anything you can do? Can you do any make-up? Or help the actors get dressed?'

'I can take photos?' I say in a small voice.

'Well, all right then. We already have a production photographer but I'm sure it wouldn't hurt to have two perspectives. You have your own equipment?'

I swing the backpack round my shoulder and show her the camera inside.

'Fantastic.' She claps her hands together. 'Get to work then!' She gives her dress a dramatic swish and strides off purposefully to intimidate some other students. I let out the long breath I hadn't even realized I was holding. Somehow, even though they're at opposite ends of the drama spectrum, I bet Madame Laplage and Mum would get on really well.

I fish my camera out of my bag and, with the other hand, send another text to Mum, Elliot and Alex, telling them I'll meet them after the performance. Then I make sure to put the phone on mute and start my 'new job'.

This is the part I love most. Once the camera's in my hands, it's almost as if I become a different person – one who's not afraid to shoot the right subject from any angle, who will do almost anything to capture a unique moment. I spot a group of the chorus huddling together, doing vocal warm-ups, and I take a snap. After that, it becomes almost automatic – point, shoot, refocus.

I only stop when my viewfinder comes face-to-face with another camera, in the hands of a tall guy with dark blond, slightly wavy hair.

He lowers the body of his camera first, and gives me a shy grin. Of *course* the production photographer Madame Laplage mentioned would be Callum!

'Hi, friend,' he says.

'Hi,' I say back, suddenly shy.

'Can you help me out? I'm having trouble getting the right settings in the low light backstage.'

And, just like that, we're back to geeking out about cameras again, and I realize how much fun it is having someone else around who's just as passionate about this stuff as I am – even if it only goes as far as a camera friendship, not a relationship.

'Five minutes until curtain up!'

'I better take my place,' says Callum. 'See you around?'

'See you later. Don't forget about that shutter speed!'

'I won't,' he says, then he heads out to the front of house to get shots from the orchestra pit. I can hear the musicians warming up now, ready to play the first few bars of the opening number. All around me, I take pictures of people in various states of nervousness, psyching themselves up for the start of the performance. There's a rustling in the auditorium now as the audience files in to take their seats, and there's a strange tension out there too – the audience's expectations of the performance to come, their hopes that it will be an enjoyable spectacle.

'Penny?'

I see Posey come out of her dressing room looking absolutely radiant. Her glossy dark hair has been curled fifties-style, and her face is thick with make-up to make her features clearly visible on stage. Woven into her hairline is a tiny microphone that hangs discreetly on her forehead. She looks every bit the star.

'Posey – or should I say *Maria* – you look amazing!'

She bites her red-stained lower lip. 'I haven't told my mum yet that I'm playing Maria again.'

'Maybe that's a good thing,' I say gently. 'Are you ready?'

'As ready as I'm ever going to be.'

Posey's not on straight away – she has to wait as the first few scenes are played. I can sense her shivering next to me, a bundle of nerves as taut as piano strings. I hold her hand and whisper, 'Remember the tree.'

'Got it,' she says.

Then, faster than it even seems possible, her cue is up. She lets go of my hand, puts her face into a huge smile, and steps out on to the stage. The first few notes that the orchestra plays seem to hang in the air for an age, but then she bursts into song like this is the very thing she was born to do.

Tears well up in my eyes.

And the applause when she finishes her first solo is almost deafening.

I feel the weight of a hand on my shoulder, and I look up to see Madame Laplage peering down at me. 'You might want to rejoin the audience now. It looks like your work here is done, and you'll be much better able to appreciate the show from down there.'

I nod.

There's no place I'd rather be than right in the middle of that audience, clapping until my palms turn red, and the only sound flooding towards Posey is that of rapturous applause.

Chapter Forty-One

There's a standing ovation.

The audience rises to their feet as one, saluting the actors on stage. The performance has gone off without a hitch and the whole cast has performed superbly. Posey is spectacular as Maria and note-perfect. Her singing has brought a tear to more than just a few eyes in the audience. For the students, it might have been a performance they've had to do as part of their course, but it felt as if they were all performing simply for the pure joy of it. Maybe that's the difference between loving something totally and only doing it out of obligation. I can see any one of them going on to successful careers one day in the West End or on Broadway – and if *I* was Madame Laplage, I'd be giving them *all* top marks.

When Posey comes out on stage to take a bow, I'm whistling loudly through my fingers and shouting 'Yeah, Posey!' before I remember myself. Beside me, Mum gives my arm a squeeze, and Elliot and Alex are beaming.

'What a show!' Elliot exclaims, when the noise finally dies down enough for us to have a normal conversation again. Even then, a low hum fills the auditorium, the sound of a satisfied audience discussing the show.

Mum's eyes are glassy with tears. 'It's like being transported straight back to my youth,' she says. 'I've forgotten how much I *love* this show. And Posey was just amazing. I can't believe she ever dropped out of the main role! But what's happened to Megan?' She looks down at the programme, confused. The cast list still shows Megan's name against the part of Maria; it's only a hastily printed slip of paper that announces the change from Megan to Posey.

'Yeah, what *did* happen to everyone's favourite snake?' Elliot asks. 'She wasn't even in the chorus, as far as I could see.'

'They discovered she'd tricked Posey into dropping out of the role – and that she was the one who leaked Leah's song. They couldn't know she'd committed copyright theft and let her get away with it. So at the last minute she was kicked out.'

'Oh, Megan!' says Mum. 'But it sounds like she got what was coming to her.'

Elliot and I both stare at Mum in surprise – normally she's Megan's staunchest defender. She shrugs. 'What? No one messes with my Penny and gets away with it!'

We file out into the foyer. I spot Kira and Amara standing with some of the other students from Brighton who'd come up to see Megan's big debut. They're all puzzling over their programmes in confusion. When the twins see me they beckon for me to join them, so I excuse myself from Mum and Alexiot and walk over to them.

'What did you think?' I ask Kira, trying to keep my voice as normal as possible.

'The show was cool, but . . . I thought we were here to see Megan. Did you speak to her earlier? What happened?'

I shrug. 'Look, it's Megan's story to tell.'

'Aw, please? Tell us,' pleads Amara.

It's tempting to give in to them, but I won't tell them what happened. I won't gossip. I've been a victim of people trying to write my narrative for me, twisting the true story until it's beyond recognition, and I won't be a part of that. Not even for my worst enemy.

Besides, Kira, Amara and the others don't have to wait long. The drama students at the Madame Laplage school – the ones who were in the show – are rushing out of the stage door and into the waiting arms of parents and friends. But, as Megan said herself, one of the major currencies at this school, as at any other, is gossip. Word travels fast. Practically the only thing everyone's talking about is the big scene between Madame Laplage and Megan Barker. Everyone knows she must have done something *really* bad in order to get kicked out of the school.

There's a tap on my shoulder. 'Penny?'

I spin round, and there's Posey standing next to a tall, slender woman with the same glossy back hair and dark eyes as Posey. 'This is my mum, Christine.'

'Oh, lovely to meet you, Mrs Chang.' I extend my hand.

Instead of extending hers back, she surprises me by pulling me into a hug. 'Thank you for everything you've done for my Posey. She said she'd never have been up there on stage tonight if it wasn't for you.'

I blush. 'Honestly, it was all her.'

'I'm not totally convinced of that. *You* brought out the courage that I knew my daughter had all along.'

'She's a remarkable girl,' I say.

'You *both* are,' says Mrs Chang. 'And I'm glad she's got a friend like you.'

I smile warmly at Posey. 'The feeling is most *definitely* mutual.'

★ ★ Chapter Forty-Two ★

When the bell rings at the end of school the next day, I can't wait to get out, so I race out of the doors. I've spent the whole day being amazed at how the tide can turn on a person – in this case, Megan – and I've even felt a twinge of pity for her. While no one knows the full details, there's a lot of speculation, and none of it is good. Everyone pesters me for answers, but I refuse to divulge any of the details.

But that's not the only reason I'm looking forward to the end of school today. This is the first proper day that I can come down the school steps knowing that I can text Noah and will be able to see him.

Hey – you around? Xxx

And when I hit send I have a huge smile on my face. It sounds like such a ridiculous thing to be happy about, but Noah and I have never been able to have that kind of normal relationship. The one where you know the person isn't a million miles away. Where we're not living for snatched Skype conversations, or navigating time zones, or looking up the price of plane tickets all the time.

This is our chance to see if we can really work. And that starts with being able to handle the ordinary stuff.

Within a few seconds, he replies.

With E & A in The Creperie. Come join? N x

Now there's an even bigger skip in my step. All my favourite people are hanging out in one place, and I'm so excited!

My school is a little bit far from the Lanes, so I hop on a bus on the way down to the sea. There are loads of people on board, including a bunch of kids from my school, all with their heads bent down low over their phones. I want to take a picture, but there's no way I can do it discreetly. Instead, I sit on my hands and will the driver to go even faster.

The tiny crêperie is down a winding cobblestone lane and almost right on the seafront. When I walk in, the waitress gives me a smile and points downstairs.

'Thanks,' I say, making my way past a table of tourists. I catch the name of a well-known star who lives in Brighton – if they hope to see him, I think they'll very likely be out of luck. I wonder what they'd say if they knew a famous American singer was just downstairs . . .?

The whole of the lower ground floor is for seating and there's a table at the back where I spot my friends. Elliot sees me first, and waves frantically at me to come over. I slide into the seat next to Noah, reaching over to take a sip of his Coke.

'Hey!' he says in mock indignation. Then he kisses me on the cheek.

'What? I was thirsty!' I grin.

'Did you know that crêpes are actually from the Brittany region of France, where they call them *krampouezh*?' Elliot says, tucking into one that's laden with strawberries and whipped cream.

'Can I get you anything, miss?' says the waitress behind me.

'Oh, just a lemonade, please,' I say.

When my drink comes, Elliot lifts his glass. 'I want to make a toast. To the *whole* gang finally being back together – and to Noah finally coming to his senses.'

'Cheers!' we all say, lifting our glasses and clinking them together.

'And . . .' A sly grin appears on Elliot's face. 'Let's say cheers to MegaNasty finally getting her comeuppance.'

'Hey, I think you should speak more quietly,' says Alex.

'What do you mean?' says Elliot. 'Ding Dong, the Mega-Nasty's Dead! And all that.'

Alex is really elbowing Elliot in the ribs now, and Elliot exclaims, 'Ow! Quit it!' with a frown. But then he looks up, past my shoulder, and his mouth turns into an 'O' of surprise.

I blink at the two of them as if they've gone crazy, but

then a shiver runs down my spine, like someone is watching me. I turn round, feeling like I'm moving in slow motion, like I'm moving through maple syrup. When I look round, there's Megan. Her hair is scraped back off her face into a ponytail and she doesn't have a scrap of make-up on. Her eyes are rimmed red from crying and her lower lip is trembling. I automatically check – but there are no milkshakes in sight.

And no wonder because following her down the stairs is her mum. If there's anyone scarier than Megan herself, it's Mrs Barker. She takes a seat at one of the empty tables near the stairs as Megan tentatively approaches us.

'Hi, Penny,' she says quietly.

'Hi, Megan,' I reply, swallowing hard. Underneath the table, Noah grips my leg, giving me a squeeze of encouragement. Elliot just glares at her.

'Kira said I might find you here. I know you probably don't want to talk to me, and I get that you might never want to be my friend again, but I just wanted to apologize to you for the things I said yesterday, and for everything I did to you, Posey and Leah. I know that it wasn't right, and I can't believe I let it get as out of hand as I did.'

'Um . . . OK,' I say, a little unsure of myself.

'I know it's hard to understand,' she continues, reading my mind. 'And I don't expect you to forgive me. But I wrote more of my thoughts out and published them on my blog. Just so that you know I'm not hiding any more.'

My eyebrows shoot up in surprise. I thought Megan would instinctively want to protect her reputation at any cost, not post a public apology for all her friends and family – the world even – to see.

'After you've read it, will you let Leah Brown know for me? I don't really have any way of getting in touch with her myself to apologize personally.'

'Yes, I'll tell her,' I reply.

'Thank you,' she says. She turns round to return to her mum.

'Wait, Megan,' I call out.

'Yeah?'

'What are you going to do now? About school and stuff?'

'Madame Laplage has suspended me for the time being, but she's letting me have my place back eventually. She's suggested I take a year out to make sure that it's what I really want before I go back. As my first year, because of missing the first major drama performance this term I'm not going to get any credits for it.'

'Taking some time off sounds like a good plan,' I say.

'Well, see you around,' she says with a small wave.

'Yeah, bye,' I say, unsure of what else to add, and she walks away.

Mrs Barker puts her hand on Megan's shoulder and escorts her back upstairs. I wonder how many other people she's having to call on just so that she can say sorry, and I hope she's already apologized to Posey.

'Holy wow,' says Elliot.

'I know! I can't believe Megan came all the way here . . .' I say, sitting back down on my chair with a bump.

'No, not that – well, yes, that – but I'm reading Megan's blog post. Want to see?' He turns his phone round so that I have a full view.

I'm sorry

Hello readers,

I know I usually use this space to show you the things I'm loving, but I have a few things I want to write about today.

I've done a really stupid thing that most of you probably know about already. I just want to say that I'm really sorry for all the hurt I caused. I wasn't thinking about anybody but myself.

I wanted that part in the school performance more than anything – but that should have made me want to work harder, to be better, not to spoil someone else's success just to beat them to the top. I did receive money from *Starry Eyes* for releasing the song but I've decided to donate that money to Great Ormond Street Hospital.

I won't be returning to Madame Laplage for a while. I need a bit of space to re-evaluate what it is I really want. A friend of mine gave me some great insight recently into finding your own feet and not relying on anybody else. For once, I think I need to take her advice on board. I can be extremely stubborn a lot of the time and I know I tend to bulldoze my way through life, grabbing everything I want. I'm really ashamed it's taken getting suspended from my dream school for me to realize this. I have risked losing some good friends and my dream career all because of one selfish act.

Again, if you're reading this and you're one of the people I've offended or hurt, I'm truly very sorry.

Comments are closed.

Chapter Forty-Three

Elliot lets out a long whistle. 'Well, you can't say the girl isn't brave,' he says.

Weirdly, reading Megan's blog post has helped release the bundle of tension that had built up in my stomach. My friendship with Megan will never be the same again, but then again it's never really ever felt like a real, proper friendship. At least now I know where I stand with her.

And, strangely, that's OK.

Maybe this whole growing-up thing isn't so bad after all.

Elliot's phone buzzes, and he frowns down at it.

'What is it?' I ask.

'It's your mum . . .'

'Mum? What does she want?'

'I don't know. She just says that you and I need to come home now. Just the two of us, if possible.'

'Huh?' I frown at Noah, just as Elliot frowns at Alex. What could it mean?

'You two don't have any strange surprises in store, do you?'

Noah holds his hands up. 'Nothing to do with me.'

Worry gnaws at my tummy. It's rare for Mum to text out of the blue, demanding that I come home. Especially now that I've started sixth form, both my parents seem happy to give me more independence.

'We'd better go,' I say. 'It might be an emergency.' I kiss Noah and let him know I'll be in touch with him later.

'OK,' says Elliot, unusually sombre.

'Call me?' Alex asks him, giving him a light kiss on the cheek. His normally calm features have a look of concern marring them. I suspect Alex feels the same unease that I do.

'Of course,' says Elliot. In typical style, he's changed his tone so that it's light and breezy, as if there's nothing to worry about. He gives me a grin and a wink, and – I can't help it – I feel better too. He slides out from his side of the bench, then links his arm through mine. 'Come on, she probably just wants my *expert* opinion on the latest wedding decor.' Arm in arm, we practically skip back upstairs and out of the door.

By the time we get home, Elliot and I are back to normal, singing 'We Are Family' and 'Ain't No Mountain High Enough' at the top of our lungs and generally being complete nutters.

The mood changes, though, as soon as we walk into the living room, where Mum and Dad are sitting opposite two stern-looking lawyer-types: Elliot's parents.

I immediately reach out and grab Elliot's hand. It feels

limp in my own. He starts taking steps backwards towards the door, and I feel his hand quiver, like he's ready to bolt.

Mum must see it too, because she stands up. 'Please, Elliot. Your parents have something they need to discuss with you.'

'I . . . I came here because I trusted you!' Elliot cries, wrenching his hand out of mine and clasping it to his chest as if it's burning him. His words are directed at Mum, but they also feel pointed at me. 'I wanted to get away from them, not have them here too.'

'We know, Elliot,' says his mum.

'Your parents –'

'My parents don't get to decide when they want to come in and ruin my life!'

'Elliot, don't talk to Mrs Porter like that,' says his father.

'And you don't get to talk to me at all, Dad.'

'See?' says Elliot's father to his mother. 'I told you this was pointless.'

'Yeah, I'm just *pointless*, as always.' And, with that, Elliot spins on his heels and hurtles upstairs.

I'm left standing in the living room, my head fizzing with emotion. I still can't believe Elliot's dad talks to him that way – but I also can't believe that Mum ambushed him.

Mum looks up at me, her face crinkled with anguish. 'Penny, do you think you can talk to him? It's really important that he hears his parents out. I know it's hard.'

I nod, feeling numb. I climb the stairs slowly, trying to work out in my head what to say to my best friend. When I approach Tom's room – Elliot's room – Elliot is angrily throwing all his worldly belongings into a suitcase. This kind of anger doesn't suit him. His face has gone splotchy with rage and I can see he's trembling.

Without saying a word, I walk up to him and envelop him in a hug. He struggles against me at first, his rage not allowing him to let go, but eventually I feel him relent and he leans his head on my shoulder. 'I'm going to have to go and talk to them, aren't I?'

I nod into him. 'Even if your parents aren't being particularly grown up here, *you* have to be.'

'Growing up sucks, doesn't it?'

I pull away from him, and wipe a tear away from his cheek. 'Yeah, big time. But Mum's a good mediator, you know. She won't let things get too bad for you. She'll protect you from your dad.'

He nods miserably. 'I think I'm going to need it. Did you see how on edge he was?'

'They're going through a hard time too. Just whatever you do, don't let them put the blame on to you. You're a victim in all of this. This isn't your fight.'

'Thanks, Pen-Pen.' He bends down to look in the mirror on the dresser, wipes away the remains of the tears from beneath his eyes, then straightens and shakes his shoulders out. 'Wish me luck.'

'Do you want me to come down with you?'

He shakes his head, then gives me two kisses on the cheek. 'No, this is something I'd better do on my own. But if I need anything, you'll be here, right?'

'You got it.'

I spend the next hour staring at the ceiling in my room,

unable to concentrate on any of my homework, my blog comments, or even on the email from Melissa that's sitting in my inbox. I just about manage to compose a reasonable-sounding text to Noah that explains why Mum called us away, and he texts back with a frowny face emoji and a promise to come over if we need anything.

Three short knocks interrupt my thoughts, the only thing that could have broken my weird trance. I roll off the bed and open my door.

There, red-eyed but eerily calm, is Elliot. 'It's happening,' he says, his voice sounding small. 'My parents are getting divorced.'

What to Do When Your Best Friend Is Suffering

Hi, everyone,

It's advice time again. As in it's time for me to ask you guys for some advice.

A friend is going through something really hard at the moment.

Something I'm not sure I can help him with.

But I know it's something a lot of you out there have had to deal with or are dealing with right now. So here goes:

How do you handle it when your parents are splitting up?

I know I'd find it so difficult to cope with. I think, in my friend's case, the atmosphere in his house has been toxic for a long time because his parents weren't happy together. So if this helps his parents be happier then it has to be a good thing for them.

But for my friend, it's shattering. I'm desperate to help, but how? There's only so many creamy hot chocolates and upbeat playlists I can force on the guy to try to make it better. That's not enough any more. I know divorce happens a lot these days, so I was hoping some of you could help me out by sharing what got you through when your parents were splitting up.

I'd be really grateful for your advice.

Thanks in advance.

Girl Online, going offline xxx

Chapter Forty-Four

'Do you swear this is a *real* British tradition, and not just something you made up? You're not pulling my leg?' Noah is in JB's Diner with me, sipping hot chocolate, and I'm trying to explain to him the ins and outs of Bonfire Night.

I giggle at his scepticism. 'Honestly, it's all true!'

'What's the nursery rhyme again?'

'Remember, remember, the fifth of November,' I recite. 'Gunpowder treason and *plot*!'

'And you really burn someone on a bonfire?'

'Sometimes they burn an *effigy* on a bonfire – a "guy" – like a man made from old clothes and stuffed with newspapers. But we don't tend to do that in Brighton. We just have a big bonfire and fireworks.'

'It still sounds pretty cool. Where did it come from?'

'For the history lesson, you're going to have to wait until you see Wiki!' I say with a laugh. 'This year Dad says he's going to build a bonfire in the garden. He hasn't done that for ages, but since you're here, he wants it to be special.'

'Your folks are the best,' Noah says with a grin.

I run my fingers along the metal edges of the table. There are loads of kids from school all around, but most of them don't give Noah and me a second look. He's just part of the Brighton scene now. 'Did you know that this is where I had my first major panic attack?' I say.

Noah raises an eyebrow. 'Seriously?' He puts his arm round me protectively, and I smile up at him. But I check all the signs: my heart rate is normal, my vision is clear and my hands are still. I'm not at risk of another attack right now.

'Yeah. Megan was there for that one too. In fact, she pretty much triggered it.'

'It sounds like it's a good thing she's out of your life,' he says. 'She doesn't exactly seem like the best influence.'

'You're probably right about that.' I frown. 'I thought the attacks were linked to when I got scared – I mean, that's what happened during the car accident.' Even now, if I close my eyes, I can picture that moment. I can't remember the details any longer – I can't even remember where we were driving to – but what forms my memory of it now are the flashes and feelings. The headlights spinning on the road. Not being able to take a breath as we turned over. And my hands, flat against the side of the car, unable to escape. 'But I think it's not just when I'm scared. It's the feeling of being *trapped*: in that car, in a place, in a . . . in a friendship.'

'Penny, you have to promise me, if you ever feel trapped when I'm around, you'll let me know.'

'I will. But it's weird – when I'm with you . . . you're like an escape route for me. I look into your eyes and . . .' I blush, feeling I must sound stupid.

Noah's finger brushes the underside of my chin, causing me to look up into his eyes. 'I know. I feel the same way.' Then he chuckles. 'Trust me, when you hear my new song, you'll know what I mean.'

'And when will that be, Mr Mysterious?'

'Soon! And don't go calling me Mr Mysterious, when you're not willing to tell me about what you've been working on!'

'All in good time, all in good time.'

There's a bustle at the front of the diner and I hear someone call my name. I spin round and see Alex. His hair is in disarray and his face is pale and wan. Something must have happened . . .

'Alex? Is everything OK?'

His eyes open wide with relief as he spots me. 'Oh thank god you're still here!'

I had a text from Alex about an hour ago asking where Noah and I were meeting after school. I assumed it was so he and Elliot could meet us again. But there's no Elliot with him this time.

He rushes up to our table. 'Have you seen Elliot, by any chance?'

I frown. 'No, but then I thought he'd be with you.'

'So, he hasn't texted you? Or called?'

I shake my head.

'Oh no. I was hoping . . .' He paces up and down by our table, too wound up to sit down.

Noah reaches out to stop him. 'Alex, man, what is it?' he says.

'It's so stupid! We had a bit of a fight last night, after everything that happened with his parents . . .'

I swallow. Elliot wasn't in a good place emotionally last night, and the last thing he'd have needed was a fight with his boyfriend. 'What did you say?' I ask.

'It's all my fault! I . . . I can be so cold at times. I told him that divorce is something some people go through and it won't be that bad. It was the wrong thing to say – it was too soon for him to hear that, and I should've known. He told me to get out of your house, so I left. But we've never had a fight that's lasted longer than a couple of hours before. After the shock and everything, I thought I'd give him time to sleep – I mean, everything seems better in the morning, right? – and then he'd be OK again. But, Penny, he hasn't answered any of my texts and, according to some of his friends at school, he didn't go in today!'

I'd noticed that I hadn't received any replies to my messages or any random Elliot factoids today as usual, but then I hadn't thought that strange, because of what he was going through.

'Have you checked his room at my house?'

Alex grimaces, then drops his eyes to the ground, his shoulders slumping. 'Of course I have. He's not there, but no one saw him leave this morning either. His bed doesn't look slept in . . . and his bag has gone.'

I feel my blood turn cold in my veins. 'You're kidding?'

'No. I wish.' A tear rolls down his cheek, and I know he must be worried out of his mind. 'His parents don't know where he is either. As if they'd even notice or care.'

'I don't think he'd have gone far without telling us,' I say, trying to inject more confidence into my voice than I feel. 'He's probably in one of his usual places. Come on. Noah and I will help you look.'

'Thank you. I'm going to go back to my flat to get some warmer clothes and grab the charger pack for my phone – the last thing I want to do is have that run out in case he's trying to get hold of me. Text me as soon as you know anything?'

'Of course.' I'm already snatching up my scarf and winding it round my neck.

Noah's grabbing his coat at the same time. 'Do you really think Elliot's run away?' he asks.

I bite my lip. 'He might have done,' I reply.

Elliot *always* runs away – whether it's from fights with his parents or a bad day at school. When he and Alex broke up, he even ran away to Paris to find me. It's what he does. I curse myself for not realizing in time that after the bad news he'd had last night this is what would happen. But he's never run away from *me*. He has never gone anywhere without telling me, or without inviting me along too.

Something about it this time feels different.

More permanent.

'We'll find him,' Noah says, full of confidence. 'He wouldn't have done anything without telling you.'

'That's what I thought. But if it's already been almost a whole day . . .' I stare down at my phone, looking at it like I don't know what it's for as there haven't been any messages on it from Elliot. I try one more time.

Hey, where are you? P xxxx

It's already dark by the time we step outside, the night falling early now that it's November. It's bitterly cold, but we're all wrapped up, my white-and-gold-flecked scarf pulled up so high the wool tickles my eyelashes. I can barely feel my fingers inside my woollen mittens.

'Where to first?' says Noah.

The bright lights of the Pier catch my eye. I think of all the times Elliot and I, when we've needed to calm down about something, have escaped there to play on the 2p machines, our nerves soothed, bizarrely, by the jangle and clatter of the fairground games.

'The Pier,' I say, and I take off at a run. Thankfully, it's not far. There are still plenty of people milling about after work because of the fireworks. We dash past groups sipping hot drinks and eating churros dipped in chocolate. I can hear the whirl of the rollercoaster and see its lights flashing brightly, its circle giving the impression of dropping all its riders into the rolling sea.

When we reach the first arcade I point to the left. 'You go that way, I'll continue down here. And after this arcade, keep going straight until you reach the end. Meet you by the bumper cars?'

'You got it,' Noah calls, ripping the beanie off his head.

Now that we're indoors and surrounded by people, the atmosphere closes in around me. I'm sweltering from running in the cold air and my heart is pounding madly inside my chest, but I need to stay focused.

Elliot – where are you?

Each time I pass one of our favourite machines I hold my breath. But there's no sign of Elliot. My heart misses a beat when I see someone in Elliot's signature trilby hat and vintage striped scarf – but it's not him.

The Pier is definitely Elliot Wentworth-less.

'Anything?' I ask Noah as I catch up with him by the bumper cars.

He shakes his head. 'No, no luck.'

I pull out my phone and give Alex a quick update.

Not on Pier. Will check a few places in the Lanes – then regroup back at my house? P x

Home's the last place anyone saw him, and if I'm not back in time for Dad's signature pre-Bonfire-Night marshmallows, my parents are going to start worrying about my whereabouts too. At any rate, at my house we can talk to Mum and Dad and think about gathering a proper search party.

Plus, something Elliot once said niggles at the back of my mind. Elliot's Great Escape Card. If *that's* gone . . . that's when I'll know to really worry.

I fill Noah in on our conversation so many weeks ago, and he nods grimly. 'Sounds like he's planned for something like this,' he says.

Tears fill my eyes unexpectedly, and Noah pulls me into a fierce hug. 'He wouldn't do this without telling me!' I sob. 'That was the deal. We tell each other *everything*!'

'He's almost seventeen . . . he'll be OK.'

'I don't care,' I say. 'I don't care how old he is; he still needs his friends. He can't just ditch his whole life . . .'

But that's exactly what Noah did – for a little while anyway. I can't think about that.

We dash around the Lanes, checking all of Elliot's and my favourite places: the crêperie, the cafe at Waterstones on the corner, Choccywoccydoodah; I'd check the library too if I could, but at this time of night it's closed. The streets are steadily filling up with revellers heading towards the big public bonfire and fireworks display.

'Come on,' says Noah. 'I think it's time we got back to your house. Who knows – maybe he's come back already and is just waiting for us there?'

'Maybe,' I say, but my trembling voice belies my real thoughts. *No, Penny. Don't give in until you know for sure.*

We take a taxi home as it's the quickest way and we're too cold to wait for a bus anyway. In a matter of minutes we're there. I walk in and see Mum's face, drawn and lined with worry. 'Have you heard from him?' she asks me as soon as I'm through the door.

I shake my head but leave Noah to answer. I can't wait any longer. I dash up the stairs to Elliot's bedroom. Alex was right: it feels empty and the bed is still neatly made. The one thing that gives me a shred of hope is that the book Elliot is currently reading is still upside down on his bedside table, his bookmark still marking his page. I'm sure he'd have taken it if he was going for good. He can't leave anything unfinished – it would drive him mad, wouldn't it?

I look inside his wardrobe and rifle through his jackets and freshly ironed jeans until I find what I'm looking for. A small black box fastened with a combination lock. I know what the combination is – the same one we both use, a mixture of his birthday and mine – and quickly set it to open.

I lift the lid.

It's empty. Elliot's Great Escape Card is gone.

The box clatters out of my hands and falls to the floor.

He's really gone.

Chapter Forty-Five

'Penny, are you OK?' Noah comes bounding up the stairs. In Elliot's room I've fallen to my knees without realizing it, and that's where Noah finds me, in a crumpled heap on the floor.

'He's taken his Great Escape Card,' I say between sobs. 'That means he *was* really serious about going. I can't believe it . . .'

'Come on,' Noah says, helping me to my feet. 'Alex is going to be here any minute and you have to tell your mum and dad what's going on.'

When I get downstairs, Mum has her arms round Alex while Mrs Wentworth, Elliot's mum, paces frantically round the room. My eyes must ask her the question I'm too afraid to say out loud, because she suddenly covers her face with her hands, saying, 'I don't know where he's gone – I didn't mean for this to happen.'

'Where's Elliot's dad?' I ask.

'He's gone too!' She laughs bitterly. 'But *that's not* a

surprise. He's gone to live with his secretary. They've been seeing each other behind my back all this time!'

'I'm sorry,' I say, my voice sounding small.

'I thought Elliot and I could start again. It seems so silly now, but I went out to buy him a chocolate caterpillar cake, the sort he used to love when he was little.' She gestures to a crumpled box on the dining-room table. 'A peace offering, if you like. But he's not a child any more. When I came back home, I found this.'

She hands me a note written on a scrap of paper ripped out of a school notebook.

Last night, you made it clear I wasn't welcome here any more. So I'm leaving. Goodbye. Elliot

My heart constricts inside my chest. 'Where did you find this?' I ask her.

'It was on the table in the hall.' Mrs Wentworth looks miserable, her face lined with concern. 'In the space of a single evening, I've lost my entire family.'

'Well, maybe if you hadn't driven him away!' says Alex, pounding his fist angrily on the back of the sofa. 'If you'd thought for a second about the impact this was having on him!' Mum strokes his arm and shushes him.

I drift over to the dining-room table and open the box with the cake. It's like having an out-of-body experience – my mind is numb; my body is acting of its own accord. *Now is not the time for a sugar rush, Penny,* I tell myself. The picture on the box is of a little cartoon caterpillar.

Something sparks in my heart and a lump appears in my throat. There's still one place we haven't checked.

Where no one but me would think to look.

'Mrs Wentworth,' I say, 'is the door to your house open?'

'No, but I can give you the keys,' she says.

'I've just had an idea of where Elliot might have gone, but I need to get something from his room.'

She nods, handing me her keys. Noah gives my hand a reassuring squeeze and I can feel Alex's questioning eyes on my back. I try not to seem too hopeful, just in case this turns out to be another dead end.

Once I'm in Elliot's house, I run upstairs all the way to his attic bedroom. The one that's a twin to mine. I know that if I could see through the left-hand wall, I'd be looking right into my bedroom.

The place looks ransacked – by Elliot's mum, and by Alex. But they don't know everything about this room, not the way I do. I know that behind his mirror there's a hidden doorway that leads through into the low eaves of the house – as there is from my room too. It's there in that space that Elliot and I used to stash away our most precious things – not expensive stuff, but the silly, only-important-to-us things that were the world to us when we were younger. Our memories – things we should have grown out of, that we promised to throw away, but never did. I kept my old diaries in there, along with too many packages of photographs to count, developed with the old wind-and-snap disposable cameras. Elliot kept all his most valuable books, along with items he was *sure* would one day come back into fashion. He'd also hung up his drawing of a giant peach (*James and the Giant Peach* was his favourite childhood book), with one of his mum's gold stars stuck on to it. Her way of telling him 'well done', and her way of showing him she loved him.

I move right to the back of the room and crouch down by the panelling. It takes me a moment to find where the catch is, but finally I manage to prise it open. The door is tiny, but still just about wide enough for me, so I poke my head through and crawl inside.

I spy Elliot curled up in the corner, his dark blond hair dishevelled and laced with cobwebs. He's got an old blanket wrapped round him and he's staring at a scrapbook I've never seen before.

'Hey,' I say quietly, not sure what else to say.

'Hey.' He looks up at me, and behind his tortoiseshell glasses I can see his eyes are rimmed with red. 'How'd you find me?'

'I know you, you goof.'

He smiles, but it doesn't quite reach his eyes. 'I was going to run away, you know.'

'I know,' I say softly. He lifts up the corner of his blanket and invites me to come in. I curl up next to him, wrapping his hands in mine.

'I meant it too,' he continues. 'I was going to run away for good. I crept back in here late last night only to grab some of my things – like my book.' He lifts up the copy of his Roald Dahl treasure, still with its cover of clear plastic to protect it. 'But then I found this. I'd totally forgotten

I'd made this scrapbook.' He flips to the inside cover, where I read:

My Family by Elliot Wentworth, aged 8, 5, 5¾, 10

I chuckle at even young Elliot's desire for factual accuracy, even when it came to his age.

'I think it started as a school project, but I kept it going for a while.' He flips through it. It starts with a family tree, with little pictures (meticulously cut out) of his grandparents, parents and himself, then it turns into a treasure trove of memories: a pressed thistle from their first visit to Scotland, various museum leaflets, cinema-ticket stubs and, best of all, pictures of Elliot and his mum and dad together. Happy.

'Look, there's you!' Elliot points to a photograph in the corner. Sure enough, there's a picture of a chubby six-year-old Penny in a pale, spotted pinafore, her arm thrown round the neck of a lanky seven-year-old Elliot. Young Penny is wearing Elliot's glasses; Elliot has one of my mum's feather boas wrapped round his neck. We look like a pair of nutters. We look like best friends.

'Oh god, look at my hair!' I groan, staring in disbelief at the upside-down pudding-bowl mop on my head.

'I think you look *très chic*, darling,' says Elliot.

'Liar,' I say, and I nudge him in the ribs.

He catches my eye and then sighs. He strokes the outside edge of the scrapbook absent-mindedly as he talks. 'I thought, this time, I'd really get away. I'm old enough now, or near enough. I could have made it. I didn't want to have to rely on anyone. I didn't want to love anyone. Love only brings you pain, right?'

I squeeze his hand.

'But then I came in here and I saw all the little things I'd collected growing up. OK, so our family was far from perfect – I mean, look at how my dad treats me now! – but there *was* love in our house. I was lucky to have that, even if it's gone now. Just because it's gone one day, it doesn't make it any less special while it lasted, does it?'

'No,' I whisper.

'Is this what growing up feels like?' he says with a small laugh.

'If you mean equal parts painful and happy, sad, terrifying and exciting, then I think you're right,' I reply.

'How do we know if we're ready to grow up?'

'I'm not sure we ever do. I don't even think our parents know they're ready.'

'Ha! Maybe that's true of your mum and dad – but look at mine. They're so set in their ways, they're basically statues.'

'Is that true? Look at the changes they're going through. They're growing too.'

Elliot sighs. 'Things are really changing now, aren't they, Penny?' He leans his head on my shoulder.

'Yeah, they really are.'

'But we'll never change, will we? We won't let what we have slip away?'

I take his hand in mine and grip it tightly. 'Never,' I say firmly.

I know we can't stay here forever, so after a few more

moments I say softly, 'Elliot, you really scared us. Why didn't you answer any of our messages? Alex has been out of his mind!'

Elliot wriggles in the blanket. 'When I came up here I was using my phone as a light and I guess I fell asleep. My phone's run out of battery, that's all. I'm sorry I worried everyone, but I just needed some peace.'

'OK. Ready to join the real world again now?'

'Do I have to?' Elliot looks up at me pleadingly.

I nod. 'You can't live in here for the rest of your life. What about that gorgeous townhouse you've dreamt of? I'm not sure this suits you . . .'

'You're so right. This isn't very chic.' He puts the scrap-book back where he found it, rearranging the blanket over his duffle bag full of things.

I crawl back out of the tiny space, then help Elliot out as well. I brush the cobwebs off his hair and the dust from his shoulders.

'Pen?' he asks, as he takes my hand.

'Yeah?'

'I'm glad you found me.'

'Wiki, I would never have stopped looking, ever.'

'I know.'

'You're my best friend in the entire world. No, you're more than that. You're my whole life. I wouldn't be able to go on without you. So you're never allowed to leave me like that again. OK?'

'Never again,' he says. 'I promise.'

Chapter Forty-Six

When we get back to my house, there's no shouting or yelling – only relief. Alex runs into Elliot's arms and showers him with kisses. When they finally remember they're in a room full of people, they separate sheepishly, Alex's hand remaining firmly gripped in Elliot's. Elliot turns to his mum, and gives her a sad smile. 'Sorry about the note,' he says.

'I'm sorry for everything,' she replies. 'Can we . . . do you mind if we start again? The two of us?'

Elliot nods. 'Only if I can have my room back?' he asks.

His mum's face lights up like a Christmas tree. 'Really? You want to come home?'

'If that's OK.'

'Of course!' Then the two of them share the most halting, awkward hug I've ever seen, but it's a start.

The expression on my mum's face is one of pure relief. 'Where'd you find him, Penny?'

I blush. 'It was actually the caterpillar cake that reminded me of the little shared space off our bedrooms. It's where Elliot keeps all his childhood memories. It used to be our favourite hiding place when we were little.'

'I remember that,' says Mum. 'I lost you for a whole day when you were a little girl. I'd forgotten that was there.' Then her eyes light up. 'Maybe that's where I can store some of my spare clothes from the wedding shop!'

'Mum!'

'So, who's up for marshmallows?' says Dad, coming out of the kitchen with impeccable timing.

'It's not too late for Bonfire Night?' Noah asks.

'Oh, it's never too late for Bonfire Night in the Porter house!'

'Righty-oh then,' says Noah, doffing an imaginary cap.

'Oh jeez, that's a *terrible* British accent,' says Elliot with a laugh.

'What?' Noah's face looks crestfallen. 'But I've been watching *My Fair Lady* on repeat!' He grins.

'Eliza Doolittle you are *not*,' retorts Mum.

I grin too, fetching a bundle of sparklers from the cupboard underneath the stairs. We all walk through the kitchen into the garden, where Dad has prepared wood for a bonfire inside a large stone fire-pit. It's not a proper bonfire, but as we're not going down into town, it will work perfectly well to toast our marshmallows on.

Dad helps us light our sparklers, and Elliot, Alex and I dance around, writing our names in lights. Then, after too many sparklers to count, I run back inside, grab my camera and take several long-exposure shots of Alex, who stands still while Elliot runs round him with a sparkler. The effect is that Alex looks like he's surrounded by streaks of bright golden light. It's epically cool.

Noah helps Dad with the fire itself, placing small pieces of wood and paper in the fire-pit to help the flames catch and ignite the larger logs. After a few minutes of prodding and persuading, the fire roars to life, bathing us all in a warm orange-red glow.

Dad throws little parcels of tinfoil on the fire, and after a few minutes, we have delicious gooey marshmallows encased in a biscuit and chocolate crumb. Totally yum.

'Well, they're not quite what we'd have back home,' says Noah. We all look at him expectantly for his judgement. 'But they are *so* good!'

Dad looks like he's just won *The Great British Bake Off* and Noah is the new Paul Hollywood. 'That might just be the greatest compliment ever!' he says, smiling from ear to ear.

'Can I help you, Rob?' Alex asks.

'Of course – come on!' says Dad.

Alex and Dad retreat to the bottom of the garden, where they begin to set up the fireworks. Elliot's mum comes out with a tray of mulled wine and hot chocolate, Mum following not too far behind with a bundle of blankets. We curl up on the outdoor chairs, huddled round the fire.

'Noah, do you have any music you can play us?' Mum asks.

'For you, Dahlia, of course!' He jumps up and hurries into the house. When he returns, he has his guitar in his hand.

Noah strokes the neck of it gently, sliding his fingers down the strings. He plucks a couple of notes, then – satisfied that it's in tune – he slips the strap over his neck.

He walks back over to us waiting for him round the fire, and Elliot and I make room for him between us.

His fingers absently pick at the strings, and I marvel at how good someone can be at an instrument, that they can make such a beautiful sound without even appearing to try. At Elliot's request, he plays some of his old hits first, like 'Autumn Girl' and 'Elements', and Mum asks for 'Brown-eyed Girl', which he plays perfectly – without missing a note.

When there's a break between songs, we hear Dad shout from the bottom of the garden: 'I think we're ready! *Three . . .*'

I lean over to Noah. 'That was amazing,' I say in a whisper. 'I'd forgotten how much I miss hearing you play.'

'*Two . . .*'

'And I'd forgotten how much I love playing for you.'

'*One!*'

As Noah and I kiss, fireworks explode all around us.

After the fireworks, Elliot's mum goes back round to her house, and Mum and Dad say goodnight. They're all exhausted, they say. So, soon it's just me, Noah, Elliot and Alex.

'We're pretty exhausted too,' says Elliot.

It's been a long, emotional day for us all. I stand up and give Elliot a huge hug. 'I love you,' I say.

'Love you too, Pennylicious.'

'Thanks for all your help today, Penny, Noah,' says Alex. 'I don't know what I'd have done without you.'

I smile. 'Just take care of him, OK? He's very special.'

'With all my heart,' Alex replies, smiling at Elliot, and I really believe him.

When it's just Noah and me alone with the stars, I want nothing more than to snuggle up in his arms. But, to my surprise, he keeps his distance. When I look sad, he smiles. 'I have one more thing I want to play for you,' he says.

'Oh?' I lean forward and shuffle under my blanket, intrigued.

'It's . . . one of the new songs that I wrote.' He plucks at a loose thread in the blanket, running his other hand up and down the guitar.

'Noah, you seem nervous!' I say with a laugh.

'I am,' he says, his eyes shining. 'I always am when someone's about to hear my new stuff. But mostly I'm nervous because I hope you like it. It's called "My Forever".'

He draws a deep breath, then his sweet, soulful voice fills the night air.

You have your life, I have mine
Plenty of reasons to deny
All these feelings runnin' round in my head
But as I . . . have . . . always . . . said . . .
We may not be good for each other
But I know we'd be great together

Can't spend forever this way
Can't spend even one more day
Away from you
Apart from you
My forever

Seasons come, seasons go
From sun-soaked days, to crisp white snow
So many things I love through the year
But as I . . . have . . . always . . . said . . .
The thing I long for most in this world
Is to be in love with my Autumn Girl

Girl, you and I may be complicated
But if you ask me, distance is overrated

Can't spend forever this way
Can't spend even one more day
Away from you
Apart from you

Far from you
I long for you
My forever

As the last note disappears into the night air, I feel like I've melted into a pool of pure liquid. 'Noah, that was . . .' But I don't have enough words to say how the song was, what I'm feeling.

'It's how I feel,' he says. His eyes lock on to mine, and he pulls me out of my chair and on to his lap. 'It's just that – Penny . . . I'm not sure forever is gonna be long enough.'

One month later

Girl Online Goes Out Into the World

Hi everyone!

This post has been a long time in coming, but I've also been really nervous about hitting publish. You guys have been my community, my heart and soul online, for the past two years and I wanted to do something to thank you. But most of all, I realized recently that I want to meet you. I want to take this little community that was built on the Internet and see if it will work outside.

I've been working on a little secret project that I haven't told anyone about – not even Brooklyn Boy or my BFF Wiki, and I want you – the readers of *Girl Online* – to be involved. You don't have to live near Brighton or even in England to participate.

Just send me your photos of your online space – your sanctuary. I want to know where you guys are while you're reading this. Maybe that means on your computer in your bedroom, or your phone while out and about. The photos can be completely anonymous (you don't even have to be in them!) and any quality.

I promise to let you know what I'm up to, as soon as I'm able to tell.

All the love as always,

Girl Online, going offline xxx

'Penny?' Noah's voice comes from my living room. I step through from the kitchen.

'Yes?'

'I just read your blog – what's the project all about?'

My eyes sparkle with the secret. 'You'll just have to wait and see, along with everybody else. Are you going to send in a picture?'

'What do you mean?'

'I want pictures of my readers in action. Where they read *Girl Online.*'

Noah slouches back on the sofa, his phone in his hand. 'You're the better photographer. Why don't you take a picture of me?'

'OK, one second.'

I run out to the hall, where my camera is in my bag as normal. Once it's in my hands, I turn back towards the living room. From this angle, Noah's face is hardly visible, but I can see the glare of his phone reflecting back off his hair. I take the shot. When I play it back on the camera's screen, I smile. It's perfect.

★★Chapter Forty-Seven★

'What is this?' Noah asks. 'Where are we going?'

'You'll see. Just trust me.'

We step off the escalator at Waterloo and see the station already decorated for Christmas. Underneath the old Victorian clock is a giant tree, covered in red and gold oversized baubles, and gathered round it a group of carol singers are bringing 'Ding Dong Merrily on High!' to life.

This is one of my favourite times of year in the capital. London seems to come alive at Christmas, with shoppers, tourists and Londoners alike all out on the streets. I think back to last Christmas, which I spent in New York. I can't believe it's been a year now since Noah and I first met. It feels like we've known each other forever and at the same time no time at all. We still have a lot to learn, and I – for one – can't wait to know every single detail.

We cut across the crowds in the station, heading through the underpass towards the Southbank Centre. There's a

German-style winter market along the banks of the River Thames. A canopy of fairy lights is strung above our heads, and all around are wooden chalets selling glühwein, gingerbread stars and carved ornaments.

'There they are,' I say. Mum and Dad, Tom and Melanie, Sadie Lee and Bella, Elliot and Alex, Posey, Miss Mills, Kira and Amara – all my favourite people, gathered in one place. They all look smart, dressed to the nines for the occasion. When they spot Noah and me approaching, they all gather round us expectantly. They all have the same question for me on their faces.

I take a deep breath. 'I know you've all been wondering why I asked you to meet me here. Well . . . the truth is, I've been working on a photo series. It's called *Girls (and Boys) Online*. François-Pierre Nouveau liked it so much, he set me up with my first gallery show here on the South Bank!'

Mum shrieks with delight, and her enthusiasm is infectious. Soon, everyone is showering me with kisses and hugs. I feel like the happiest girl on earth. It's been absolutely killing me, keeping this secret for so long, but I know it's been worth it just to see their delighted reactions now.

But it's even more than that. This is going to be the first ever real-life *Girl Online* meet-up. I'm finally going to be putting faces to the names that have been with me for so long. Names like Pegasus Girl, for example.

My cheeks tingle with a mixture of excitement and cold – it's freezing standing outside.

'Can we go in and see?' Elliot asks, stamping his feet impatiently.

'Of course! After you, guys.'

Everyone crowds in, but I take Noah's hand and hold him back until it's just the two of us.

'I'm so proud of you,' he says.

I squeeze his hand tightly. 'It took me a long time, but I finally found something that was *uniquely Penny*. And I want you to share it with me.'

'And I want to share all these moments with you,' whispers Noah, his head leaning so close to mine, his breath tickles my lips.

'Then let's do it,' I say. 'One day at a time.'

We step inside the entrance to the huge Southbank Centre, which is packed with people milling around the foyer, waiting for a concert to start or just enjoying a drink in the cafe.

Over in one corner, there's an area that's marked off by a velvet ribbon, a small crowd of people already inside: I spot Melissa right away, in a chic black dress. With her bright earrings and long plaits piled up in an intricate knot on top of her head, she looks every inch the glamorous gallery manager.

'Welcome to your first ever main show, Penny Porter!' Melissa says, stepping forward to kiss me on both cheeks.

'Thanks, Mel! This is Noah,' I say, gesturing behind me.

Melissa's eyes sparkle mischievously. 'Yes, I guessed as much. Hi there. There's a great photo of you in here – a late addition to the collection.'

'I can't wait to see,' he says.

I introduce Mum to Melissa, then I take a moment to look

around. My own little show! In its own corner of a huge, iconic space. Right in the centre of the show, blown-up and standing alone, is the photograph that inspired the collection. The self-portrait I took that day with Leah, of me working on a blog post. My face is a picture of concentration, and my laptop looks like it's casting a shadow – but of light. Like the light I hope to send out into the world with *Girl Online*.

That's the message of the collection. All around me are photographs of teens – kids, like me – who live their lives as much online as off. And while some people might bemoan wasted youth or wonder why we aren't outside getting fresh air, I hope my photos offer a different perspective.

There's the boy on FaceTime, connecting to his grandparents back in India.

There's the group of girls taking a selfie and posting it to Snapchat, sharing the moment with all their friends.

There's the French school group at the National Gallery, looking like they're absorbed on their phones, but really learning so much about the paintings in front of them.

There's Noah, on his phone, reading my blog.

It's not just the photo of him, though. His photo is enlarged in a collage of others – the photos that my blog readers sent in. I must have received over five hundred images, and all of them are up on the wall. These are my tribe. My #TeamInternet.

'Penny, this is so cool!' says Miss Mills, hurrying over to me. 'But don't expect to automatically get top marks. You still have to work for those A levels,' she says with a wink.

'Don't worry, I know,' I say with a smile. 'Besides, there's something else I want to do now.'

'Oh? What's that?'

'I thought maybe I could help people who are like me. People with anxiety.'

Miss Mills's face relaxes into a reassuring smile. 'I think you'd be great at that, Penny. As soon as we get back to school, we can plan how you can achieve that goal too.'

After Miss Mills, the next person to come up is clapping his hands loudly. 'Pénélope, *ma chérie*!'

There's only one person in the world who calls me 'Pénélope'. François-Pierre Nouveau, the world-famous photographer and the man who made this gallery show happen – with lots of help from Melissa, of course.

'Didn't I tell you I'd give you your first solo show? But only if you found your true style.' His eyes shine as he looks around at the photos. 'And I think you've done it. A voice of your generation! Something so . . . *uniquely you*.'

'Thank you, Mr Nouveau,' I say, feeling bashful.

'You shouldn't be thanking me – thank your inspiration! Some of them are here today, are they not?'

'Just one,' I say. She's the one person I'm looking forward to meeting most of all.

'Well, go, go! And well done. I hope to see you back in my studio next summer.' He flutters off in a whirl, searching for people who might be interested in buying my photographs. It's strange to think of my art being hung on the wall in other people's houses.

I spot a girl gazing at one of the photos, her red-and-white striped scarf still wrapped round her neck so she looks like a candy cane. She has a navy blue coat on over a dress with several layers of neon-bright petticoats, and beneath them thick black tights dotted with gold-thread stars. On her feet are classic Doc Martens. She looks incredibly cool but I can see the shyness in the way her shoulders hunch forward and her fringe falls over her face like a curtain. Then she turns round and I can see her necklace: a thick acrylic pendant of a white horse with wings. *Pegasus Girl.*

She looks up at me at the same time as I look at her. She's been my online confidante since the early days of *Girl Online*, and I feel like she knows me as well as anyone – even Elliot.

I walk over to her, feeling as if my feet are barely touching the ground.

'Hi,' I say, the word hardly seeming adequate.

'Hi.'

In one swift movement, we fling our arms round each other, like long-lost siblings – friends who've finally met at last.

Girl Online has finally come offline – and it's just as amazing as I could ever have hoped.

31 December

New Year's Eve

What a year it's been! From calculating managers to jealous friends and one boy I just couldn't get rid of. (Brooklyn Boy, if you're reading this – which I'm sure you are – I'm glad you stuck around like that annoying piece of gum on the sole of my shoe – ha ha ☺)

When people tell you life is a path, and that path is sometimes very bumpy and winding and you really aren't sure where it's taking you, it can be very daunting. I'm a firm believer that everything happens for a reason, so whatever downs you may encounter, the ups will even them out – and everything will work out in the end.

If you told me a year ago that I'd be spending another New Year's Eve with Brooklyn Boy, I'd have laughed (let's not forget how incredibly unlucky I usually am). It feels so right – I honestly can't imagine life without him in it now. He's become as permanent as the white cliffs, and I don't have one single doubt in my mind that this will be a lasting relationship. I know this probably sounds crazy, but we just fit.

In fact, everything in my life feels good right now: I've distanced myself from some negative friendships, and formed new, healthy ones that bring me nothing but joy. I still have my best friend, my biggest cheerleader, and it makes me so happy that he's also in a loving and open relationship with one of the nicest guys I know.

I think the main thing that helped make everything better was choosing to work on me before anyone else. How can you be truly happy with someone else when you aren't in the best place you can be for you? So I think I've made great progress this year in terms of my personal goals. Sure, I managed to get myself a photography show for F-P Nouveau, but that happened because something else clicked inside me. I was more determined than ever to prove to myself that I CAN do whatever I want if I really put my mind to it. I didn't need anyone else doing it for me; I didn't need the media, and I didn't need a guy (dreamy guitarist or not), and I definitely wasn't going to let my anxiety get in the way. Once I started accomplishing more, the other bits fell neatly into place.

After the overwhelming response to my call for photos I want my space here on *Girl Online* to continue to be our little hub, our community, where we can all be involved in helping one another and spreading positivity. We can all be part of supporting one another to reach our own personal, individual goals in life; none of us are travelling alone along the path that leads there.

Hope you all have the best night tonight. Let's be full of hope and promise as we all raise a little toast to the year we're leaving behind and the new one waiting just round the corner for us. And, as always, thank you so much for all your support.

I love you all.

Girl Online ... always online xxx

*** Acknowledgements **

I want to start here by thanking my amazing editor and friend, Amy Alward. This book would not be as beautifully put together without her help. *Girl Online* has been such a huge part of our lives for two years now and I'm happy that it brought us together. We chuckled over cheesy name suggestions, ate far too many strawberries and bopped along to many a Spotify playlist. As well as guiding me through the writing process, she has been a loyal and caring friend and I couldn't have asked for a better editor. In fact, I don't think one even exists!

To the rest of the brilliant team at Penguin who have brought *Girl Online* to life: Shannon Cullen (my publisher and one of the nicest ladies I know), Tania Vian-Smith (who ALWAYS knows how to save the day – she is the fairy godmother of PR and book tours), Clare Kelly (Queen of PR), Natasha Collie (Marketing Guru), Jacqui McDonough and Becky Morrison who create such beautiful front-cover designs, Wendy Shakespeare who is also part of my editorial team, and everyone else at team Penguin who make it happen behind the scenes. Thank you so much for making this such an enjoyable and smooth experience for me and allowing me to share my story and characters with the world.

To the Gleam Team: Dom, Maddie, Phil, Meghan, Ange and my PA, Carrie. Thank you for everything you do to enable this to be as straightforward as possible. I am beyond grateful that I get to share this exciting journey with you all right beside me.

My friends and family: you all know how much your continued support and love encourages me every day to carry on stepping out of my comfort zone. Thank you for always believing in me and joining me on this crazy journey. I feel like the luckiest girl in the world having such a solid support network around me. Even though half of you haven't finished *Girl Online: On Tour* yet, I forgive you. Just make sure you let me know what you think of this book in four years' time, OK . . .?

I also want to mention my friend Mark, who I met for the first time at my book launch for *Girl Online: On Tour*. At a time in my life where things felt a little difficult, he was like a light at the end of the tunnel. I didn't realize I had space in my life for a new friendship until I met him. I was laughing until my sides hurt, dancing in my kitchen and sharing one too many Wagamamas with someone who was so like me, we could be twins. He recently asked me if I ever realize how much I've changed his life. After this, I thought about the way in which he has also changed mine. I am more confident, a lot happier and so much more carefree since I met him. Hold on to the friends who make you feel something; they are so rare and so special.

Alfie Deyes. The main man in my life. My rock, my world and my biggest fan. I love you xxx

Girl Online

HAVE YOU CAUGHT UP WITH THE WHOLE SERIES?

Send us your shelfie!

GirlOnlineBooks

Girl Online

Now on Snapchat:

girlonlinebooks

Add us for exclusives, sneak-peeks, competitions and much more . . .

Search '**girlonlinebooks**' in Snapchat and add us

OR

1. Open Snapchat
2. Point your camera over the image below and tap the image

girlonlinebooks

Listen to
Girl Online

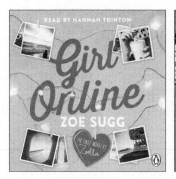

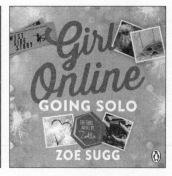

http://po.st/
ListenGirlOnline

http://po.st/
ListenGirlOnlineOnTour

http://po.st/
ListenGirlOnlineGoingSolo

read by the brilliant
HANNAH TOINTON

For all the latest news about

Girl Online

www.girlonlinebooks.com